The Lightfir

Born and raised in Sheffield, Joanne lives in the coastal village of Laxey in the Isle of Man with her husband, children, dogs and other assorted wildlife. She has worked in print, radio and broadcast journalism in the north west for the past three decades and is now a full-time writer of historical fiction set in nineteenth century Sheffield.

Also by Joanne Clague

The Sheffield Sagas

The Ragged Valley
The Girl at Change Alley
The Watchman's Widow

The House of Help for Friendless Girls

The House of Hope
The Lightfingered Lass

The
Lightfingered
Lass

Joanne
CLAGUE

CANELO

Penguin
Random
House

First published in the United Kingdom in 2025 by

Canelo, an imprint of
Canelo Digital Publishing Limited,
20 Vauxhall Bridge Road,
London SW1V 2SA
United Kingdom

A Penguin Random House Company

The authorised representative in the EEA is Dorling Kindersley Verlag
GmbH. Arnulfstr. 124, 80636 Munich, Germany

A CIP catalogue record for this book is available from the British Library.

Print ISBN 978 1 80436 800 8
Ebook ISBN 978 1 80436 801 5

This book is a work of fiction. Names, characters, businesses, organizations,
places and events are either the product of the author's imagination or are
used fictitiously. Any resemblance to actual persons, living or dead, events
or locales is entirely coincidental.

Cover design by Rose Cooper

Cover images © Shutterstock, Arcangel

Printed and bound in Great Britain by Clays Ltd, Elcograf S.p.A.

Look for more great books at
www.canelo.co
www.dk.com

For Jess, Olivia and Tom

SPRING 1888

Chapter 1

Stepping into the street, Ned Staniforth inhaled the smoky scent of the bowl of the town, slung his jacket over his shoulder and set off for home, one amongst the throng coming off the day shift. He shoved his cap into the back pocket of his britches, relishing the breeze that tickled the hairs on his forearms and lifted his fringe away from his forehead. Fishing out a none-too-clean piece of flannel from his waistcoat pocket, he wiped the worst of the grime from his face and neck.

Pounding footsteps sounded from behind, and a breathless greeting.

' 'Ey up, Ned.'

He turned to find the apprentice of one of his fellow furnacemen running to catch up. The kid was a tall sapling, not yet muscled from the work.

'Have a gander at this,' he said, his eyes shining. He showed Ned the raw, mottled welt that ran from the pale skin on the inside of his wrist, wrapping around his arm up to the elbow. 'What's tha think?'

'Looks sore,' said Ned.

'Aye, 'tis. Caught in a chain.'

'Tha's been lucky, then.'

'Too right.' He rolled down his sleeve. 'I'm goin' to the Castle wi' some o' the lads for a pint, if tha fancies it.'

'Aye, I might do.'

The apprentice skipped ahead – 'See thee in a bit then' – and was gone.

A pot or two of ale along with a story that would be embellished into the lad nearly losing his arm sounded a better prospect than returning to his lodgings, but Ned was bone tired. Working in a steel mill was a young man's game and he'd been at it twenty years, and lucky to have no more than the occasional scald or scratch to his name. At thirty-five, he was starting to feel the strain in the bones and ligaments of his back. There was a permanent whine in his lugs from the clamour of the factory floor, and everything, from a foaming jar of ale to a plate of kippers, came with the peculiar, almost garlicky, odour of molten metal.

Each completed shift drove him nearer to accepting the offer that Jacob, his second cousin, had made to go halves on a forge by Malin Bridge. This was a plum ripe for the plucking – a thriving family business with no relatives able or interested in taking it over, located where the Loxley and Rivelin rivers converged. Small fry compared to the steel mill. The difference was that he'd be his own boss. There was one obstacle to that plan that he kept trying and failing to fathom out – where would he find the coin to invest? He'd no savings to speak of. The father of an acquaintance had offered to put up Ned's half and sit back, no interfering. This man would just take his cut, until such time as Ned could settle the balance. It would put him in the debt of the notorious Prescott family. This concern was the reason he hadn't yet given an answer.

Ned reached the foot of Snig Hill that led up to Angel Street and the high street of the town beyond. It was a shortish road with narrow pavements cluttered by the awnings, swinging signs and display trays of the shops that lined both sides. The premises of the Pack Horse Inn dominated one corner. Ned paused outside the drooping Tudor buildings on the opposite corner, debating whether to pass by the foot of the hill or take up the offer of a jar or two at the Castle Inn. The tavern sat at the top of Snig Hill, a road named for the wooden wedges – snigs – drivers put on the wheels of their wagons to stop them rolling away. Though his grandmother had always reckoned the moniker came from the slang for eels and that there had once been an eel – or snig – pond right where he stood.

A wagon belonging to Tennant's brewery was parked outside the Pack Horse Inn, the dray facing up, the driver remonstrating with another man on the pavement and pedestrians giving them a wide berth. Ned stepped closer to the overhang of the crumbling wattle and daub wall to allow a heavily laden double-decker omnibus, pulled by two straining horses, to make the ascent.

He made his decision. He'd filch some grub from his landlady – she had a soft spot for Ned – and get his head down. Tomorrow was the last twelve-hour shift of the week then he had a day off, though he never knew what to do with himself except spend his earnings in the Castle or the Blue Pig. He was turning to set off towards his lodgings at West Bar when the sound of a whistle being repeatedly blown reached his ears.

Ned looked towards the direction the constable's shrill command seemed to be coming from, guessing it was somewhere beyond the municipal buildings at the top of the hill.

Then he saw her, a woman tearing full-pelt down the middle of Snig Hill. Elbows akimbo, both hands bunched in her skirt so she would not trip over the hem, she dodged around the double-decker bus within a hair's breadth of the horses, earning a mouthful of abuse from the driver. Without slowing, she hopped onto the pavement, running past the giant banners of the Bombay Tea Company and Wilson's toy warehouse. Pedestrians blocked the way outside Meek's drapers, forcing her to leap back onto the cobbles.

As she drew nearer, Ned could see she was laughing. He had time for the fleeting thought that she ought to be saving her energy, before she risked a glance over her shoulder and ran straight into him. Instinctively, he grasped her upper arms and braced himself or they would have both gone tumbling.

'Take your hands off me!' She stepped back, pushing thick and unruly auburn curls away from her face. Her eyes were blue, set above high and rounded cheekbones, and her lips were red – painted, he thought – above a strong jawline. A streetwalker, maybe, caught touting for business. A looker, for definite.

'Clumsy oaf,' she said. She was breathing heavily.

Ned laughed. 'Tha ran into me,' he said.

She gave him an appraising look, one that made him wish he'd wiped more of the grime from his face, then seemed to remember she was being chased and whipped her head around to look back up the hill. Ned followed her gaze. The road and pavements were busy with vehicles and pedestrians and the constable was nowhere to be seen. But the increase in volume of his whistle was unmistakable.

'Tha'd best scarper, love,' said Ned, retrieving his jacket from where he'd dropped it on the cobbles when he'd caught her by the arms.

Straightening up, he was almost thrown off balance for a second time when she pulled him towards her, her eyes

6

sparkling with mirth, and tickled his ear with a whisper – '*Don't tell.*' She planted a kiss on his cheek then darted across the road and onto the pavement behind the brewery wagon, where she fell into a crouch behind the wooden spokes of the rear wheel. Ned remained where he stood, open-mouthed. When she waved her arm at him in a gesture that told him to stop staring, he grinned and looked away.

Now he could see the constable who was in pursuit running down the cobbles, his police helmet swinging from one hand like an empty bucket. A young bobby, with embarrassment written all over his face. He stopped alongside Ned at the junction, looked in both directions then replaced his helmet on his head and put his hands on his knees, panting heavily. His whistle hung from his neck, swaying gently.

'Been outrun by a girl, then?' said Ned, innocently.

'See which way she went?' The bobby lifted a hand to point one way then the other.

Ned risked a glance across the street. She was visible through the back wheels of the wagon, crouched low, her dress bisected by the spokes, but she might look like a blue cloth sack to the casual observer. He turned away to watch the junction.

'Nah,' he said, wondering how much the bobby had seen. 'She barged right into me and I dropped me jacket, so I weren't really lookin' to see where she went. Long chase, were it?'

'Aye.' The bobby stood upright, giving Ned a defensive look. 'From Portobello Street. I've run a mile, practically.'

A horse whinnied and Ned looked around to see the brewery wagon driver wave off the fellow he'd been debating with and hoist himself back onto the box. The dray horse flexed its muscular neck in anticipation of the climb up the hill. Ned held his breath. Any minute now, the wheels would begin to turn, exposing the woman's hiding place.

The driver tapped the reins on the animal's broad back. 'Gee up, then.' The dray horse strained forward, and the wagon moved an inch, then two.

Ned coughed into his closed fist and pointed to the left of the junction. 'She might've gone that way, come to think o' it.'

The bobby obligingly turned his back on the wagon and peered in the direction Ned had indicated. He shook his head. 'No sign of her.'

'I think tha must have lost her then,' Ned said regretfully.

A youth approached them, grinning all over his face. He nodded over Ned's shoulder. 'Lookin' for summat?'

Ned turned around reluctantly. The woman with the auburn hair was rising from her crouch, exposed for all to see as the horse slowly clopped away. She looked at Ned, her eyes still merry, and held out her hands in surrender. Her pursuer wasted no time, striding across to pin her arms behind her back. She yelped in pain.

Ned had been about to continue on his way but found himself trotting over to the constable and his quarry. 'Is there need for that?'

'She's putting it on. At any rate, you can give me your opinion once you've chased her halfway through town.'

An audience was gathering. The bobby made to tug her away but the woman stood her ground. 'I've not done anything wrong,' she said, loudly. 'I'm the victim here.'

'What's she meant to have done?' somebody shouted.

'None of your business.' The bobby's cheeks coloured. 'If you must know, she's a pickpocket. I witnessed it myself. She snatched a gentleman's purse right out of his hand after begging him for coin.'

Another voice from the crowd. 'Not a pick*pocket* as such, then, eh?'

And a third. 'Got nowt better to do than chase after poor young lasses?'

The woman's eyes flashed in delight. She twisted her neck to glare at the bobby. 'Search me, why don't you? You'll not find anything.'

Ned had recognised she wasn't a local lass when she first spoke to him. Now, he realised her rounded vowels and soft intonation belonged to the West Country. They had an immigrant from Penzance at the steelworks and he recognised the cadence.

'You'll have chucked it in the gutter, that's what you'll have done.' The bobby gestured up the hill and one or two youths drifted off in that direction, their casual stride belied by the eagerness in their eyes. 'Have you pockets in that dress?'

The woman nodded and he released her arm so that with a flick of her wrist she could turn out a seam pocket in the skirt to hang like a rabbit's ear. Empty. 'See?' She plucked at the sleeves and the collar of her dress, and ran her hands down the sides of her bodice. 'Nothing to hide.'

A shout from the crowd. 'Check under her skirt!'

This was followed by wolf whistles and applause. Ned stepped closer to shield her from view as much as possible and she turned her blue eyes on him. She was breathtakingly beautiful. And her lips weren't painted, after all. They were naturally red and full and Ned was overcome by an urge to bend his neck and kiss them. So entranced

9

was he that he thought the bobby's next comment was directed at him.

'There'll be none of that. Be off with you, the lot of you.' He shook the woman's arm. 'Where d'you live?'

'Nowhere. I mean, I have no home to go to.' Ned could have listened to her leisurely drawl all day long. 'That gentleman was going to take advantage of me.' Boos from the crowd. 'He thought he'd do as he liked, didn't he?' Several people gasped. The woman's chest hitched in a sob but she cut her eyes at Ned, so quickly he almost missed it too.

The bobby kept his grip on her arm. 'Why did you run then?'

'I'm sorry to say I became panicked.' Her eyes swept over the onlookers. 'I don't know a soul in this town. I was afraid of what might happen to me.'

'Well.' He looked nonplussed for a moment. 'Disturbing the peace of this town is…'

A shout from the crowd: 'She's stretched thee legs. Leave it at that, eh?'

'Who said that?' The constable looked around, his eyes settling on Ned, who shook his head and held up his hands. Ned met the woman's gaze, the humour in her eyes that seemed meant for him alone, as if they were sharing a secret.

An older, well-dressed woman stepped forward. 'Might I say that I agree locking her away is not the answer. Perhaps you ought to take her over to the house for friendless girls. Are you quite alone, my dear?'

She nodded, a slight frown creasing her brow.

The woman continued. 'It's only a short distance…'

'Aye,' the bobby said. 'I know the place. It's on my beat. I've brought lasses there before.' He let go of the woman's arm and she rubbed at it ruefully. 'Don't run, all right?'

'I haven't the breath left. Where are you taking me?'

The older woman smiled. 'You've no reason to be fearful. What's your name?'

'Nan Turpin.'

'Your age?'

'I'm twenty-six or thereabouts.'

The woman raised her eyebrows. 'Hmm. And you have nobody will take you in?'

Nan Turpin shook her head.

The woman seemed satisfied. 'If they have a bed at the house, they'll give it to her.'

'I'd sooner just go on my way,' she said, but it seemed only Ned was paying attention to her words.

The bobby directed her to walk ahead of him. 'Back the way we came, now, but not at a clip, eh?'

Nan Turpin didn't look back. Ned watched the two of them until they were out of sight, certain that at the last moment she would turn, acknowledge him with that secretive smile. He remained where he stood as the crowd dispersed. She was gone, leaving him with a curiously hollow feeling, as if she'd taken all the colour of the day with her.

He'd have that drink after all.

The low-ceilinged snug inside the Castle Inn was hazed with pipe smoke, ale fumes and the buzz of conversation. Ned greeted his workmates and nodded to the landlady, a woman in her fifties whose diminutiveness disguised the fact she was capable of lifting drunks off their feet by the scruff of the neck and turfing them out.

'Me usual, love.'

'You took yer time, din't yer?'

Ned turned to the man who had spoken, whose wife would be along soon to fish him out and kick him home. It was a daily tradition. He grinned. 'I just got floored by the woman o'me dreams. She were bein' chased by a bobby. A thief, he reckoned.'

The others laughed.

'Woman of yer dreams, eh?'

'Thought you were never goin' to let another lass hook thee?'

'Aye, well.' He picked up his pint pot and eyed the contents, his guts shrivelling in the beat of awkward silence that followed, knowing they were all thinking the same thing, his shame at being cuckolded, and by his best mate too. It was the reason he was in lodgings and another man lived in his house with his former wife, leaving Ned forever branded with the stigma of divorce.

The landlady put her elbows on the bar and leaned towards him. 'Tell us, then, Ned. Who's this girl that sounds like she'd be nowt but trouble?'

Ned was a good storyteller and enjoyed having a rapt audience listen to his tale. He ate a meat and potato pasty and a pickled egg and drank a second pint of porter before bidding his fellow drinkers farewell. It was still light out, the birds in the trees making their clatter, but the temperature had cooled. Ned stood on the threshold of the tavern, nodding a greeting to a couple of men who were entering, and pulled his cap from the back pocket of his britches.

'Tha's dropped summat,' one of the men said.

A tooled leather coin purse with a fat brass clasp lay on the pavement. It was a fancy item, nothing Ned would ever waste his coin on. He opened his mouth to say the purse didn't belong to him, then realisation dawned.

'Ah, reight. Thanks.'

He retrieved the purse and walked a few steps down the hill, stopping in the shelter of the first shop doorway he reached. He glanced around furtively before unfastening the clasp. A handful of coins lay inside. Ned shook them into the palm of his hand. A few bits of silver and copper. The purse itself looked like it was worth more than the meagre hoard it contained. He stirred the coins with one finger. Ah, here was a guinea. And another. He slid the coins back into the purse.

Now he knew why she had not acknowledged him as she was led away. By tucking the purse into the folds of his cap, she had made him complicit. She must have done it immediately after they had collided, when she had pulled him towards her and whispered in his ear. *Don't tell.* She hadn't wanted the constable to think they were in collusion.

He rubbed his cheek where she had kissed him.

'Nan Turpin, you little varmint.'

Ned set off for his lodgings. The people he passed seemed uncommonly cheerful. Perhaps it had to do with the stupid grin he couldn't seem to wipe off his face. Another twelve-hour shift to endure, then he had – for once – something to do on his day off. He would be paying a visit to the House of Help in Paradise Square.

Chapter 2

Name: Nan Turpin

Age: Twenty-six

Address: No fixed abode

Occupation of nearest relatives or friends: Unknown

Further Particulars:

Hetty Barlow, warden of the House of Help for Friendless Girls, laid down her pen and sat back in her chair, tapping her lower lip. What ought she to write under *Further Particulars*? The girl had been unforthcoming in her interview and seemed not to care that she had spun inconsistent stories to the staff at the house. She'd told Cook she was running away from a violent husband, but she wore no wedding band and referred to this husband, according to Cook, only as *Mr Turpin*. Cook hadn't pressed her, telling Hetty she didn't want to further distress the girl. Nan Turpin spoke to the deputy warden, telling Hope of a house at the edge of a cliff at Carn Kez on the south-westerly edge of England. It was a wild place, she'd said, a place to roam and think of distant lands. Meanwhile, Clara the maid was offered the tale that she'd been orphaned at an early age and had been on the move from town to town, fending for herself, since the age of sixteen. She'd only fetched up at the House of Help because of an unfortunate misunderstanding between herself, a gentleman and his purse. The alternative had been a police cell.

She had been correct on that final point, at least.

'All we've got is our stories,' she'd said, when Hetty challenged her. She had widened her eyes in an appeal for sympathy. 'If I decline to tell you mine, will you throw me out?'

Hetty had sighed. 'No, a'course not. D'you have any training? Have you ever been in service?'

'I have to say...' her reply was a drawn-out descent, as if she was rejecting the very idea but as tactfully as possible. 'No.'

Now, alone in her quarters with the ledger open before her, Hetty picked up her pen, blotted the nib and wrote. *She was brought to us by Constable Goodlad, who had caught her in the act of stealing a purse but thought our intervention might bring about a better outcome than the magistrates' court.* He'd obviously had his head turned, to shift from chasing her through the streets to wishing her his very best on the doorstep of the house. *She has no training.* Hetty dipped her pen. She was going to take a liberty here but she could only hope. *Miss Turpin is willing to learn.* There was an option, provided the girl didn't disappear as suddenly as she had arrived. *A place might be found for her at the servants' home in Gell Street, where she can be trained in domestic service. Our Deputy Warden is investigating this.*

Hetty had asked Hope to draw the truth out of the girl. Hope had a way with the women and the girls who fetched up at the house. It probably had to do with the fact she was an ex-resident herself. But Nan Turpin had merely spun Hope more fabulous tales, claiming her own mother was a baby farmer she had reported to the police after one too many infant deaths. She had been on the move ever since and had come to Sheffield in search of her roots. Her father, she reckoned, was notorious criminal Charles Peace, hanged nine years earlier for murder. Fabrication piled upon fabrication. Hetty shook her head. She had only so much space on the narrow-lined page of the house ledger.

She wrote the final line. *She has spoken of escaping from a violent marriage and also purports to be an orphan who has always fended for herself.*

Hetty decided she would also omit Nan Turpin's further claim to be a descendant of the infamous highwayman. She smiled to herself. The audacity of the girl. Hetty blotted the page and closed the ledger, stowing it in the top drawer of her desk. Sitting back, she gazed out of the ground-floor window that looked onto the cobbles of Paradise Square. There were still plenty of people about, enjoying the spring evening. She could hear muted piano music coming from the parlour across the hall and, if she strained her ears, the voices of those residents tasked with cleaning the kitchen after the evening meal. Above her head, feet skipped and pounded on the floorboards. This would be the youngest of the residents chasing each other about. Soon, an older woman would demand they stop and get on with something more productive, like mending. The house was only ever quiet in those few hours before dawn when the occupants of its three storeys and attic space were lost to sleep. It didn't mean Hetty would not be disturbed, even in the dead of night. The warden's quarters were conveniently placed beside the front door, where requests for entry were made at all hours of the day and night. The original receiving room had been converted into a bed-sitting room. An antechamber served as her office.

Hetty rubbed at the frown line between her eyes. She'd been in post almost a year now, and the trustees had declared themselves satisfied with the way she ran the place. No, the reason for the permanent crease on her forehead was that her life here was built on a lie. Her qualifications were fabricated and the discovery of that seemed only a matter of time. And there was the bigger falsehood that had to do with Amelia, and that sat in the pit of her stomach like a stone. Hetty had rescued Amelia from the clutches of their aunt and brought her here, and appealed to the trustees to secure her the job of housekeeper. *We are siblings, and orphans, and Amelia has nobody but me.* Truth and deception mixed, and now curdled.

Amelia had hated the house and become engaged to the first man who came along, although Hetty had kept her counsel, or thought she had.

She pushed back her chair, got to her feet and left the room, closing the door to her quarters behind her. She walked down the hall towards the kitchen, deciding that while in this unsettled mood she would mash a pot of tea for herself and make sure those residents tasked with clearing up weren't poking around in the pantry. Amelia was responsible for the stores but, lost in the fog of grief, had not yet returned to her housekeeping duties. Hetty had resolved to give her all the time she needed, and to pray Amelia would remain with her.

As she descended the short staircase that led down to the kitchen, Hetty heard Nan Turpin's gently musical voice floating from the ground-floor dormitory across the hall. Curious, she turned her feet in that direction instead.

'He seemed like such a kind old gentleman,' the girl was saying as Hetty entered the room. Nan Turpin looked up and bestowed upon Hetty a wide smile. Hetty nodded a greeting. The girl sat, legs stretched before her, on the floor at the end of the bed she had been allocated. Amelia was sitting on the mattress behind her, trying to tame Nan's wild hair into a braid. She glanced at Hetty, irritation in her eyes.

'Go on,' said Amelia.

'Well,' said Nan. 'He helped me into the carriage. He offered to stow my bag away, and then, well, it's a sorry tale, let me tell you. When it came time to leave the train there was no sign of my bag and no sign of this kind gentleman either.'

'That's terrible,' said Amelia. 'So you've lost everythin'?'

The corners of Nan's mouth turned down. 'Everything.'

Hetty sat on the edge of the bed nearest the door, facing the two young women. 'Why Sheffield?'

Nan frowned, as if she was pondering the question. 'Why not? Seems as good a place as any.'

'You told my deputy you came here looking for your father's family,' said Hetty. 'Searching for your roots or summat like that.'

Nan tilted her head as if this was a theory she was hearing for the first time, and Amelia gently straightened it again. 'Hold still, Nan.'

'Where did you get the train from, that brought you here?' said Hetty.

'Well.' Nan drew out the word. 'One railway station is like the next. I've been all over, haven't I? Travelled far and wide.'

'I wouldn't know.'

Amelia spared Hetty a brief glance. 'Leave her be, sister.'

'Oh, you two are sisters?' Nan Turpin's eyes sparkled. 'I can see the resemblance now. That's wonderful. And you the warden, Miss Barlow, and you, Amelia, working here too. And how did that come to pass?'

Amelia gave Hetty a challenging look before returning her attention to tugging at Nan's curls. 'Hetty brought me here,' she said, 'to get me away from mad old Auntie Gertie after our mother died. She's a lot older than me, is our Hetty. Thirty-eight, aren't you? She thinks it gives her the right to rule my life.'

Hetty shook her head. 'We should leave that in the past, love. Least said, soonest mended.' She spoke gently, but her heart was pounding, in fear and in frustration too. She would not discuss their circumstances with this stranger who had been dropped into their midst. Hetty might have expressed her displeasure, but she had Amelia's bereavement to consider. She got to her feet. 'I'll leave you be.'

'Oh, don't leave us.' Nan reached around to pat Amelia's knee. 'Your sister has been confiding in me about losing her betrothed to the smallpox. What a terrible thing.'

'Aye,' said Hetty, shortly. 'It was. Amelia.'

'What?'

'I'm going to mash a pot of tea.' It was an appeal for Amelia to join her. On the day Amelia had returned to the House of Help with the news of Linus's death, she had fallen into Hetty's arms. Hetty had hoped this initial rapprochement would continue, but Amelia's coldness now radiated from her like an icy blast. Hetty was rocked by it, and knew she could not reveal the biggest secret she carried in her heart. Not yet.

'A pot of tea sounds very agreeable,' said Nan.

Hetty ignored her, fixing her gaze on Amelia, who was frowning at the top of Nan's head.

'You have the thickest hair I've ever seen,' Amelia said. 'Birds could nest in this.'

It was time to admit defeat. She would try to speak to Amelia later, in the warden's quarters. She felt, confusingly, that there were very many things to say and, simultaneously, nothing at all. Helpless in the face of Amelia's grief, Hetty turned away. How could she burden her further, with a truth that might destroy their already fragile relationship?

The thought occurred to her, as she walked across the hall and into the kitchen, that Nan Turpin had successfully deflected all the attention away from herself.

Hetty measured tea leaves into the strainer, enjoying the comfort that focusing on a simple task brought, and was lifting the kettle from the range when the door knocker sounded. Two strong raps. She replaced the kettle with a sigh and pinched the skin on the bridge of her nose. There was no peace to be had in this house. Three more raps. 'Hold your horses,' she muttered. It would likely be a police constable or the station porter, or one of the agents for the house. Women in need tended to approach her door more cautiously, with timid knocks, and she had gone to leave the house on more than one occasion to find a woman sitting on the steps, having not alerted the house to her presence at all. Regardless, the first thing Hetty did whenever the knock came was to mentally tally up the number of unoccupied beds. Presently, there was one cot to spare, in the attic space. The dormitories on the ground, first and second floors were full.

If there were no vacancies, Amelia would be prevailed upon to share Hetty's bed. The deputy warden was the third and final member of live-in staff, although Hope had an open invitation to lodge at the Master Cutler's mansion in the bucolic surroundings of Ranmoor, since her well-to-do parents had become acquainted with the Master Cutler and his wife. The moneyed always found one another. Hope opted to live at the house but could be persuaded to give up her bed if necessary, and endure the hardship of being waited on hand and foot at Tylecote.

Of course, it might be Mr Wallace. The treasurer of the house trustees was given to dropping by and a friendship had developed, and had prompted Amelia – in happier times – to tease Hetty about the genial widower having designs on the warden of the house. What nonsense. Hetty stopped on her way to the door to examine her reflection in the hallway's wall mirror, tucking a stray lock of hair under her cap.

But it wasn't Mr Wallace on the doorstep, nor a woman in need. A man about Hetty's own age stood there in working clothes, doffing his cap to reveal thick dark hair that was parted neatly in the middle. He was olive-skinned with large brown eyes, and ruggedly built. He could be a navvy or a foundryman.

' 'Ow do, love.'

Hetty drew herself up. 'I'm Miss Barlow, the warden of the house. Can I help you?'

'Aye, I reckon so.' He wore an expression on his face that was both apologetic and hopeful. Perhaps he had broken the heart of one of the women in her charge. He didn't look the guileful type. But looks could be deceiving. 'I'm 'ere to visit wi' one of your lasses. She's called Nan Turpin.'

He moved forward a step. Hetty folded her arms.

'I can't allow you in,' she said, 'but you can leave your name and reason for visiting.'

He stepped back again, abashed. 'No point leavin' my name, love. She dun't know it. We bumped into each other, t'other day.' He fished in his jacket pocket and brought out what looked like a wages packet. 'I've got summat for her.' Something seemed to occur to him and disappointment flitted across his features. Hetty had never before met anyone who wore every thought so openly upon their face. 'That is, if she's still 'ere?'

Hetty cocked her head. 'Mr...'

'Staniforth. I'm Ned Staniforth.' He coughed and opened his mouth to say more, then closed it again.

'Mr Staniforth. We run a respectable house. If you and Miss Turpin have an acquaintanceship...'

He interrupted her. 'So she is 'ere then?'

'...but she does not know your name, and you come here, offering cash.' She waved at the envelope he was clutching, and rolled her eyes in exasperation. 'You should try your luck on Love Street. You've come to the wrong house.'

His eyes widened in understanding. 'Nah, tha's got the wrong idea completely.' He opened the envelope and took out a sheet of paper. 'I've written her a note.' He tucked the paper away again. 'I were goin' to come sooner. I've got summat belongs to her.'

'Miss Turpin was brought here on the day she arrived in town, by a police constable.'

'Aye. Like I said, that were the day we bumped into each other. She nearly sent me flyin'. The bobby carted

22

her off an' I saw she'd dropped summat.' His tongue was running away with him, as if he was anticipating Hetty closing the door in his face. 'I couldn't come 'til now. There was an explosion at the mill and I've been coverin' for a couple of injured lads. Back-to-back shifts.' He paused for breath and spread his hands. 'But look.' Hetty obligingly took in his clean-shaven cheeks, white collarless shirt, waistcoat and trousers. 'I'm 'ere now.'

'What did Miss Turpin lose, when you pair collided? She reckons all her possessions were stolen, by a man she encountered on the train.'

'Train?' He shrugged. 'I know nowt about that. I were hopin' to show her about the town a bit.' His eyes flashed with inspiration. 'It's a ring. That's what she dropped. I'm keepin' it safe for her.'

Hetty snorted. 'Looks like she's put a ring in your nose to lead you by.'

He merely shrugged and smiled.

'That girl,' Hetty muttered. She held out her hand. 'Give me the note then. After all, I've nowt better to do with my time than pass messages along.'

'Thanks, love. Is she allowed out, if, say, I wanted to take her for a stroll?'

'I don't run a prison,' said Hetty, 'but I can't allow you inside the house. I can't speak for Miss Turpin, neither. Have you this ring on you?'

'No, I forgot it.' He offered a crooked smile. 'I'll come back on Sunday, at three o'clock.' He skipped down the steps. 'It's in the note.'

'I'll make sure she gets it.' Hetty stepped back into the house and closed the door, and stood for a moment, tapping the envelope in her hand. Clara, the maid of all work, came down the hall swinging a commode bucket by its wire handle.

'All right, Miss Barlow?'

'Aye. Woolgathering, that's all.'

'Need owt?'

'No. Thank you, Clara.'

She watched the maid disappear upstairs and sighed.

The weight of her deception lay as heavy as a thick blanket across her shoulders. She wanted to console Amelia, to share the burden of her grief as only a mother could. But Amelia believed her mother was dead, and Hetty had not gathered enough courage to take the girl's hands, look into her eyes and tell her that her mother stood before her.

Chapter 3

'There,' said Amelia.

From her position on the floor at the foot of the bed, Nan Turpin twisted at the waist to peer up at the housekeeper of the House of Help. 'What would you say if I asked you to undo it and start all over again?'

The smile on Amelia's lips did not reach her eyes, which were shadowed by fatigue. 'You want me to yank at that mop all day long?'

Nan laughed. The last time she'd felt fingers on her scalp they had belonged to a portly gentleman she'd contrived to collide with in the gutter of a quiet side-street. She'd picked on the wrong man. He had seized hold of her by the hair and pulled her into a narrow alleyway. She'd been surprised at his strength but his breath smelled like he had a quart of whisky inside him. A swift kick to his private parts and he'd crumpled like newspaper thrown on the fire. She'd liberated his pocket watch and made off.

Nan gingerly touched her head. 'Nobody has ever braided my hair for me.'

'Not even your mother?'

'I never knew…' She stopped speaking and cocked her head towards the door, which stood ajar. Voices floated down the hall, Miss Barlow's and the deeper tones of a man.

'If it's not the bobby or station porter wi' a girl in tow,' said Amelia, 'it'll be the husband or father of one o' you lot. Don't worry theesen. My sister'll see them off.'

'Oh, I'm not concerned.' She laid the palm of her hand against her chest as if that might calm the thudding of her heart. 'You and your sister seem at odds with each other.'

'Aye, well. She's glad I'm back, an' I'm not.' Amelia pushed gently at her shoulder. 'Let me up. I could use some fresh air.'

Alone in the dormitory, Nan sat on the edge of the bed they had given her, playing her fingers over her lips. She was thinking about the man she had collided with on her first day in this town. His bicep had been strong under her grip when she had pulled him towards her and whispered in his ear, his cheek rough with stubble where she'd kissed him and slipped the coin purse into his back pocket. She'd lost the money, lost all her possessions thanks to the crook she'd encountered and would be stuck in this halfway house until a solution presented itself. So why did an involuntary smile spread across her face whenever she thought of their encounter? Her aim had been only to distract him so he wouldn't notice her hand dipping into his pocket, albeit in a reversal of her usual manoeuvre. The frisson of excitement that coiled through her body when her lips touched his skin was entirely unexpected.

He had saved her from the police cells. She wished she could have seen his face when he discovered the purse.

Nan remembered the words of the boy who had taken her in all those years ago and taught her how to survive. He'd begun with a warning. *You can't do what I can do. You're not grey enough. Your talents lie elsewhere.* She'd been sixteen or so, begging in the rain, the filth of London running down the gutter, and saw him – this pale, thin

26

creature about her own age, perhaps a little older – swipe food from the trolley of a street vendor, a theft that went unnoticed. He'd caught her eye, and then her wrist, and she'd gone with him to his lodgings, not fearing him at all. She had stayed with him for three years before one day the rent collector came by and said her boy had been caught, his own clasp knife turned against him. He'd never be coming back and the landlord had found somebody for the room who was willing to pay a higher rent. He'd jiggled the coin in his pocket and told Nan he knew a house would take her in, a fine-looking wench like her.

You'll never pass unnoticed in a crowd, her boy had told her. *So use that beauty. Charm their pants off, distract them and learn to run fast.* In all the time they had shared the same bed, he'd never so much as touched her. Seven years had passed since she learned he'd had his throat slit. She missed his company every day.

'I've jobs you can do, save you ligging about here.'

Nan jumped to her feet at the sound of Miss Barlow's voice. The warden had entered the room and was holding an envelope in her hand.

'This came for you.'

Nan took the envelope from her and turned it over in her hands. There were numbers and letters pencilled on the rough paper. 'What is it?'

'There's a note inside.' Miss Barlow smiled thinly. 'It's from a man. You bumped into him, so he says. Dropped summat he wants to return.'

Nan lowered her eyes to avoid the woman's sharp-as-scissors gaze and opened the envelope. 'I did drop something,' she whispered. She drew out a folded scrap of paper.

'Not a purse, were it, by any chance?' said Miss Barlow. 'A gentleman's coin purse?'

Nan forced a shaky laugh. What had that fool of a man told the warden? To buy time, she unfolded the note and frowned at the pencil scrawl, aware of Miss Barlow waiting for her response. Eventually, Nan sighed and raised pleading eyes to the warden. A little deflection was required.

'I have a confession to make,' she said.

'Oh aye?' Miss Barlow folded her arms.

'I'm not able to... I'm ashamed to say I can't read.'

'Nor can most o' the women here.' Miss Barlow narrowed her eyes. 'Didn't you tell our deputy warden that you could read and write, and quite adequately? Self-taught, an' all, I'm sure she said.'

Nan shook her head. 'I was too ashamed to admit it to Hope. She's so clever.' Her eyes brimmed and she blinked quickly to nudge a tear onto her cheek. 'I lied. I'm very sorry.'

She sniffed and handed the note back to Miss Barlow. Sunday at three o'clock. This man, this Ned Staniforth, wanted to take her for a stroll, show her the town. Nan covered her mouth to hide her smile.

'Can you tell me what he's written down, Miss Barlow?'

'There's nowt much to it,' the warden said. 'He wants to come here at three o'clock on Sunday and take you out for a walk.'

Nan pretended shock. 'Is that allowed?'

'That's the very question he asked.' The warden turned away, pausing on the threshold of the room. 'You have my permission, provided you don't get yourself in any bother.

I won't tolerate owt that reflects badly on the house. Do you understand?'

Nan clasped her hands before her. 'Yes, I do. Thank you, Miss Barlow.'

It was unsettling, being under rigorous scrutiny for the first time in over a decade, and by people who claimed they had only her best interests at heart. Nan told Hope that she was disinclined to go to the servants' training home. The two women were strolling companionably back to the house, Hope carrying a basket of eggs donated by the headteacher of a private school in the square. He had shown Nan the hens he kept in a wire pen at the back. This pen, the headteacher explained, was for their benefit, serving as protection from foxes and thieves. The hens were excellent layers and he couldn't afford to allow them to roam free. Nan imagined cutting the wire and watching them scatter in all directions.

'You know, the servants' home will find you a good position,' Hope said. 'It's very highly regarded.'

'I'm not training to become a live-in slave,' said Nan.

Hope laughed. 'It's not slavery. It's honest work and a roof over your head.'

They entered the house, stepping out of the path of one of the residents who was transporting a large vase of flowers to the front parlour.

Nan waited until the woman had passed. 'I'm not spending my life kneeling in front of a filthy grate worshipping the God of cleanliness.'

'It's next to godliness.'

'I don't care what it's next to. It's not for me.'

Hope put her hand on Nan's arm, stopping her in the act of opening the kitchen door. The sound of laughter and women's voices came from within.

'Why did you come here, Nan?'

'It was this or jail, you know that. I have no means to support myself. My luggage was stolen.'

'No, I mean, to Sheffield.'

'I have a connection, perhaps family, perhaps the only family I have left.'

Nan pushed open the door before Hope could reply.

Several of the women of the house were busy preparing plates of sandwiches and buns, putting teacups on trays, sugar in bowls and milk in jugs, all under the supervision of Amelia. She nodded to Hope. 'Will you do the Bible reading? The vicar's not comin'. Again. Hetty's not in the mood an' nor am I.'

'Yes, of course I will.'

Amelia turned to Nan. 'When's your fancy man arrivin'? Got time to butter some bread?'

Nan arched her eyebrows. 'Fancy man?'

Cook laughed. 'Tha can't keep a secret in this house, love.'

'Oh, he's only someone I ran into who wants to check on my wellbeing.' Nan smiled at Cook. 'Those cakes smell delicious.'

'Here.' Cook plucked a marzipan slice from a plate that was being carried from the room and handed it to Nan, to a chorus of disapproval. 'Well, she won't be 'ere for the bunfight, will she? Poor lamb.'

'You can borrow one o' my bonnets, if you like,' said Amelia. 'Have a gander in the chest next to my bed.' She waved a bone-handled knife in the air. 'Butter us this bread first?'

Nan bit into the cake, nodding appreciatively. 'I ought to go and get ready. I will look at the bonnets. That's very sweet of you, Amelia.'

In the blissfully deserted dormitory, Nan peered side-ways at herself in the mirror, tilting her chin this way and that. The midnight-blue felt hat with the little feather flattered her auburn hair but was too sombre for Nan's liking. The summer bonnet with the wide satin band would be more appropriate for walking out. Exactly how much coin was in that purse? The purse itself was prob-ably worth a fair bit. Amelia would know where a good pawnshop was located. With money in her pocket, she could skip off and find a room somewhere, a place where she wouldn't be pestered, and set about replenishing her fortunes. She might not return to the house at all, once she'd got her hands on that purse. She had no need to come back. All she possessed were the clothes on her back.

She might have gone off with a new hat, but neither sat right. Nan discarded them on the bedcovers and stepped into the hallway. The house was unusually quiet. She crept to the door of the front parlour and listened. She could hear the deputy warden's voice. This would be the Bible reading, to be followed by afternoon tea in the presence of one or more of the house trustees, perhaps a benefactor too, who would be fawned over, and any past residents who had returned to crow about their success. This was how Amelia had explained it to her, in bitter tones. Nan felt sorry for the girl. Amelia had pinned all her hopes on a man who had up and died on her.

Nan's eye was caught by a paisley shawl hanging on the coat hooks by the front door. She took it down, draped it around her back and over her arms and stepped outside.

He was waiting at the foot of the steps, smiling up at her.

''Ow do, Miss Turpin.'

Nan remained where she stood, looking down on him. 'Good afternoon. I think you have something of mine.'

'Oh aye?' He laughed. 'Belongs to you now, does it?'

'I should say it does.'

'I'm Ned Staniforth.' He stuck out his hand and Nan descended the steps to shake it.

His grip was warm and strong and when their eyes locked, Nan looked away first, finding she could not hold his guileless gaze. She glanced up at the house in time to see the net curtain in the front parlour swing back into place. He'd unsettled her, and she wasn't used to that. Sweeping her gaze across the square, she took a breath then met his eyes.

'Well then, Ned Staniforth, where are you taking me?'

Chapter 4

Until now, Ned had never wasted his coin on a trip on a horse tram. They were an expensive way of getting around town, for one thing, and in his opinion the boxy car looked too bulky for the small and narrow metal wheels upon which it balanced. But he'd been told the ride was smoother than the omnibus, and the wheels hardly ever jumped the grooves of the track.

The passengers already seated on the exposed top deck peered down at Ned and Nan as they approached. His eyes were drawn to the advertisement emblazoned across the upper deck for some fancy tailor's shop in Fargate. The destinations of the tram were painted beneath the windows of the lower deck – *Moorhead, Sharrow, Nether-Edge.*

He had in his head the notion Nan would enjoy a trip on a newish form of transport that was continuing to spread over the town like a spider's web. He'd never been near Nether-Edge, but was told it was a lovely spot, up and coming, plenty of the lush greenery that covered the seven hills of the town, and he wanted to impress Nan. What he really wanted, he supposed, was for her to fall in love with these surroundings and by extension with him.

Nan grasped the rail of the curved staircase and ran up to the top deck, calling back that she wanted the bird's eye view. Ned paid their fare to the conductor standing on the cobbles at the back of the tram, who had put one hand to the upturned brim of his bowler as Nan passed, following her up the steps with his eyes. A second conductor, identically dressed, stood at the front of the tram, on the step beside the driver's empty stool. The two horses waited, their reins hooked over the brass rail ready to be taken up and the command given. One of the beasts stood stock-still, head slightly dipped. The other seemed a bit skittish to Ned, chafing against his harness, snorting and stamping.

Ned trotted up the staircase and gestured to the man sitting beside Nan on the wooden bench that ran down the centre of the upper deck, who shifted over to allow Ned in. Nan smiled at him and rested her hand, palm up and fingers lightly curled, in the space between their bodies. He fought the urge to fold his fingers over hers. She'd bowled him over, this lass. He'd been telling the truth to the landlady of the Castle. But he wasn't kidding himself. She wouldn't be sitting beside him if he hadn't brought the thing she wanted.

On the edge of Paradise Square, she had taken the coin purse from him with those long, delicate fingers, and he'd returned her secretive smile, forgetting for the moment that she'd stolen this purse, and that he was colluding in her crime. He'd reminded himself that hers had been an act of desperation, and he'd been overwhelmed by a feeling of protectiveness. When Nan was his, she'd never have to put herself in danger again.

He leaned towards her so that their shoulders brushed and she turned to him, smiling. Ned spoke in a murmur, self-consciously, hoping none of the other passengers were earwigging. 'I thought, if tha's thinkin' about stayin' in town, tha'd like to get a good look at the place, a bit away from the factory smoke.'

'That's a fine idea,' she said, and he grinned with relief.

All the passengers were now onboard and an anticipatory silence had fallen. Eventually the man who'd moved to allow Ned to sit beside Nan took off his cap and scratched his head. 'Are we goin' or what?'

From further down the bench, another man leaned forward. 'Gone for a wazz, han't he? O'er there.' He pointed to the public house at the end of a terrace of houses. 'Bet he's sinkin' a quick pint, an' all.'

Nan laughed but Ned shifted on the seat, uneasily. One of the horses – the restless one – was flicking its thick and matted tail from side to side. A ragged cheer rose when a man Ned assumed must be the driver emerged from the pub. The man stopped on the edge of the pavement to allow a wagon to pass, the driver perched atop one of several large sacks that filled the cart bed, sitting sideways like a lady riding side-saddle, and evidently in no hurry. Ned heard the conductor shout to the tram driver – 'Hurry up, will ya! We're behind't timetable.' – and then curse loudly as the tram jerked forward – 'Whoah now!' There was a hoot of nervous laughter from inside the lower deck. At the same time, a furious jangle of bells and pounding hooves heralded the arrival, hurtling around the corner towards the tram, of a fire cart. Startled, the wagon driver steered his load towards the tram to allow the cart to pass. It raced by, men in uniform hanging from the sides, with a hair's breadth to spare. A sack toppled from the back of the wagon, exploding in a dense cloud of flour.

The horses bolted.

Ned hadn't time to brace himself. Along with the rest of the passengers, he was thrown sideways and then pitched forward, landing on his knees on the floor of the top deck. He whirled around, thinking to catch Nan, but she was already on the floor beside him, on her hands and knees, her mouth wide with shock. With shouts of alarm ringing in his ears, Ned lifted her, his hands around her waist, and sat her on the bench, steadying himself with his hands on her shoulders. 'All right?'

She laughed shakily. 'Yes, yes.'

Ned went to the rail to peer over. They were moving at a clip down the hill. He looked back up the road. The driver stood in the middle of it, waving his bowler at them, shouting unintelligible words. Ned shook his head impatiently. *Fat lot of good you are.* Most of those on the top deck had regained their seats and were reaching forward to hold onto the rail, although the tram ran as smoothly as promised, albeit at speed.

Ned pushed through to reach the staircase at the front and jumped down to the lower deck, glancing inside where one of the conductors was tending to a man on the floor who had a thin trickle of blood on his face. The other conductor, hatless now, was pulling on the reins. The driver's stool lay on its side. Ned righted it and the conductor sat, panting heavily.

'Can't you stop 'em?'

'That fucken' fire cart. Think they can do owt they like.' The conductor swiped at his hair, his eyes round with fright. 'Not the first fucken' time they've startled the 'orses.' He glanced at Ned. 'Aye. They'll stop at the foot o' the hill, I'll wager. Won't want to drag this lot up the other side if they don't 'av to.'

Ned nodded. 'Owt I can do?'

'Sit theesen back down.'

The tram was already slowing. Ned breathed a sigh of relief. He took the steps to the top deck two at a time, thinking to reassure Nan, but she was sitting calmly, her arm around a woman whose head was buried in Nan's chest. 'She's all right,' said Nan. 'She's just a bit shaken, aren't you, dear?'

'Are *you* all right?' said Ned.

'Why, yes, of course I am.' Nan laughed. 'What an adventure, hey?'

The landlord of the Swan looked like all his Christmases had come at once when a large party of people stumbled into his premises, the men loudly demanding a drink, the women and children dropping into seats. Ned stood off to one side with Nan. He felt her stiffen when a police inspector entered in his blue cape and bowler, accompanied by the tram driver who was remonstrating with him.

Nan reached up to whisper in Ned's ear. 'Shall we make our escape?'

'Aye. Why not?'

He took her to Weston Park on the omnibus that climbed – sedately, thankfully – towards the gardens at Crookesmoor. These gardens – Canada and Holy and Hollow Field – were made up of acres and acres of allotment strips rented by working men who lived in the industrial bowl of the town. Ned had often thought of renting a plot to grow vegetables. Thinking about it was as far as he'd got.

Her shoulders swaying in time with the rhythm of the road, Nan had turned her head to look out of the window. This meant he could safely gaze at her.

As the bus slowed to a halt, Ned coughed. 'This is us. Park's just up the lane.'

He took her hand to help her down from the 'bus. 'We won't need a horsecar back into town. It's all downhill from 'ere. Twenty minutes an' I'll have thee home.'

'Ned, we've just arrived and you're already thinking about putting me back in that house.'

He loved the sound of his name on her lips.

They strolled through the park gates and onto a gravel path shaded by large oaks and sycamores. People sat on benches or knelt on picnic blankets on a large, sloping green. Ducks floated on the pond beneath the carved arch of a wooden footbridge. A statue of a famous townsman – an iron foundry owner whose name Ned couldn't recall – stood on a tall plinth higher up the path. Behind it, in the distance, stood the ionic columns of a large mansion.

'That's a museum now,' said Ned, nodding towards the building. He pointed to a flat patch of ground. 'O'er there, they're talkin' about fixin' up a bandstand. Weekly concerts.' He breathed in. 'Can tha smell that?'

Nan looked at him expectantly. He could drown in those blue eyes. 'What?'

'Exactly. We're not in Nether-Edge but we're out o' the stench up here.' He took another deep breath. Always the faint tang of molten steel. 'What does tha think?'

'I'm wondering why you kept the purse,' said Nan. 'Why not hand it in?'

'Well.' Ned paused, caught off guard. 'I din't want them thinkin' I were in it wi' thee. An accomplice.'

Nan squeezed his arm. 'Is that the only reason?'

'I think gettin' that purse back is the only reason tha's come out wi' me.'

She lifted her chin. 'Maybe not.'

'Stop messin' wi' me, Miss Turpin. Come on.'

He took her hand and began to run, pulling her towards the pond. Nan's laugh was like birdsong, easing the constant whine in his ears. 'Don't forget, lass, I've seen thee run like the wind.'

'Like runaway horses!' she called.

They stopped, breathless, on the planks of the bridge, Ned shading his eyes against the glinting water. Nan leaned over the handrail. 'Oh!'

He looked down to see a straggling line of ducklings follow their mother under the bridge. He raised his eyes to the weeping willow on the far bank.

'There's a bench over yonder wi' nob'dy on it.'

They sat on the bench in the shade of the willow tree, watching a child poke at the muddy riverbank with a stick.

'Where've you come from, then?' said Ned.

'Oh.' Nan smiled. She was still watching the child so he could look at her lips and imagine kissing them. 'Here, there and everywhere.'

'I've never been out o' this town,' said Ned.

'It's good to have roots.' Nan turned her gaze on him. 'Tell me about yourself.'

Ned shook his head. 'Nowt to tell, really.'

'What about your parents?'

'Never really knew 'em.' He paused. 'I'm not feelin' sorry for mesen, don't get me wrong. I were raised by me nan. She passed, not so long back.'

'What was she like?'

'Lovely,' said Ned. He was surprised to find his throat was closing. Nobody had ever questioned him like this before. 'Aye, a good sort.'

'What happened to your parents?'

'Well, me mother run off an' me father…' Ned paused. 'He were a sailor. Is a sailor still, maybe. Nan allus said they both suffered wi' wanderlust. It were in their blood.'

Nan laughed gently. 'Not in yours then?'

Ned smiled at her. 'I'm stayin' put and makin' my fortune here.'

'You're a catch, Ned. I'm lucky to be in your company.'

'Get out of it.'

Her laughter rose into the canopy above, more musical than any birdsong. Ned wished he could bottle that sound.

'So what's it like?' he said. 'In the house they brought thee to?'

Nan rolled her eyes. She patted her waist where she had tucked away the coin purse after checking its contents. 'It's full of nosy sorts. I'll pawn this tomorrow and that'll give me enough to stay in a respectable hotel. Do you know of any?' She didn't wait for his reply, her voice rising indignantly. 'That warden, Miss Barlow, wants to put me in the servant training school.'

'I feel reight sorry for anybody tryin' to tell thee what to do.'

She dug him in the ribs, gently. 'Shall we have a wander?'

'Aye.'

They strolled along the path that ran the length of the edge of the park. Ned asked her to wait a moment and ducked onto Winter Street, returning with hot sugared codlings wrapped in newspaper from a street vendor, which they ate with their fingers. They walked on, cresting the brow of the hill that would lead them back down towards the centre of town.

'Are tha warm enough to walk home?'

'Yes.' Nan turned her face to the sky, basking in the sunshine. 'I wish I didn't have to go back there.'

'Better than bein' locked up, though, eh?' He dodged away from her raised hand, laughing.

They stopped at the wrought-iron gates to allow a horse rider through. Nan bent to examine a rose bush. When she straightened, one of the white blooms was tucked into her hair. He wanted to tell her there was no need to gild the lily. 'The gardener'll be after thee,' he said.

On the street, Ned pointed the way back to town.

'Thank you for bringing me to the park,' said Nan. She sounded wistful. 'Is there a longer road back that we could take?'

Ned thought for a moment. 'Tell thee what, we can allus stop off at the Ball in Campo Lane. It's in your neck o' the woods.'

Nan squinted at him. 'The ball?'

'The Golden Ball. Tha can enter, provided tha's got a male escort.' He spread his hands. 'Always at your service, Miss Turpin.'

–

Inside the public house, he guided her to a chair at a table in the corner, the only one not occupied by patrons, mostly male, eating and drinking. It was a cosy room, even without the fire lit, with a fern-patterned carpet on the floor and varnished panelling below the dado rail. A dusty glass pendant light hung from the yellowed ceiling and the wood-framed paintings on the walls – bucolic scenes and race-horses – were bookmarked by brass wall lights.

Nan took her seat, seeming not to notice the stems of pipes turning towards her like water diviners. A pint of porter and a small beer were placed before them. Ned looked up to mumble a thank you and yelped in surprise.

' 'Ey up, Frank.'

The man who towered above them had a pink slab of a face, like a cut on a butcher's block, that belied his relative youth. He was grinning from ear to ear, his eyes disappearing into the flesh around them.

'They're on the house. Can I join thee?'

This wasn't a question, and Ned knew that he couldn't refuse. 'Aye, 'course tha can.' He turned to Nan, who was smiling politely as Frank dragged out a chair and sat down heavily beside her. 'This is a mate o' mine.'

'Frank Prescott.' He stuck out his hand.

'Nan Turpin. Pleased to meet you.' She shook his hand and looked past him, around the room. 'I didn't think it would be so busy, being a Sunday.'

Ned took a swallow of his porter. 'Factories go seven days a week and so do the pubs. You could say these're our places o' worship.'

'It's thirsty work, bein' a furnaceman,' said Frank.

'Not that tha would know owt about a hard day's work.' Ned clapped Frank on the back, to show him he spoke in jest.

Frank smiled at Nan. 'I've not seen thee around before.'

'I've just arrived here,' said Nan. 'A scant few days ago.'

'Oh aye? From where?'

Ned leaned forward. He'd not wanted to pry but if a third party was willing to ask the question, he was keen to hear the answer.

'Here and there,' said Nan. 'I've come to see the sights. We've just been to Weston Park, an' before that we were on a runaway tram.'

'Oh aye?' Frank looked at Ned, who nodded and shrugged. 'An eventful day then. I can tell from the accent tha's not local.'

Frank waved to the landlord, who was peering through the serving hatch. 'I'll be round in a sec.' The man nodded, and withdrew. 'Aye, thirsty work. Has tha thought any more about me father's offer, Ned? I know he'll ask me when I tell him I seen thee.'

'It's generous of him,' said Ned, 'to offer.'

'Aye,' said Frank. 'It is that, an' he's after an answer.' He drained his glass and smacked his lips. 'I know he can be tricky but I'd be keepin' an eye on things, keepin' it amongst friends. Tha'd be daft to turn him down. Our young 'un thinks it's a grand idea.' He rubbed his hands together. 'She's been askin' after thee, Ned. Still carryin' that torch, like many o' the lasses o' this town.'

'Who's this?' said Nan.

'Me sister,' said Frank. 'Felicia. Ellie, for short. I'll have to tell our Ellie he's taken, won't I, love?'

'Ned's not my property,' said Nan, tartly.

'Other way round, it should be,' said Frank. 'You're his.'

'Knock it off, Frank,' said Ned. He had already decided to ask Nan whether he could court her. This lumbering oaf might put her off the idea.

But the exchange had made him wonder. What did he have to offer? He'd not even his own place, only a room in a house. He'd be a better prospect as the owner of a forge. His cousin had his own house and a large brood, so Ned would get the pretty riverside cottage that came with a large garden. And he wasn't getting any younger. This might be his last chance – at love and business.

'Tell the lass what tha planning then,' said Frank, his tone conciliatory.

'All right.' Ned cleared his throat. 'There's a forge for sale, an' I'm thinkin' of goin' in wi' me cousin. We'll be runnin' our own business, should be set up for life.' And just like that he made his decision. 'Frank's father is lendin' me the money.'

Frank clapped his hands together then leaned on Ned's shoulder to get to his feet. 'We've summat to celebrate now, an' I need a word wi' the landlord.' He cracked his knuckles. 'He's fallen behind wi' his payment. Gormless sod.'

Nan waited until Frank had exited the room. She wrinkled her nose. 'Is he a good friend of yours?'

Ned laughed. 'He's all right, is Frank.' He tapped his knee. 'I've known him since we were this high.' He rolled his shoulders, and tried to ignore the tension squirming in his gut. 'I were raised by me grandmother and the Prescotts were good to her. I've reason to be grateful to them.'

The money he needed wasn't going to drop in his lap any other way. Ned folded his lips. The dubious look on Nan's face had shaken an already unsteady conviction. But he'd look a fool telling Frank he'd changed his mind, having only just made it up.

A large pig snuffled into the room, staggered into a patron's leg and was nudged away, and dropped onto its side near the hearth, snorting gently. Nobody paid it any attention, except for Nan whose mouth had dropped open in surprise.

'That's Lucy,' said Ned. 'The pub pig. Khalied as usual.'

'Kay-lied?'

'Drunk. She likes her ale but she can't handle much more'n a saucerful.'

Nan's face lit up when she laughed. Ned could watch her all day long. But here came Frank, striding over and dropping a stack of sovereigns onto the tabletop. Ned tore his eyes away from Nan and looked up expectantly. 'I weren't expectin' a donation this quick.'

'Nah, six sovereign wouldn't touch the sides, would it?' Frank fell into his seat, lowered his voice to a whisper and leaned towards Nan, who, to Ned's surprise, moved forward conspiratorially, raking her hair with her fingers to shake some of the thick curls loose. 'It's what I'm due from this place, love.'

Ned sighed. Frank was about to unwittingly confirm Nan's opinion of him.

'Do you work here?' said Nan.

Frank leaned back and roared with laughter. 'No, love. Well, in a sense, aye, I suppose I do. Landlord pays me to stop trouble before it starts.'

Nan leaned an elbow on the table, rested her chin in her hand and regarded Frank with interest. 'Nasty things can happen when protection money isn't forthcoming.'

Frank looked delighted. 'Got it in one, love.'

Ned had heard enough. If he was to accept coin from the Prescotts, the last thing he needed reminding of was this sort of business. He was jealous of the attention Nan was giving Frank, although this was harder to admit to himself. And he didn't like the way Frank looked at her, either.

Ned rose to his feet. 'Think we'll be off, all right, Nan? Before they send out a search party for thee.'

Frank leapt to his feet to pull Nan's chair out. She murmured her thanks. He lifted up the stack of coins, dropped them into his palm and frowned down at them.

'What's up?' said Ned. A suspicion was beginning to form in his mind.

Frank spread the sovereigns on his outstretched palm, three showing the Queen's profile. The stamp of the Royal Arms was face up on the remaining two.

'Must've dropped one,' he muttered, his eyes roving over the carpet.

Ned took advantage of the opportunity to glare at Nan, giving a tight, almost imperceptible, shake of his head. When Frank dropped to his haunches to look under the table, Ned made the gesture for a slit throat. Nan spluttered with laughter that she disguised with a cough.

She turned her back on Ned and bent to examine the green and gold hearth tiles.

'Bleedin' hell,' said Frank, straightening up.

'Here she is.' Nan stood at the same moment, holding the gold coin between thumb and forefinger. Ned let out the breath he had been holding. It was impossible to keep the corners of his mouth from twitching in response to Nan's mischievous smile.

'There you go, Frank,' she said. 'You couldn't see her for looking.'

Chapter 5

Hetty's hand trembled as she picked up the saucer and cup brimming with hot tea. The china rattled when she placed the saucer down on the doily that sat in the centre of the small rosewood tip-table. She had brought out the Sunday tea set for her guest.

'Thank you, Miss Barlow,' said Mrs Calver. 'Goodness. There's no room for milk.'

Hetty had overfilled the cup.

Mrs Calver picked up the saucer, lifted the cup by its dainty handle and blew gently on the contents. 'I sometimes prefer it this way, depending on the strength and flavour of the leaves.' She returned the cup and saucer to the table and leaned forward, her eyes bright in their network of wrinkles. The blue hat she wore was the latest style, small and fitted to the top of her head like a chimney pot, contrasting handsomely with her white chignon. She was a striking woman, and knew it. No widow's weeds for our Mrs Calver.

Hetty smiled enquiringly.

'I've come to help you,' said Mrs Calver. 'We must put our heads together if we are to provide the best care the house can give. You and I have experience of making the most of meagre budgets, wouldn't you agree?'

'I would, aye.' Hetty dropped her gaze, terrified the truth she was hiding must be written on her face. Unlike

Mrs Calver, Hetty had never been matron of a hospital. The common bond this woman thought they shared did not exist.

Hetty clasped her hands in her lap, squeezing her knuckles. Where, now, was the house crisis that on any other occasion she would be called upon to resolve? She had what her mother used to call the guilty jitters. Hetty's experience running a hospital had secured her the job of warden, and it was true she had worked in that environment for many years, but not as the matron she'd claimed to be. Hetty had spent her time on her hands and knees scrubbing floors, beneath the notice of the likes of the woman sitting opposite her now. Matron Calver would have, no doubt, run her hospital along firm but fair lines. She had the authoritative quality about her that had the unfortunate effect of reducing Hetty to a childlike state. She'd never been able to lie to her mother, not even when a lie might have saved – or at least cushioned – her fall from grace.

Hetty had no illusions about what would happen if Mrs Calver discovered the truth. She would be out on her ear, and so would Amelia.

'Miss Barlow?'

Hetty snapped out of the downward spiral of her thoughts. She had vowed to herself that she would remain vigilant in the former matron's company.

'Excuse me, Mrs Calver.'

'I was only remarking that I think it might be an idea to place an advertisement in the newspaper, with a view to resolving the present shortage of clothing and shoes.'

Hetty breathed out. 'P'raps you could come up with the correct wording.'

'Yes, indeed. I understand how exhausting your role here must be. But a woman like you, in her prime, should not look so careworn.'

Careworn? Hetty cleared her throat, at a loss for what to say.

'Forgive me,' said Mrs Calver. 'Tact was never my strong point. I would wish to share some of your burden. That is what I'm trying to say.'

Hetty blinked in surprise when Mrs Calver threw her arms wide in a declamatory manner. 'Open your wardrobes, ladies! Make a bundle of clothes you do not intend to wear again and deliver them to the house. Dresses, linens, boots and bonnets!' She laughed. 'Yes, you can see I've already given this some thought. This should be the text for the advertisement.'

Hetty smiled tightly. 'Then I think I can prob'ly leave it in your capable hands.'

Mrs Calver beamed, then took a sip of her tea. 'This does require milk, after all,' she said. 'No, no, I can manage. So.' Hetty braced herself against Mrs Calver's penetrating gaze. 'You seem preoccupied. I know the work you do here can be highly challenging, and perhaps you feel taken for granted by the trustees.'

'No, no,' said Hetty. Once again, she couldn't think of anything else to say. This woman continually wrongfooted her.

'Believe me when I say,' said Mrs Calver, 'we are fortunate to have someone with your expertise. Our dear Mr Wallace spends most of our time together singing your praises.'

'Does he,' said Hetty faintly. She wondered what *our time together* implied, not that Mr Wallace's doings were any of her business.

'I imagine that dealing with the unfortunate children and ladies here is not so widely separated from dealing with patients.' Mrs Calver took another sip. 'That's better, though rather cold now. I am correct in thinking, you were at a women's hospital, were you not?'

'Aye.' Hetty cleared her throat. 'Yes. Many aspects are similar.' She scrambled for common ground. 'Finding bed spaces can be a challenge.'

Mrs Calver sighed. 'It was ever thus.'

'We are full again, I'm afraid.'

She had steered the conversation onto house matters and was determined that was where it would remain. Hetty told Mrs Calver about that day's arrival, a girl of fourteen who'd been removed from the workhouse and given a live-in job as a domestic in a tavern. On her second night, she'd been told to bed down with a patron or leave the house without pay or references. She had refused, and spent a terrified night in the bedroom she shared with another girl, a chair wedged under the doorknob.

'It was a bawdy house,' said Hetty.

Mrs Calver clucked her tongue and shook her head sorrowfully. 'Poor, poor child.' Her eyes were bright with eagerness. 'What happened next?'

'She ran away, the next morning,' said Hetty, 'and reported them to the police, which was brave of her.'

A wise nod from Mrs Calver. 'Exceptionally brave. And the other girl?'

Hetty shrugged. 'I gather she'd stayed behind. I'm told the couple who run the house have been arrested and it seems our girl will have to give evidence in court. I'll accompany her, or Hope will.'

Sarah Bramhall. Hetty prided herself on never forgetting the name of any of the girls and women who passed through the house. Young Sarah Bramhall had had a poor start in life, but that did not mean she couldn't better herself. Conversely, Hetty had been raised in a loving and secure home, had received a rounded education and had squandered it. She had been the age Amelia was now when her head was turned, and her life changed forever. It would change again if the truth was ever revealed.

'What will happen to her?'

'Pardon me?'

'To the girl you have,' said Mrs Calver. 'What will become of her?'

'Oh. Well, I've told her we'll find her summat, a respectable position, save going back to the workhouse.'

'That poor child.'

'Aye.'

'Well.' Mrs Calver stood, prompting Hetty to get to her feet. 'I shall let you get back to your duties, Miss Barlow.'

'Thank you for calling,' said Hetty.

'It's been pleasant,' said Mrs Calver.

Hetty dutifully nodded her assent. She followed Mrs Calver into the hall, where the older woman hesitated, then turned and took her hand.

'Perhaps we should make this a weekly occasion, where you may enjoy half an hour of peace and conversation?'

'If time permits, that would be grand.'

Hetty dropped the smile that had been fixed to her face as soon as the door closed on Mrs Calver's heels. Her jaw ached from effortful politeness.

And what was that smell, coming from the kitchen?

She had taken two steps down the hall when an ear-piercing scream echoed around the house. What now, and why could it have not come half an hour earlier when the interruption would have been welcomed? Hetty hurried into the kitchen, which was fogged by smoke and the acrid smell of something burnt. As if she had conjured her up via her conversation with Mrs Calver, Sarah Bramhall was kneeling on the floor by the range, her hands tucked under her armpits, tears streaming down her face. What looked like a rock, black and caved in the middle, lay on the hearth tile.

Amelia stood over Sarah, breathing hard. Hetty saw the red mark that covered one side of the girl's face.

'Did you strike her?'

Amelia pressed her lips together. She looked on the verge of tears.

'Go on. Wait in my quarters. I'll come an' see you in a bit.'

Amelia fled, without a word.

Hetty crouched by the girl, who raised her tear-streaked face, pleadingly. 'I din't mean to. Am sorry.' She showed Hetty the palms of her hands. There were angry red marks on the fleshy pad of each thumb and across her fingers. These burns would blister, later, but all things considered it could have been worse.

Hetty got the story from the girl in fits and bursts. Amelia had told her to take out the bread once it was baked but she had been scrubbing the sink and sides in the scullery and forgot all about it until the smell reached her nostrils. She'd rushed into the kitchen at the same time as Amelia, and tripped over her own feet, and ran into Amelia, who walloped her. She'd been so panicked that she spun around and took the tin out of the range with her bare hands. Was the bread all right?

Hetty looked at the blackened loaf. From behind her, there came a peal of laughter.

'It makes a fine piece of coal.'

She looked up to see who had spoken. Nan Turpin was observing the scene from the doorway, with three other residents craning their necks behind her.

'It's about time you made yourself useful,' said Hetty. 'Go to the top shelf in the back of the pantry. There's a square glass bottle with a cork stopper. The label's come off but the stuff inside looks like a layer of custard on top of a layer of chalk. Fetch it here.'

Nan returned moments later and handed over the bottle, pulling a face. 'I wouldn't want to drink that. What's in it?'

Hetty took the bottle from her and gave it a good shake to mingle the contents. 'Lime-water and linseed oil. There should be a roll of lint in that drawer behind you.' She turned to the girl. 'I know it's reight painful but the burns aren't bad.' She uncorked the bottle and shook some of the liquid onto the lint. 'We'll wrap up your hands. Nan here can feed you your tea.'

'I would, gladly, of course, except I won't be here for tea tonight,' said Nan. 'Ned is calling for me.' She crouched beside the girl. 'I'm sorry I laughed, but when you asked about the bread, oh my goodness.' She went off into fresh peals of laughter, raising a tremulous smile from the girl. 'Oh dear. It's tickled me. Well, worse things happen, I'm sure you'll agree.'

'It hurts,' said Sarah Bramhall.

Nan patted her shoulder. 'She might benefit from a nip of whisky.'

'We've none of that, not in this house,' said Hetty. 'Help her upstairs an' then you can clear up the cups and plates in the parlour. An' come an' find me after breakfast in the morning, Nan. Seeing you has reminded me, we need to get you sorted with a proper job if you're goin' to be stayin' on.'

Hetty ignored the scowl on Nan's face and left the room, her pace slowing as she walked down the hallway, wondering how she might discipline – and whether she even ought to – a girl in the deepest throes of grief.

Hetty closed the door to her quarters behind her and leaned against it. She could see Amelia sitting in the ante-chamber, at Hetty's desk, idly leafing through the ledger. Amelia had been only semi-literate when she came to the house. It had been Hope who taught her how to read and write to a higher standard. It was another bone of contention between Hetty and Amelia. Hetty's parents had scrimped and saved to send Hetty to a fee-paying school, an expensive education that had come to naught. Amelia had been kept at home, out of sight, and never told the reason why. How difficult it must have been living with the older women – Hetty's mother and aunt – after her father had died, as a servant to them in all but name. No wonder she railed against her job here. But what choice had Hetty? None, that was the truth of it.

'You shouldn't be readin' that.' She wanted to take the words back as soon as they were out. 'I mean to say, put it away, and come and sit with me.'

Hetty went to the two-seater settee by her bed, wincing at the sound of the ledger being slammed shut and the drawer it was kept in being roughly opened and closed. Amelia stalked in and sat beside Hetty, arms folded.

'I din't mean to hit her,' she said.

'I know, love.' Hetty put her arm around Amelia's shoulders and was grateful the girl allowed it. 'You lashed out. It had nowt to do with Sarah Bramhall.'

'I've got a pain, in here.' Amelia put her hand over her heart. 'When will it go away?'

'I don't know, love.' Hetty sighed. 'But I've been wonderin', how about resuming your duties, in the morning? You need summat to do, and we can't manage without you.'

'You did, though, when I went to Linus.' Amelia stopped, swallowing hard. 'You never liked him.'

The girl's mood changed with the wind. She shrugged off Hetty's arm and went to the window, looking into the square. The late afternoon light was soft against her cheek.

'I gave you my blessing,' said Hetty.

Amelia lifted her shoulders, dropping them with a sigh. 'None o' that matters now.'

'What can I do, to help you?'

'There is summat.' Amelia turned to face her, the halo of light that framed her head making her dark hair blacker. Her features were shadowed, her expression unreadable. 'Summat I've been thinkin' on.'

Hetty smiled encouragingly. 'What is it, love?'

'I know you dislike her, but you have to put that aside. I have to see Auntie Gertie.'

'Gertie?' Hetty said faintly. 'What for?'

'She can help me.' Amelia stepped towards Hetty, until she was standing over her. Her jaw was set. 'She has the gift. I have to hear his voice. He's waitin' for me, I know it.'

Hetty's stomach plunged. She spoke in a whisper. 'No, Amelia. You're not going where Linus has gone.'

Tears poured freely down Amelia's cheeks. She let them fall. 'I'm not sayin' that. You know Auntie Gertie talks to them, the spirits. You've seen her do it.'

'She's a charlatan.'

But Amelia wasn't listening. 'What if Linus has a message for me, an' I don't get to hear it?' She swiped at her cheeks, and swooped like a bird to sit by Hetty and take her hands in fingers that were hot and sticky. Hetty shook her head, her gut twisting in fear. 'Don't say owt, Hetty. For once, listen to me. I'm goin', whether you like it or not.'

Amelia lowered her head onto Hetty's shoulder. Hetty put her arm around the girl and stared into space as Amelia sobbed. Gertie knew the truth, and was malicious enough to speak it, had threatened to speak it the last time Hetty had encountered her. Hetty couldn't allow Amelia anywhere near the malignant crone.

'I mean it, sister.' Amelia choked out the words. 'She'll help me. She's family.'

Hetty squeezed her more tightly. 'Then I'll come too. We can leave Hope in charge for a day or two. We'll organise a trip.'

Amelia raised shining eyes to Hetty's face and smiled weakly. 'He's still close by. I know you don't believe in it, in the spirit plane and all that, but I've seen what she can do wi' my own eyes.'

Hetty risked the truth. 'It's nonsense, love. An act to steal money from the gullible. And your father's sister is not a friend to us.'

'But you'll let me go, an' you'll come too?'

'All right. If you're set on it, all right.'

Amelia sat upright and stared into Hetty's eyes. 'Do you mean it, sister?'

'Aye.' The lie broke her heart. 'Aye, 'a course I do.'

Chapter 6

Nan glanced up at the gas lamp on the corner to confirm she'd reached Gibraltar Street, although reading the lettering painted on a strip of metal beneath the clouded glass lantern wasn't strictly necessary. The three balls of the pawnbroker emblem were already in view, hanging like golden fruit over an entranceway not a hundred yards away.

She entered a small cobbled courtyard through an iron gate that would be kept locked at night to secure the various premises inside, but now stood open. The pawnshop was on her left, the items in its barred window each telling their own tale of poverty and misfortune. Nan passed by the display and pushed down on the handle of the door, which triggered a tinkling bell. The room inside was cluttered and dingily lit and smelled of sweet decay, like dead mice. Behind a none-too-clean glass counter stood a heavyset man who compensated for his bald pate with a pair of fulsome sideburns. He was rubbing a cloth over the rosewood casing of a mantel clock, and paused to acknowledge Nan.

' 'Ey up.'

Nan laid the leather coin purse on the counter. 'How do you do? How much?'

The broker bent to look at it, and peered up at Nan. 'Is this thine?'

She nodded. 'It belonged to my father, rest his soul. We've a plot to pay for.'

The man grunted and picked up the purse. He sniffed at it and felt inside, examining the stitching and the brass clasp. 'It's a nice piece o' work but tha won't get a box nor hearse out o' it.'

Nan shrugged. Whether he believed her story or not was irrelevant. He would either allow her to pawn the purse or send her on her way. By his demeanour and the scruffy state of the shop, she guessed the former.

'I will be returning to collect it in a week's time,' she said.

The man smirked. 'Is that right?'

She decided to take the risk. 'I may, from time to time, have other items I'd wish to leave in your safekeeping, items I'd not be returning to collect.'

The broker lay the purse on the counter between them. 'Hold thee horses, lass. We've not become acquainted yet. For the purse, I'll give thee a shillin' an' sixpence.'

'It's silk-lined and, as you say, finely made. Why not take another look?'

Instead, the man's eyes travelled over the buttons of her blouse, moving up to rest on her mouth, his tongue creeping out to lick the corner of his lower lip, before meeting her eyes. 'Oh, I'm lookin', all right.'

Nan held his gaze.

'All reight. Tha's caught me in a good mood. Two shillin' an' if we're keepin' up the pretence I'll need to tell thee I'll want two an' six back.'

Nan made a moue of disappointment. 'The interest doesn't concern me, but the purse is worth more than that, sir.'

'I say it's not. Why not take the coin an' the ticket an' let's see if we can do a little bit o' business again, eh? Nowt too pricey, though. I don't want tha bringin' in owt that'll come back on me.'

Beggars, as the saying went, could not be choosers. Nan accepted the offer. The pawnbroker went back to polishing the clock after their business was conducted, without offering a farewell.

Rain was spotting the paving stones when she emerged into the courtyard. Amelia had done her a favour by directing her to a less-than-respectable broker, although Nan was certain the girl had simply chosen the nearest establishment to the house. Amelia had shown no interest in Nan's errand, which Nan had been counting on. The warden or her deputy would have pounced on her with their questions. There had been an awkward moment when Nan wrapped across her shoulders the paisley shawl she'd taken to wearing. 'That's mine,' said Amelia. Then she had shrugged and said in a toneless voice: 'Take it. Tha can have it.'

Standing under the shop sign, Nan lifted the shawl to cover her hair and gazed at the crumpled ticket and two shillings in her hand as if the coins might magically multiply. It was time to set off back to the house, before she was missed and questions were asked. First, she ducked into a deserted alleyway to add the shillings to the copper, silver and guineas she was carrying in a tie-on pocket concealed under the folds of her skirt. It was a start.

–

Fourteen-year-old Sarah Bramhall had been found a position in a townhouse as a maid of all work but would remain resident in the House of Help until her probationary period was completed. Another girl – an orphan – was being put on the train to York, to live with distant relatives who had agreed to take her in, while an older woman who had been recuperating from a hospital operation was returning, somewhat reluctantly, to the bosom of her family. A girl called Maisie, a shy creature Nan had passed the time of day with when they had arrived at the House of Help within a day of each other, had been apprenticed to a seamstress in the town. It was a live-in post, and Maisie would also be leaving today.

'The poor girl was brought here by the station porter,' said the deputy warden. 'She ought to have been collected from the train by her employer but there was some confusion over the date. She was left sitting by the platform for hours.'

Nan made a non-committal sound. Hope had cornered her in the porch, where she was holding steady the stepladder Clara the maid stood on, feather duster in one hand, chamois cloth in the other. Nan had been tasked with cleaning the fanlight over the front door and removing cobwebs from the ceiling and coving. She had gone to Clara for help and the maid had agreed it would be quicker to do it herself, if Nan held the ladder for her.

'Still, all's well that ends well,' said Hope. 'We have three empty beds.'

'Not for long, I can tell thee that for nowt,' said Clara, from above. 'We'll soon be full again. Then Miss Barlow'll turn her attention to thee, Nan.'

Nan had the impression the two women were colluding against her. 'I'll be out from under your feet soon enough,' she said. 'There's a cottage for rent on the edge of town, with gas and running water, and it even has a small garden, all for only five shillings a week clear. I've to apply to the agent in Figtree Lane.' She looked over her shoulder at Hope. 'Where is that, do you know?'

Clara snorted. 'How will you afford rent, when you've nowt but the clothes on your back?'

'I believe,' said Hope, 'that Miss Barlow is hoping to set you on the correct path, by finding legitimate work for you, and a good home.'

'Or tha'll end up bein' slung in the workhouse,' said Clara, 'an' still get sent out to slog, but for half the pay and double the shame. And next time tha gets caught thieving I doubt they'll let you back in here. I can't see your beau hangin' about once you're locked up in jail.'

Hope clicked her tongue. 'That's not helpful, Clara.' She turned to Nan. 'Ned seems a steady sort.'

Nan put her hand on her waist, her fingers stroking the material that concealed the coin pouch. 'Oh, you approve, do you? I'm glad I'm doing something right.'

'I catch sight of him every evenin',' said Clara, 'hurryin' into the square to meet his beloved.' She tickled Nan's head with the feather duster. 'Like Romeo and Juliet. Star-crossed lovers.'

Nan laughed and shook the ladder, eliciting a shriek from Clara. 'D'you know where Figtree Lane is, or not?'

'How *will* you afford the rent?' said Hope.

Clara leaned down and spoke in a whisper. 'I don't know about Figtree Lane. I can direct thee to Love Street. Plenty o' beds there but I doubt tha'll get much sleep.'

Nan shook her head. 'And I don't know about you, but I've never had to open my legs to get my way.'

Hope gasped. 'Nan Turpin!'

Clara laughed along with Nan. 'Good thing Miss Barlow's not in earshot.' She climbed down from the ladder. 'Well, I've still the lavatory to clean. Tha can take the ladder back to the scullery for me, Nan.' She continued to mutter as she walked away. 'At least the rain's cleared off so as I can hang the washin' out. Bouncing down it were, before.'

Left facing Hope, Nan held up a hand. 'I've looked after myself for the past ten years,' she said. 'Alone, for the most part. I'm answerable to nobody and I've no intention of toiling my life away in the service of others. I'm due to come into some money—'

'But I thought you had no people.'

'—and then I'll find accommodation and I'll trouble you no further.'

Hope rubbed at her forehead. 'It's not a trouble, having you here, Nan. We only want to help.'

'I know that and I'm so grateful I was brought here, instead of being locked up.' Nan took the middle rung of the ladder in her hands and lifted it up, creating a barrier between the two women. Hope stepped back, flattening herself against the wall to allow Nan into the hallway. 'I'm not one of your causes, Hope. As I say, I can look after myself.'

Hope spoke quietly as Nan walked away. 'You've stolen money.'

'A little,' she said, keeping her voice light, and whispered, once she was out of earshot, 'not quite enough, yet.'

–

Set back from the road and positioned beside a small copse, the gentleman's residence was an architectural hodgepodge, like a church that thought it was a castle, or vice versa. Elaborate stonework framed the leaded panes of arched windows on either side of a large, blocky porch. A raised turret on one corner gave the building a lopsided look. Standing at the foot of an expanse of sloping lawns halved by a wide gravel path, she counted four tall brick chimneys. Idle wisps of smoke rose from one of them.

She set off up the path at a brisk pace, her hair tied back tightly under a mop-cap that was covered by a grey, crocheted shawl, hiding her face. She wore a plain cotton dress over a chemise, petticoats and stockings, and boots, all borrowed from the House of Help's clothes donation box. Her own dress and undergarments were being cleaned, and it was her intention to leave the house as soon as she had them back. The garment she was wearing had no pockets but she had her linen tie-on with her collected hoard safely tucked inside it. The boots were a poor fit and, after nearly an hour's walk, she was limping in discomfort. This suited her ends, as a limp would feature in any description, should she be witnessed.

The edge of a stable block was visible behind the house, and she caught a flash of movement. A boy was brushing down a horse, his back to her. She kept her head down and hurried on towards the house. The front door stood ajar, revealing a wedge of red and yellow mosaic tiling. She pushed the door wider with the tips of her fingers and stepped onto the tile.

A cloaked figure stood in the corner. She had taken a sharp breath and a step backwards before the figure coalesced into a hat-stand. Wrapping her hand around the handle of the inner door, she looked for movement beyond the opaque glass. Everything was still. The door opened silently on well-oiled hinges.

She stepped onto the polished, mahogany flooring of the lobby and drew a folded piece of newspaper from her sleeve, a politely enquiring smile playing at the corners of her mouth. The walls were similarly decorated in dark wood and gave the space a closed-in and foreboding aspect. On the wall at the top of a red-carpeted staircase hung a larger-than-life-size portrait of a scholarly looking man sitting at an escritoire, pen in hand, gazing haughtily at the observer. This was indeed a gentleman's residence with no evidence of a woman's touch, exactly what she'd anticipated. The advertisement in the *Sheffield Telegraph* had helpfully spelled it out. A banker lived here alone, with a small staff. His household had advertised a vacancy for a maid of all work, a live-out position as the gentleman of the house valued his privacy. The hours were six o'clock in the morning to seven o'clock in the evening, six days a week, and the position would suit a young, strong girl not afraid of hard work.

She stood perfectly still, the scrap of paper containing the newspaper advertisement in her hand, and waited to see whether anybody would come. Finally, she moved forward slowly across the hall. An open door to her left revealed a dining room, dominated by a round mahogany table. A silver epergne sat in the middle of the table. She allowed herself a brief smile, imagining smuggling a five-foot-high centrepiece that must be worth at least a hundred pounds into the House of Help, unnoticed. She moved on. The door to the room beside the dining room was closed, as were the two doors on the opposite side of the lobby. No sounds came from within. Narrow corridors on either side of the staircase led towards the back of the house, ending in an uncarpeted flight of stairs leading down on one side and a closed door on the other.

She walked down the corridor that led to the closed door and knocked gently on it. There was no call to enter from within. She twisted the knob.

The door opened onto a study. Her lips widened into a genuine smile. She had struck lucky and would not need to investigate the upstairs rooms, where her presence would be impossible to explain. The study was in an orderly state and contained a desk, a leather chair on casters, drawers, book shelves and a wall clock with a gold face, beneath which a pendulum swung gently. *Tick, tick, tick.* The grate was cold, the mantelpiece bare other than a pair of empty brass candlesticks. Glancing through one of the two windows, careful not to disturb the thick velvet drapes, her heart rate accelerated. The view was of the stables but there was no sign now, of the boy. She would have preferred to know where he was. The field behind the stables was dotted with sheep, the shadow of a cloud scudding across it.

She had reached the point of no return. Taking a deep breath, she strode over to the desk. She found the bankroll in the bottom drawer on the left side. These gentlemen were so much more predictable than they believed themselves to be. She unrolled the slim rubber band from the tube of paper and fanned out Bank of England five-pound and one-pound notes. She let out a low whistle, withdrew three five-pound notes and four one-pound notes, rolled up the rest, replaced the band and tucked the roll back into the corner of the drawer. From the desk, she picked up a silver letter opener, wrapped it in the notes and slipped the package into her sleeve. A gold fob watch on a delicate chain lay on the blotter. She examined the face and held it to her ear. It was exquisite. What would Ned say if she presented this watch to him? She smiled at the thought. He'd have conniptions.

His friend, Frank Prescott, would have no such qualms about accepting stolen goods. She'd encountered many Franks in her time, had tricked some of them, as she'd tried to get the better of Frank by stealing a sovereign from him. She smiled again, recalling Ned's horrified expression, the set to his handsome jaw, the appeal in those large brown eyes. He seemed vulnerable in a way that made her want to protect him from the world. And reticent too. Before the tram had run away with them, she had rested her hand on the bench between their bodies, certain he would take it, and would interlace his fingers with hers. He hadn't.

A scraping sound from above, like a chair being moved, shook her from her reverie. She couldn't afford to have Ned invade her thoughts, not at times like this when she needed all her wits about her. Moving quickly, she laid the watch back on the blotter – its disappearance would be too obvious – and flipped open the lid of a blue lacquered snuff box. It was empty, obviously an ornamental item. The snuff box went up the same sleeve as the letter opener wrapped in bank notes. She tightened the cuff of her blouse.

It was time to leave.

She was a few steps from the front door when the sound of laughter came from the floor above. Stopping and turning, she once again arranged her features into those of a humble girl looking for work. The sound of male voices drifted down. It might be wishful thinking but the conversation seemed to come from the back of the house, rather than one of the rooms at the front, where she might be observed leaving. Walking backwards, she opened the door to the porch and slipped through, closing it gently behind her. She remained on the front doorstep for a moment, debating whether to make her presence known, in which case she'd have to go through the rigmarole of pretending she was there to apply for the job, or take a risk.

She took a risk.

Her feet crunched on the gravel as she walked, shoulders deliberately stooped, away from the house. The back of her neck prickled in anticipation of a shout, or the thud of pounding boots. She bit her lip, and breathed in quick pants, preparing for an encounter. *I saw the advertisement for the job, in the newspaper, but, oh sir, this house is too big. It daunted me. I'm sorry to have troubled you.*

But there was nothing.

On the street, a group of boys hung from the limbs of a pear tree behind a low stone wall. They looked alarmed as she approached and began clambering down. Nan laughed and held up her hands. 'Throw me one here and let's agree to say I haven't seen you thieving.'

It was the juiciest pear she'd ever tasted.

Chapter 7

Ned stepped around a lumpy sack of spuds propped against the wall like a drunk. Just beyond the potato dealer's premises was Gebhardt's pork shop, its interior obscured by a curtain of marbled meat hanging from hooks behind the window. Frank had assured him there would be something to eat at the coffee house but Ned didn't half fancy one of the butcher's famous pork and apple pies. His stomach rumbled loudly in agreement. He'd gone back to his lodgings after work to put on a clean shirt and collect the satchel his cousin had given him. It contained documents pertaining to their new business venture but wearing it across his body made him feel like one of the hapless conductors from the runaway tram.

The Workman's Rest cocoa and coffee house was another five hundred yards or so along the wide slope of Pond Street. The meeting was to take place there to cater for the senior Frank Prescott's sensitivities. The man was a teetotaller. Frank liked to tell everybody this meant his father never forgot a kindness – or a slight. And here Frank junior stood, waiting for Ned outside the door to the coffee house. The two men greeted each other and Ned followed Frank inside, into what looked like a regular ground-floor saloon with a constellation of tables around a central bar. Most of these were occupied by groups of men whose chatter and pipe smoke curled and eddied around the room.

Ned looked around. 'Where's Mr Prescott then?'

'He's upstairs,' said Frank, 'in the news room, keepin' abreast o' the town's doings. He'll be back in two shakes.'

He left Ned sitting at a table, returning a few minutes later with mugs of coffee. He disappeared again and came back with plates of ham sandwiches and pickled eggs.

'Ta,' said Ned. He would be buying that pork pie on the way home. Maybe two. He might even pop into the Blue Pig for a pint of porter, as the hour would be too late to walk up to Paradise Square. He'd only be sent away by the warden with a flea in his ear. Tomorrow was Saturday and he'd arranged to call on Nan during the afternoon, after he'd finished work. Any free time spent away from Nan seemed like time wasted, including this meeting with Frank and his father. But if it went according to plan, tomorrow he would be taking Nan to see the forge. He intended to ask her whether she could see herself living in a cottage on the riverbank, a nice spot where the burbling waters of the Rivelin and Loxley met before joining the sluggish brown flow of the Don. She'd never again need to thieve to survive. Ned would look after her.

' 'Ey up, son.' Frank Prescott senior pulled out a chair and sat beside Ned, jerking him from his reverie.

' 'Ow do, Mr Prescott.' Ned half-rose and shook the man's outstretched hand. Frank's father was a slender, fox-faced man, and the butt of a long-standing joke about his son's parentage – not that anybody would ever suggest this to the man's face.

Mr Prescott sent Frank to fetch more coffee and sat back, munching on the pickled egg he'd filched from

Ned's plate. He looked around the room and back at Ned. 'Tell me what tha's thinkin' then.'

Ned sat up straight. It seemed they were getting down to business straightaway.

'Well, first off, I'm grateful to thee for…'

'Nah.' Mr Prescott cut him off. He twirled his finger in the air. 'This place. Honest opinion.'

'Oh.' Ned made a show of looking around. 'Seems all right. Busy enough. Ah, here comes Frank.'

'It's sandwiches and the like down 'ere but there's a proper dining room upstairs, an' a news room—'

'Aye, Frank mentioned tha were reading the papers.'

Mr Prescott frowned at the interruption. '—*And* a mission room. It's been set up by the church an' will help fund our Lord's work in the parish.'

Ned felt a nod of approval was required.

Mr Prescott smiled. 'Don't worry, lad. I'm not expectin' thee to start prayin' on tha knees. All this,' he gestured around the room, 'is to the betterment of the working man. Coffee house is as good a name as any, eh? Nob'dy would come if they thought they were steppin' inside a church.'

Frank set down the mugs and laughed. 'Ned's thinkin' this'll never compete wi' the Blue Pig or the Castle when you're lookin' to quench yer thirst. An' I can't see many like him trottin' upstairs for a prayer session, neither.'

What Ned was really thinking was that Mr Prescott had deliberately put him in his place by letting him know there was a restaurant upstairs. They could have eaten there, but the message was clear. Ned had come with his begging bowl and would have to make do with saloon bar pickings.

Mr Prescott jabbed his finger at Frank, who recoiled. 'Tha'd do well to lay off the liquor, an' all.' He turned back to Ned. 'There's plenty that need a rest from the wife's naggin' but do they want to squander all their hard-earned coin in a public house, losin' their senses and gettin' in fights? Nah.'

'I do,' said Frank, too quietly for his father to hear. Ned hid his smile behind his coffee mug.

'Nah,' repeated Mr Prescott. 'They can come 'ere instead. Save their coin an' their temper.'

'Aye, reight enough,' said Ned. If he had Nan waiting for him after a hard day's graft, he wouldn't want to be anywhere but at home. He took a swallow of coffee. This bitter stuff was no match for a pint of porter, either.

'Our Frank says you've a lass on the go. Would I know her?'

Ned shook his head. 'She's new to the town, but aye.' He found he couldn't keep the daft smile off his face. 'She's a reight lovely girl.' He wouldn't say any more, not to these men, would not tell them how completely Nan had captured his heart. They'd only scoff. He certainly wouldn't be admitting that they'd gone no further than hand-holding and kissing, like lovestruck kids. The resulting teasing would be unendurable.

Mr Prescott let out a low whistle. 'A man who swore off women, an' all. She must be summat special. But dun't tha want to find theesen a good Sheffield lass, instead of somebody tha knows nowt about?'

So Frank had told him that too. Nan's past was a closed book. Ned wished it weren't so and did not want to be reminded of it.

Frank leaned forward, mischief in his eyes. 'Our Ellie's still moonin' over thee, Ned.'

So tha keeps sayin', thought Ned. He glanced uncomfortably at Frank's father but his eyes were on the satchel that lay on the table between them. Mr Prescott clapped his hands.

'Reight then, lad. Let's see what we can do for each other, eh?'

—

Two women were reclining on the steps of the House of Help, eyes closed, their faces turned towards the sun. One he recognised as Clara the maid, her hand resting lightly on the handle of a sweeping brush. The other, leaning back on her elbows, he'd never seen before. She sighed deeply, stretching her neck like a cat.

Ned peered into the bucket of soapy water between them. 'Don't work theesens into an early grave, now,' he said.

Clara's eyes snapped open. She gave Ned a relieved smile. 'Cheeky beggar.'

The other woman shaded her face and looked him up and down. 'Aren't you a sight for sore eyes. Warden's not in.'

'Aye, I'd say that's evident.'

Clara got to her feet. 'What did I tell thee, Molly? Can't get two minutes peace around here.' She turned to go into the house. 'You'll be wantin' Nan. I've not seen 'er today. I'll go an' look.'

'Reight enough.' He grinned, barely able to contain the joy which must surely be written all over his face. He had been promised the loan, although the interest and ongoing protection payments – hinted at, but not spelled out – would be an elephant on his back. Mr Prescott had further suggested there might be times when Ned, and Jacob too, would be required to turn a blind eye to certain, as-yet unspecified events. Best not to think about that. It might ruin his mood. Bar the paperwork, he and his cousin were owners of their own forge, making him an attractive prospect for the woman he was determined to win over, and marry.

The mousy-haired girl named Molly was observing him, a speculative look on her freckled face. 'Somebody's in a fine mood.'

'Aye. So what's your story, love? D'you work here, or are you bein' looked after, like Nan?'

'Hidin' out, I s'pose you could say. The brute I'm married to put me in the infirmary this time, an' I were advised to come 'ere while he's tried on account of him still bein' at home an' me havin' a smart mouth. Homeless is better n' dead.'

'Ah.' Ned scuffed his boot against the step. 'Lovely day, in't it?' he said.

Molly laughed. 'I'd say so, aye.'

He felt sorry for this poor lass sitting in his shadow, but he couldn't think of anything to say to her.

She squinted up at him. 'Nan's gone, tha knows.'

'Eh?' A finger of unease crept up his spine. 'Gone out, tha means?'

Molly stood, smoothing her hands down her apron. 'No. Gone for good. Scarpered. She's a fiery creature, that one. Get yer fingers burned wi' her.'

'She's expectin' me, though.' Ned peered through the open door into the deserted hallway, reluctant to enter a domain where he'd been forbidden. 'Clara would've said summat.'

'Clara never 'eard her havin' a go at the warden. I did.'

'What happened?'

'It were reight after breakfast an' she took herself off.'

'Why?'

The girl shuffled along the step, away from him. 'You're in my sun.' She turned her face up to the sky.

'Never mind the sun.' Ned struggled to keep his voice level. 'What did she say?'

The girl shrugged. 'That she'd rather be livin' on the street than be somebody's slave. Miss Barlow had found her a place at the training school. That's what kicked it off. Off she ran.'

He'd never find her. She was gone from his life as suddenly as she'd entered it.

'Did she say owt… did she mention me?'

A soft chuckle in Ned's ear made him gasp. He spun around. Nan stood there. Without thinking, he clutched her upper arms, as he had the day they'd met to prevent them tumbling to the ground together. She smiled up at him, and he knew she was recalling that moment too.

'Unhand me, sir,' she said.

He didn't. 'I thought you'd scarpered.'

'Like you told me to? Do you remember?' She dropped her voice an octave. '*Best scarper, love.*'

Ned laughed. He wanted to kiss her. He would have, too, if Molly hadn't been watching the pair of them. 'Is that what I said?'

He released her and Nan took both his hands in hers. 'I'd never go without saying goodbye to you.'

Ned frowned. This was not exactly what he wanted to hear.

Molly piped up. 'But tha told…'

Nan looked over Ned's shoulder at the girl. 'I exchange cross words with Miss Barlow every single morning. You were hearing it for the first time, is all.' She turned back to Ned. 'I am leaving this house, in a day or two. But I'm staying in town. I've found a cottage.'

He squeezed her fingers. 'I've got a different proposal,' he said, 'if tha'll hear me out.'

–

Nan went along happily with his suggestion they walk the two and a half miles north-west to reach the forge. The two of them strolled downhill from Paradise Square, past the tall brick façades of factories, shops and tenements on West Bar and Gibraltar Street, and on to Infirmary Road, where he took Nan's hand to guide her across a busy intersection, her fingers slender and warm entwined in his. For a few moments, until a man walking briskly in the opposite direction came between them, they walked hand-in-hand and for Ned everything dropped away – the sights, the smells, the noise of the street – and all he was aware of was the touch of her skin against his.

His grandmother had always said that walking without purpose – without an end destination – was a waste of energy, but Ned could have strolled along all day long with Nan beside him, even if they hadn't the forge to see. He had never really explored the hills and crags that flanked the town on all sides and decided that one day soon he would take Nan to High Stones, where they could look down on the landscape spread beneath their feet and plan their future together.

He smiled at her. 'Want to hear summat?'

She tilted her head. 'Of course.'

'I were wi' Mr Prescott yesterday, an' he told me he'd heard a description of this town, an' it stuck wi' him.'

'What was it?'

'That it's a mucky picture in a golden frame.'

Nan laughed. 'It's mucky, no question about that. So tell me, where's the gold?'

'Soon be in my pocket.'

Nan wrinkled her nose. 'So you're accepting a loan from him, from Frank's father?'

'Aye, looks that way. He's not all bad, tha knows.'

Nan bit her lip. 'I'll have to take your word for that. Still, it's a shame to be beholden to people like that.'

They walked on in silence for a few minutes. Ned decided to keep to himself the information that both Frank junior and Frank senior had served time for petty offences, that they supplied men when somebody needed a warning, and guns when more than a warning was required. Nan had cottoned on quickly to the fact that the family extorted money from publicans on the pretext of keeping premises safe. It was best she remained innocent of their other rackets.

'Wonder if a man like Mr Prescott might have known Charles Peace?' said Nan.

'Charlie Peace?' Ned frowned. 'We all know of 'im. Notorious, he were. Long dead and gone, now.'

'Does he have any family remaining, I wonder?'

'None that'd admit to it, although Frank reckons his father and Charlie were thick wi' each other. Peace were hanged, tha knows, nine year since. Murder. You'd 'av been a little kid at the time.'

'Sixteen.'

'Tha can't 'av known him, surely? He moved about a bit.'

'No, I never did.'

'So why's tha so interested in him? Good riddance to bad rubbish, I say.'

'No reason. One of the women at the house was talking about him, that's all.' Nan rubbed her nose. 'I've caught the sun, I think. Tell me about this forge.'

'All right, I will.' Ned reclaimed Nan's hand. 'I hope tha'll love it as much as I do.'

A mile on, he steered Nan off the gentle incline of Infirmary Road, and up and down a series of short, steeper roads flanked by cottages and small shops. He bought bottles of ale from a beer-house on the corner of Thoresby Road and breadcakes and cheese from a grocer's shop. They sat on a low stone wall to eat, looking down at the smoke that rose from the lead mills, saw grinders and iron forges lining the banks of the Rivelin and Loxley rivers where the two rivers converged. Nan took off the straw bonnet she was wearing and tucked curls that had escaped from her braid behind her ears. She exclaimed over the pink blossoms falling from a nearby cherry tree but Ned couldn't tear his gaze away from her face. Nothing else in nature was as fine.

She smiled at him. 'Is it always this lovely in spring?'

'Aye.' Ned grinned. 'Wi'out fail.'

He jumped down from the wall and offered his arm. They walked down the hill via Watersmeet Road to the foot of the valley, where the sound of rushing water competed with the chug and clang of the metal industries. These factories were the smaller cousins of the mighty behemoths in the middle of the town. Ned had explained to Nan that he and his cousin had purchased a thriving business from an anvil maker whose ill health had forced him to retire. The man had no sons and intended to spend the proceeds of the sale on a little house in Scarborough, right on the shore, with a skiff to row across the bay. Ned and his cousin had agreed this sounded like a fine life, and when did he intend leaving for the coast?

He led Nan through a set of iron gates and down a grassy path carpeted in daisies and dandelions. A short distance away, two men were guiding a wagon and horses into the middle of a cobbled yard fringed by brick and stone buildings. Ned raised a hand in greeting and the men doffed their caps in return.

'We're makin' anvils, vices, sledge hammers,' he told her. 'But I'm takin' thee to look at summat else before I show thee round the works.'

He'd rehearsed what he wanted to say but now his mind was as blank as a freshly whitewashed wall. Too quickly, they emerged into a well-kept garden that sloped down to the river in one direction and up towards an ivy-covered cottage with a red-painted door in the other. Two wrought-iron chairs sat on a small brick patio, facing the river. Early potato and cabbage leaves grew from a raised vegetable bed below the patio. Climbing roses tangled up the sides and over the top of a pergola built around a sundial on a metal plinth.

'My goodness!' Nan skipped towards the cottage over the flagstone path. She stopped when she reached the patio and looked back at Ned, hands on her hips. 'This is lovely, isn't it? Does this belong to you now?'

Ned ambled towards her, a casual gait that belied the churning of his gut and gave him a few moments to get his thoughts in order. Nan was looking at him expectantly, waiting for his answer, before seeming to realise that something was up. She sat on one of the wrought-iron chairs and he dropped into the other and coughed nervously into his fist. He didn't know how to start. The one thing he was sure of was that he was going to make a hash of it.

Nan looked around the garden and at the walls of the cottage behind her before her eyes came to rest on his face. Ned smiled weakly. The silence grew.

'Do you remember,' said Nan, eventually, 'you told Miss Barlow it was a ring I dropped, that day we met? She asked me where it was the other day, and I had no answer for her.' She laughed. 'It's not often I'm caught out like that.'

Ned let out the breath he'd been holding. 'Tha dun't seem too concerned.'

'Oh, I'm not.' She examined the back of her left hand, flexing her fingers. 'What sort of ring might it have been?'

Ned gulped. He cleared his throat and scratched his head and wished the ground would swallow him up.

Nan said: 'Once I'd collected myself, I told her I'd pawned it.'

'Did she believe that?'

Nan shrugged. 'It's of no account.'

'Would tha wear a ring I gave to thee?' He blurted it out, as good as proposed to her, and he cursed himself for not giving the speech he'd had in mind, when he'd had a mind to think with.

Nan folded her hands in her lap, her eyes lowered. 'I might consider it.'

The words tumbled out. 'I know tha's allus looked after theesen. I'm askin' whether tha'd allow me to look after thee. We'd have a good life here, Nan.' She looked up at him, offering a glimpse of those blue eyes through her lashes. He rushed on. 'Tha'll have a maid, an' a washer-woman comin' in. A bunch of bairns to keep thee busy. There'll be no need for the thievin' and the lyin'.'

Nan frowned. 'I beg your pardon?'

'Don't get the monk on. Aren't you ready to stop runnin' from place to place?'

'How many bairns?'

Ned laughed. 'As many as tha wants.'

She surprised him by getting up and clamping her hands on his shoulders, lowering her head so she could look directly into his eyes. 'I'm not like your friend Mr Prescott. I only take from those who can afford to give.'

'They're not givin' though, are they?' He stared into her depthless eyes. It didn't matter to him, the life she'd led before. *Then shut yer trap, lad.* 'Not willingly.' He couldn't seem to stop his mouth.

'I can't tell which it is, Ned. Are you picking a fight with me?' She leaned closer, so that when she spoke again their lips were tantalisingly close. 'Or are you asking me to marry you? Which is it?'

He had only to lean forward a fraction of an inch for their lips to meet. Hers were warm and soft and parted gently as their kiss deepened. Ned put his hands on her waist, moving his fingers over her narrow back and into her hair, as her grip on his shoulders tightened and a soft moan escaped her throat.

After a few moments, he pulled away, and cleared his throat. 'The second one.'

Chapter 8

All the residents had taken their turn trying on the beautifully soft cape and all agreed, even the warden, somewhat grudgingly, that the vibrant green suited Nan best. She had prevailed on Amelia to braid her hair into an intricate crown on top of her head and one of the younger girls had gasped when she'd put the cape around her shoulders and told her she looked like a princess.

Nan watched as Clara folded the garment carefully back into the trunk of donated clothing. The maid said, with a sigh: 'Who'd give up such a lovely thing?'

'Well, none of you lot should be seen gadding about in that,' said Miss Barlow, 'lookin' like we've money to spare to dress like peacocks.'

Hope nodded thoughtfully. 'I imagine it might come in useful to loan out for an occasion where one of us might wish to impress our company.'

'I don't like it,' said Amelia. Nan realised she was the only woman in the room who had declined the opportunity to try it on. 'Green is bad luck and I've already had enough o' that.'

Miss Barlow pinched the bridge of her nose. 'Nan, perhaps you'll help Clara lift the trunk up to the attic. Hope can sort through the contents later, if you will.'

'Of course,' said Hope. She tapped her chin with one finger. 'You know, I wonder if we can make a dress from that cape, something more practical for one of our younger residents?'

'Or gift it for a wedding present,' said Nan. Everyone turned to look at her. 'I've accepted Ned's proposal. We're getting married.'

Hope kissed her. 'That's wonderful news, Nan.'

Surrounded by women congratulating her, only Nan saw Amelia slip from the room. Typically, it was the warden who restored order and dashed Nan's hopes.

'The clothing is donated to the house,' she said, 'for those that are in need. I'm not sure you qualify now.'

'You're right, of course,' said Nan. 'I wasn't serious. I just wanted to let you all know that I'm getting married, and we will have a wedding party to which you're all invited.'

This set them all chattering again. Nan stood in the centre of the group, a warm glow in her belly. She could see herself settling down with Ned, having a family. She wanted to have children, despite, or perhaps because of, her own miserable childhood. But a new life here would be on her terms and they did not include the Prescott family. She would extricate Ned from those dealings the only way she knew how. When the room began to empty, Nan went to the mirror that hung on the wall above the mantelpiece. Perhaps Amelia would recreate this style for her wedding day. It flattered her long neck and high cheekbones. Although today, of course, that wasn't the point of it at all. Today this elaborate style would serve a different purpose.

Miss Barlow came up beside her and the two women exchanged looks through the mirror. The warden was a dozen years older than Nan and it showed in the fine lines that fanned out from the corners of her eyes, and in the slight softening of her jaw. She was a handsome woman who, in Nan's opinion, could do with un-pursing those lips from time to time. She had barely completed the thought when Miss Barlow's mouth curved into a smile.

'You'll have to be careful a bird doesn't mistake that for its nest,' she said.

Nan tilted her head from side to side, and was satisfied the style would hold. Amelia had done a good job. 'I fancy it looks more like a crown,' she said.

'Oh, aye, so you're royalty now.' The disapproving look had returned. 'I do know you think an honest day's work is beneath you. You haven't lifted a finger in all the time we've had you. How will you manage married to a furnaceman?'

'Ned is starting up his own business,' said Nan, watching through the mirror as Amelia came into the room and walked towards them. 'We'll have help.'

'I can just see you dishin' out orders to a lady's maid,' said Miss Barlow.

'Leave her alone, sister,' said Amelia. She tried to smile at Nan. 'Sorry I disappeared when I should've been congratulating you.'

Nan embraced her, feeling the sharpness of her shoulder blades beneath the thin material of her blouse. 'You need to look after yourself, my love.'

Amelia had rejected Nan's offer to wash and style her hair in return for the favour she had done Nan. It hung down her back in a loose, greasy plait. Nan saw the pain and helplessness in the warden's eyes when her gaze shifted to Amelia. It gave Nan a moment's pause. She needed Amelia's company on the jaunt she had planned but did not want to add to the girl's burden. Hopefully, the role she had assigned to Amelia would never come to light.

'Amelia and I are going to walk down to Market Place,' she told the warden. 'Do you need us to fetch anything back?'

'Are we?' said Amelia. She glanced out of the window. 'It's raining.'

'A brief squall,' said Nan. 'And already nearly blown over.'

The warden smiled encouragingly at Amelia. 'She wants to show off your work, and I have to say that you could use the fresh air, love.'

Nan turned from the mirror to hide her smile of satisfaction. She was going to do something for Ned. He had told her he wanted to look after her, and she had been overwhelmed by his words, and by the kisses they had shared and the barely controlled hunger in his eyes. She'd come to this town in search of her past, looking for family ties that might be stronger than the ones she'd severed ten years earlier. What she had unexpectedly found was Ned.

She was going to show him that they would only ever need to rely on one another. Were her days of roaming and living on her wits really behind her? The idea made her stomach squirm. She did not know whether this was in anticipation of a new, settled life, or whether she lived in fear of it.

'I'll meet you outside,' she told Amelia. 'Just give me five minutes.'

Nan enjoyed the look of surprise on Amelia's face when she emerged from the house wearing the green cape. Hope had been easily persuaded, and Nan had needed a few moments only to make the necessary adjustments to the lining of the cape. She would be able to carry more than she had planned. And she had been correct about the squall, which added to her feeling of invincibility. All would be well.

Nan's heartbeat quickened when they walked onto the high street and turned towards the striped awnings that stretched into the distance, shading shop fronts and all but a thin strip of the pavement on the south side of Market Place. What treasures were concealed beneath those cotton canopies. The fancier awnings had scalloped edges stencilled with the proprietor's name and trade – hosiers, tea emporiums, toy shops and jewellers. The pavements were crowded with pedestrians, the road busy with carriages, carts and barrows, and every nook and corner noisy with the shouts of costermongers.

The breeze that had chased away the rain now carried the peppery scent of a nearby herb seller's tray to her nose. A tendril of hair blew onto her cheek and she touched her head, gingerly. Amelia, just ahead, had stopped to chat to a woman with grey hair and a rounded back who was perched on one of the long wooden handles of a two-wheeled barrow. The barrow was laden with a jumble of second-hand shoes and boots. A barefoot boy stood nearby, his eyes on Nan. He was wearing a too-tight jacket and filthy scarf. The left leg of his trousers flapped open like a wound, a rip running from thigh to calf. The boy didn't return Nan's smile but accepted the coin she offered and held it in his clenched fist. She came abreast with Amelia and they walked on.

'That woman stayed at the house a bit,' said Amelia. 'Her bloke's a bad 'un, bashes her about, but she's gone back to 'im. He's on the ale while she does his day's work for 'im.'

'She should leave him,' said Nan.

'Sometimes that's easier said than done.' Amelia sighed. 'Oh dear. I sound like my sister.'

They passed a straggly-bearded man leaning against the wall outside a tavern, playing his grubby fingers over a wooden whistle. A dog lay beside him with a bowl between its paws. Nan took another coin from the seam pocket of her dress and dropped it into the bowl.

Amelia turned to look at her, frowning. 'You're free wi' the donations today.'

Nan grinned. 'I'm in a generous mood.' She put her hand inside her bodice, where her linen tie-on pocket was secured, and came out with a piece of paper that she unfolded into a one-pound note, enjoying the amazement on Amelia's face.

'Did Ned gi' you that?'

'Where else would I get it?'

In a flash, she was back in the hallway of the mansion, listening to men's laughter from overhead. It was entirely possible that the gentleman who dwelled there remained ignorant of her intrusion. Nan had learned what could be safely taken, and how much, so that burglary would not be her victim's first thought. She imagined the man seated at his desk, wondering where he had mislaid his letter opener, which was now in the pawnshop in Gibraltar Street, keeping his snuff box company. Perhaps a suspicion might form in his mind, and he might reach down to open the drawer of his desk, and, spying the roll of banknotes still in place, close the drawer again, satisfied.

Nan tucked her arm through Amelia's. 'It's my intention to buy Ned a gift, a wedding gift.'

Amelia dropped her head. 'You're lucky to 'av him.'

Nan nodded solemnly. 'I am. And I'll be leaving you. Today.'

'What?' Amelia looked up. 'Goin' to live over the brush with him?'

'We'll be married soon enough. Why wait?'

'I can imagine what my sister would have to say about that.'

Nan patted Amelia's arm. 'I'm jesting, of course. Ned won't hear of it. He says he won't have people gossiping about me.'

'So where're you goin'?'

'The cottage at the forge. Ned will stay in his lodgings until we're wed.' Nan steered Amelia across the road. 'You'll come and visit, and we'll find you a new fiancé, my love. A blacksmith, perhaps, to put a bit of fire in your belly.' Amelia shook her head, but she was smiling. 'Now, let's take a look in here.'

A bell tinkled when Nan pushed open the door to the jeweller's shop. It was quiet inside, the sole customer a woman wearing a pale linen dress, a matching parasol hooked over her arm. She was turning over in her hands a silver calling-card holder, debating with the bald, bespectacled man behind the counter whether she ought to purchase it. He murmured that her husband would think it a fine gift, particularly if she had it personally engraved for only a small additional cost. He looked up briefly to smile a welcome at the two women, then returned his attention to his customer. Nan was aware of Amelia hanging back, near the door, as Nan walked slowly around the room, stopping to peer at this or that, waiting for the customer to complete her purchase and leave.

After the woman had paid for the card holder, and left it with the jeweller to be engraved, Nan approached the counter and drew out a one-pound note. She glanced at Amelia, wondering why she was so reticent in coming forward. Nan ignored the finger of doubt that crept up her spine and lay the note on the glass counter.

'I'd like to purchase a small token to thank my dearest friend Amelia,' – she saw Amelia's head jerk up – 'for taking such good care of me. Perhaps a tasteful decoration for her beautiful dark hair? What do you have?'

Amelia raised an eyebrow but came forward when the jeweller went to a cupboard and lifted out trays of hair combs and slides, arranging them neatly on the countertop, and obediently bent her head to pore over the trinkets. 'Here you are, my dear,' the jeweller said to her, 'I'm sure you'll find something to admire.'

Nan walked over to a display of cufflinks and selected a silver pair inset with garnet stones. She put the box on the counter beside the trays. 'A wedding gift for my fiancé,' she explained.

The jeweller nodded and placed the box on the ledge of a metal cash register. 'Of course.'

'Take your time, Amelia,' said Nan. 'Find something beautiful. You deserve it.'

'No hurry at all,' said the jeweller.

Amelia nodded. 'All right, then. Thank you.'

Nan watched her return her attention to the trays, lifting out a comb decorated with a small enamel butterfly, then wandered to the window and peered outside. 'I think we're in for more rain,' she said. She folded her hands inside the green cape. 'I wonder if our warm spell is over for a while.'

The jeweller nodded absently and continued to watch Amelia's fingers hover over the trays.

Nan remained standing by the low brass rail that separated the window display from the rest of the shop. She leaned forward, ostensibly examining the cloudy sky, then dropping her eyes to the items on display. Some of the brooches, watches and necklaces were pinned firmly to large cushions but others lay loosely inside individual open boxes, and there were several trays of rings nestling in slotted beds. Nan rested her hands on the rail. She could hear the jeweller exclaim over something Amelia had pointed out she might like, provided it wasn't too expensive. Nan adjusted the folds of her cape and messed a couple of times with the pins holding her hair in place, where the warden had suggested a bird might roost.

Finally, she turned towards Amelia, smiling happily. 'Have you made your choice?'

When the jeweller spoke, Nan's chest clenched in panic. 'Amelia has found a lovely comb, haven't you, my dear?'

Then she remembered, she had spoken Amelia's name aloud, when they entered the shop. For a horrible moment, she had believed the two of them were acquainted with each other. That would be disastrous. She laughed lightly, to hide her relief, although her heart continued to gallop. 'I'm so glad.'

'Amelia, I am very sorry for your recent loss,' said the jeweller. 'I hope you don't mind my saying, but a young lady from your institution came in to thank us for our donation to the spring bazaar, and I asked after you.' He looked up at Nan and gestured to the window. 'Amelia used to come and watch the time ball drop. I've missed her, lately. I'm very sorry for the reason you've been absent.'

The polite smile Nan was maintaining froze on her face.

Amelia's eyes brimmed with tears. 'Thank you, Mr Brown,' she said. She turned to Nan. 'That would've been

Hope callin' in.' She wiped her eyes. 'Don't expect to keep your business to yourself in this town.'

'It's a small world, indeed,' said Mr Brown. 'Thank you, young ladies, for your custom.'

—

'Amelia?' The call came from the front parlour. The warden's voice. 'Is that you? We've got guests.'

Nan shook her head. 'I don't feel well,' she whispered. The urge to hurry past was overwhelming. She had to divest herself of her haul, hide it until she could get herself free of this house without arousing suspicion. On the pavement outside the jeweller's she had suggested they return to the house but Amelia had wanted to continue shopping, having faced her grief in public and found the experience manageable.

Nan moaned aloud as Amelia took her hand – 'Yes, sister.' – gave her an apologetic look and pulled her towards the room.

'You can be my excuse,' said Amelia. 'You're poorly an' I need to go and look after you.' She searched Nan's face. 'You do look pale.'

In the parlour, the warden was sitting opposite an older, rotund man with a kind face, who rose to his feet when Nan and Amelia entered. Alongside the warden sat a handsome, white-haired woman who regarded Nan with interest.

'This is Miss Turpin,' said Miss Barlow, 'a newcomer to the town who has been staying with us and I believe is now ready to depart.'

Nan heard the unspoken words *and not before time* and nodded in agreement.

Miss Barlow continued. 'Mr Wallace is our treasurer and Mrs Calver our new trustee and widow of the surgeon general.'

'How do you do,' said Nan.

'May I take your cape?' said Mr Wallace.

'No, no thank you.' Her hands fluttered around the collar and she made a conscious effort to still them. The warden's lips were pursed but Nan was certain she would not ask how the cape came to be on Nan's shoulders, not in the presence of guests. Nan shivered. 'I think I'm developing a chill.'

'Aye,' said Amelia. 'She's taken sick. Let's go an' find you a hot drink.'

'In a moment,' said Mrs Calver. 'First, tell us, where have you two young ladies been this fine morning?'

Amelia unwrapped the delicate hair slide from its packaging and showed it to the others. 'Nan gifted me this.'

'Did she now?' said Miss Barlow. 'Where'd you get it?'

'Sister!' Amelia gave the warden a thunderous glare. 'I were there when she bought it wi' her own coin from Brown's.'

Nan tried to laugh. 'No offence taken.' She stepped back towards the door, throwing a pleading glare at Amelia. 'Excuse us.'

Mrs Calver held up a hand to stay her. 'I'm sure that you'll remember the kindness extended to you here, Miss Turpin, and if life is kind to you, perhaps you might furnish us with a donation at some point in the future? At the very least, return to regale us of your successes.'

'Of course, I will,' said Nan. 'It was lovely to meet you.'

Mrs Calver hadn't finished. 'One moment. Amelia, my dear. Have you ever visited the botanical gardens at

Endcliffe? Our treasurer is planning a jaunt for the residents of the house. I'm sure it will do you a world of good to join us.'

Amelia frowned. 'P'raps.'

Mr Wallace coughed gently. 'I hope you might consent to coming along too, Miss Barlow? You and I might travel together, while Amelia and perhaps Mrs Calver – yes, yes, the two lovely ladies working as a team – can supervise your charges?'

Nan saw the way Mrs Calver bristled at this suggestion. Mr Wallace hadn't noticed. He was too busy hanging on Miss Barlow's reply.

'How might the household travel?' said Mrs Calver.

'I'm more than willing to stump up for a transport,' said Mr Wallace, 'being cognisant of the house finances and not wishing to cause any further strain. I believe an outing will be most beneficial. What do you say, Miss Barlow?'

Miss Barlow shook her head. 'That's a reight kind and extremely generous invitation but—'

'Then it's settled.' He clapped his hands together, a whip-crack to end the debate.

Nan reached for Amelia's hand but was shaken off. 'Me an' Hetty have a trip of our own to plan,' said Amelia. 'Don't we, sister? We're goin' to Grimsby, to see our aunt.' She raised her chin. 'Very soon. In the next day or so. Hope'll be in charge while we're away.'

'Well then,' said Mr Wallace. 'We shall have to visit the gardens on your return, my dear.'

Amelia smiled. 'I think we could get a train to Grimsby in the mornin'. Why not, Hetty? I'll fetch the timetable, shall I? From your office?'

The warden looked from Amelia to Mr Wallace and back again, her cheeks flushed. She seemed not to know what to say. Despite her present crisis, Nan was intrigued by Miss Barlow's blindness to Mr Wallace's obvious admiration of her, and curious about Amelia's obsession with contacting her dead fiancé. But these were not her dramas. She had enough of her own. Nobody was paying her any attention. She slipped through the door, closing it gently behind her.

Amelia was continuing to appeal to the warden in a high-pitched, excitable voice as Nan paused in the hallway, gathering her thoughts. After a moment, she walked quickly towards the kitchen at the back of the house. She would go now. No farewells. She passed the ground-floor dorm and glanced inside. It was empty, her bed and all the others neatly made up, a task that had to be completed before breakfast could be eaten. She would never see the inside of this room again.

Nan had almost reached the steps leading down to the kitchen when a fusillade of raps on the front door knocker rooted her to the spot.

Chapter 9

'Shall I get that?' said Amelia.

She had been telling Hetty that she would take up her housekeeping duties as soon as the two of them returned from Grimsby. She would replace the coins she'd taken from petty cash when she flew to be at her fiancé's side in Tamworth. A confused look crossed Mr Wallace's face but he let the petty cash theft pass without comment when Amelia went on to tell Mrs Calver how she had found her Linus dying of smallpox.

She'd been interrupted by the hammering at the door.

'I'll go,' said Hetty. 'Why don't you see whether the teapot needs replenishing? No.' She stopped, her hand on the doorknob. 'Find Nan and see what's up wi' her.'

The girl might have smallpox. It crossed Hetty's mind that this would be the perfect excuse to put off a visit to Grimsby. She scolded herself. What level of desperation had she reached to wish ill on another in this way? No, Amelia was determined to see her aunt, and take part in a blasted séance, and would not settle until this transpired. Hetty was convinced the malicious old bat would tell the girl the truth about herself. This meant Hetty would have to come clean, before encountering Gert again, and what she ought to be thinking about now was how and where to have that conversation.

The *when* was dealt with, if Amelia insisted on setting out the following morning. It had to be tonight. And the last thing Hetty needed to give her consideration to was a day trip to the botanical gardens to look at ferns. She would have to insist on accompanying the women, rather than travel with Mr Wallace. Hetty was seeking Mrs Calver's approbation, not to become the target of misplaced jealousy. And it was misplaced, wasn't it? What interest could dear old Mr Wallace have in someone so far beneath his class? They got along, true, but there was also the age difference to consider. It was ridiculous, and anyway she hadn't the time to think about it.

Hetty straightened her cuffs and was reaching to open the front door when the door knocker was lifted and dropped again, once, twice, thrice.

'All right, all right, I'm here,' she muttered, and opened the door to find Constable Goodlad standing on the step.

Hetty had last encountered the young police officer when he delivered Nan Turpin to the house. He'd been all smiles, then. Hetty peered behind him. He was unaccompanied, no woman or girl standing meekly in his shadow. When he'd brought Nan, the pair of them had been shoulder to shoulder on the doorstep, a bashful smile on Nan's face, while the constable had looked as happy as if he'd been standing alongside her at the wedding altar.

Now, his eyes were wary, his mouth set in a thin line above the chinstrap of his helmet. Nan Turpin was somehow involved in this unexpected visit by the police. If Hetty was the gambling sort, she would lay odds on it.

'May I come in? It's an important matter.' He paused and she could swear his chin wobbled. 'It has to do with a flagrant theft, carried out by one or more of the women of this house.'

Hetty hesitated. It was her misfortune that two of the house trustees were sitting a few feet away in the parlour. She might be accused of not keeping her charges under control. She ought to never have accepted Nan Turpin into the house. Maybe her claim to be related to the famous highwayman had some truth in it. Maybe it was in the blood. She didn't doubt that Nan was at the root of this upset.

'Aye, you'd better come in,' said Hetty. 'I have company.'

Showing him into her private quarters was out of the question. Perhaps she could keep him in the hallway or put him in the kitchen.

The constable removed his helmet and cleared his throat. 'Then I'm very sorry to bother you but there is some urgency.'

At that moment, Amelia emerged from the parlour, carrying the teapot.

'Ah, the other Miss Barlow,' said Constable Goodlad. He chuckled uncomfortably. Hetty smiled thinly.

'I'm goin' to refill this,' said Amelia.

The constable held up his hand. 'Please, wait.' He addressed Hetty, more gravely. 'Amelia is the person I've been told I need to speak with.'

'Me?' Amelia stared at him. 'What about?'

Mr Wallace poked his head out of the parlour. 'Is everything all right?'

Hetty shook her head in exasperation and gestured for the constable to enter the room.

Planting his feet on the carpet and clutching his police helmet stiffly in both hands, Constable Goodlad looked, to Hetty, like a boy who had stolen his father's moustache and was trying on his clothes for size. The constable ran a finger under the high collar of his dark blue police tunic, fiddled with the polished silver button at the base of his throat, lurched over to the sideboard upon which he placed his helmet, and patted his pockets, bringing out a small notebook and pencil. During all this fidgeting, he gave the reason for his call. A jewellery shop in Market Place had been burgled, earlier that very day, right under the proprietor's nose. Mr Brown had discovered his window display was depleted when a boy, running down the street, had flattened his hand against the window when he stumbled, leaving a dirty smear behind. Mr Brown had gone outside to polish the glass.

Fortuitously, the shopkeeper was familiar with the culprit or culprits, hence the constable's timely arrival at the House of Help.

'Miss Barlow,' he said, directing his words at Amelia. 'You're acquainted with Mr Brown, I believe.'

'I stop for a natter, sometimes,' Amelia said. 'I were there today.' She looked at Hetty. 'Wi' Nan.'

'Indeed, you were inside his shop today, with another person. A woman, about your own age. You spent some time browsing.' He presented these as statements of fact, rather than questions. 'Mr Brown made his discovery soon after you had left his premises.'

Hetty's blood ran cold. She turned to Amelia, whose mouth had dropped open.

Amelia looked from the constable to Hetty and back, incomprehension on her face. 'I've not stolen owt, if that's what you're gettin' at!'

Hetty nodded. There was no doubt in her mind that Amelia was telling the truth. She kept her voice as level as possible. 'I know you haven't, love. Run and fetch Nan, would you?'

'Ah, no. I'm sorry,' said the constable. 'If you don't mind, I'd prefer it if the young lady remained in this room. I'm here to make an arrest and to retrieve the stolen goods.' He gulped, his Adam's apple bouncing in his throat. 'The inspector's been sent for. I need you all to co-operate until he arrives.'

Amelia groped for Hetty's hand, as a child would seek her mother's touch. Hetty squeezed her fingers and when she spoke, her voice was thick with emotion.

'My—' She stopped herself uttering the word daughter in the nick of time. 'My sister was with Nan Turpin. You know Nan, don't you? You brought her here. D'you remember?'

Comprehension dawned on the constable's face. 'I chased her when a gentleman raised the alarm. Ran through half the town.'

'Aye,' said Hetty. 'She's the one you want to talk to.' She couldn't prevent her voice from roughening. 'Amelia hasn't got owt to do wi' this, I can tell thee that!' She glanced at the two trustees. Mr Wallace had re-seated himself beside Mrs Calver. They were both leaning forward, as enthralled as a pair of theatre-goers at the climax of a play.

The constable's face reddened. 'I ought to speak to Miss Turpin. Where is she?'

'Well, I *were* sendin' Amelia to fetch her,' said Hetty.

'She was here only a moment ago,' said Mr Wallace. 'She is a most prepossessing young lady.'

Mrs Calver rose to her feet. 'Why don't I go and find her?' she said. She paused at the door. 'That is, if I'm permitted to leave.'

The constable looked flustered. 'What? Oh. And who are you, ma'am?'

'I'm a trustee of this house and the widow of the surgeon general, a former matron who—'

The constable interrupted. 'Yes, please go and collect Miss Turpin and bring her here.'

Mrs Calver bustled out. Hetty darted for the door, pulling Amelia along with her, and called to the woman's retreating back. 'Look in the ground-floor dorm, first, then the kitchen. She'll either be liggin' about on her bed or pesterin' Cook for summat to eat.'

She led Amelia to a chair. The girl sat compliantly, and Hetty stood behind her, a reassuring hand on her shoulder. Constable Goodlad drew up a chair and sat before Amelia, pencil poised.

'Tell me about your visit to Mr Brown's shop,' he said.

Amelia took a deep breath. 'All right. Nan wanted to go in, to get summat for Ned, that's her fiancé. She wanted to buy him a present. An' she bought one for me too.' She unfolded her hand to show him the hair ornament. 'She bought me this.'

Amelia closed her fingers over the comb when the constable reached to take it from her palm. 'I saw her pay for it!'

He withdrew his hand and consulted his notebook. 'I'm looking for a number of diamond rings, several jewelled brooches, gold and silver necklaces. It was a large haul, all taken from the window display, swiped from right under the jeweller's nose. Many thousands of pounds' worth, according to Mr Brown.'

Mr Wallace whistled, then apologised.

Constable Goodlad continued. 'He shut up shop and came to the station immediately to report it. Did you see Miss Turpin pick anything up, while you were in the shop?'

Amelia shook her head. She looked up helplessly at Hetty. 'I would've stopped her, if I'd thought she were tryin' to thieve. But I don't think she was. It must have been somebody else, who came in after us. I'd never steal owt from Mr Brown. Nan did pick up summat...' Her voice trailed away.

The constable pounced. 'What?'

'A pair o' cufflinks. I saw her pay for them, an' all.'

'Amelia is innocent,' said Hetty. 'I don't know about that other one; she's a wily one.'

Mrs Calver, her hat awry, ran back into the room to announce that she had caught up with Nan in the scullery, and that she had called out to her but the girl had ignored her, and had walked out through the back door, as serenely as a saint.

'Give chase!' said Mrs Calver excitedly. 'You can't miss her in that cape.'

Chapter 10

Nan cursed herself.

She had been reckless. She had been impatient and greedy. Her mind raced with *if onlys*. If only the shop proprietor had greeted Amelia by name when they entered, if only he hadn't been busy with a customer, if only Nan had chosen a different shop. If only she wasn't wearing a green cape with a lining stuffed with stolen jewellery.

'Stupid, stupid,' she muttered as she swept through the kitchen, grimacing when Cook greeted her with a cheery smile.

'What's the rush, love?'

'I need some fresh air,' she said.

'In this town?'

With Cook's laughter ringing in her ears, Nan crossed the flagstones of the scullery, alert to the quick tap of footsteps from the kitchen. A female voice, a voice accustomed to its commands being obeyed, called out – *Miss Turpin. Miss Turpin, stop!* Without hesitating, Nan opened the back door into the yard and stepped outside. Clara was pegging washing on the clothes line, facing away from Nan and partly enfolded in billowing sheets. Nan glided silently past as Clara turned her head in the opposite direction, towards the house, to see who was making all the commotion. The timing was perfect and Nan allowed herself a small smile of triumph as she reached for the latch of the wooden gate at the rear of the yard.

The gate stuck in its frame for a heart-stopping moment, then she was through and closing it behind her.

Now in the narrow gennel, with damp brick walls on either side, Nan trotted the short distance to the street, checking with her fingers that the contents of the cloak sat beneath the rip in the lining. A bubble of hysterical laughter rose in her throat. How would it be if she left a trail, like Hansel and Gretel in the wood? It would be a trail of baubles rather than breadcrumbs. No shouts came from behind her. Nan increased her pace until she was almost, but not quite, running. The bright oblong of light at the end of the gennel grew until it filled her vision and, finally, she was on the street.

Now she was out in the open, horribly exposed, and another dilemma presented itself. The warden had Ned Staniforth's full name. Nan herself had told Amelia and Hope – and Clara and Cook and Jenkins the cat, for goodness' sake – about the forge and the cottage with the red door on the outskirts of town. The police would waste no time in tracking her down. She had a decision to make that would involve losing Ned, but only temporarily. After all, she was only trying to improve the life they would share. She knew with deep and unshakeable certainty that they would spend their lives together. One day soon, she would return for him, creep back into town, seek his forgiveness and they would run away together. Ned would have to go with her, because another unshakeable truth was that her time in this town was finished.

A shout, a man's voice.

'*Stop! Halt there!*'

It was time to run. Anywhere. To run like the wind and find a place where she could hole up. She'd locate a bawdy house where they'd take her money and not ask questions. Which street had Clara named? Love Street. She would first put some distance between her and the House of Help and then seek directions to Love Street. It was the best she could come up with. Nan bent to bunch her skirts in her hands when she felt the back of her cape snag on something. She whirled around, praying she had caught the material on the wall behind her, that it was held by a nail or a piece of brick. She found herself staring into the eyes of the same police officer who had chased her through the town the day she met Ned. *Oh, Ned, I'm so sorry*.

The constable took her by the elbow, his grip like a vice, and pulled her abruptly back down the gennel, so that she stumbled before she could find her feet. Tilting her head as coquettishly as she could, under the circumstances, she pasted on a smile.

'My goodness. What on earth is going on?'

At first, she thought he wouldn't reply. He glanced at her then back towards the house in the distance. Finally, he spoke. 'I think you know the answer to that, don't you?'

'I'm sure I don't. Can you slow down?'

He didn't react. Nan tried again. 'I think we've met before, haven't we?'

'Aye, and I'm not letting you gallop off again this time.'

'I wouldn't dare.' She laughed but he did not join in. 'You've made a mistake but I won't hold it against you. You're just doing your job, aren't you?'

Again, he failed to engage with her and Nan's chest hitched in a sob that surprised her. She blinked back tears.

What now, for her and Ned? Had she ruined everything? *Hold your nerve, girl.*

'Turning on the waterworks?' the constable said.

She had no tart reply. A leaden feeling was rising from the pit of her stomach, solidifying into a hard knot that tightened her throat and prevented her from speaking, and finally filled her with a heavy despair. It was fear, and she must not succumb to it, or all would be lost.

The kitchen was empty. He pulled her through the house. In the parlour sat the warden, Amelia, Cook, Clara and Mrs Calver. Mr Wallace stood beside the mantelpiece, fiddling with the chain of his pocket watch.

'Goodness,' said Nan breathlessly, as the constable steered her ahead of him into the room. 'Are all of you waiting for me? I'm afraid I haven't prepared any enter-tainment.' She glanced at each of their faces, hoping to find an ally amongst them. 'I never learned to play the piano and my singing voice is like a bullfrog's.'

Only Clara offered her a faint smile. Amelia would not meet her eyes. The warden was glaring at her. Cook looked confused, while the expressions on the faces of Mr Wallace and Mrs Calver were apologetic and fascinated, respectively.

Nan raised a hand to touch her hair then thought better of it. 'I don't understand what all the fuss is about. I was feeling unwell and went for a walk.'

'Were you going in search of another jeweller's?' said Miss Barlow. 'There's plenty to choose from. Shame you picked the wrong 'un.'

Nan could not prevent her eyes from flashing in anger. The warden was spelling out her error. She cursed herself again. The fault didn't lie with Miss Barlow. It would have been so simple to ask Amelia if she was acquainted with the shop owner before they entered. This was not the large, anonymous town she had anticipated but was instead like a village where everybody knew each other's business.

'Perhaps,' said Mr Wallace, 'we oughtn't to jump to conclusions. Certainly, the young ladies visited Mr Brown's premises today but that doesn't preclude their innocence.'

'Amelia *is* innocent,' said Miss Barlow, her voice tight with restrained fury. 'I should never have let this vixen,' she pointed at Nan, who widened her eyes innocently, 'into this house.'

'Nan,' said Amelia. The hurt in her eyes was difficult to bear. 'Tell him you din't steal owt from Mr Brown.'

Nan shook her arm free from the constable's grip and rubbed her elbow. 'I didn't steal anything from Mr Brown,' she said. Her heart shrivelled under Amelia's pleading gaze. She could only pray this would be her lowest ebb. Once again, she told herself to hold her nerve.

'D'you have pockets in that?' Constable Goodlad pointed at her cape.

'No, there are no pockets.' She took the cape off and draped it over the back of a chair. 'This belongs to the house. I borrowed it, is all.'

'Would you mind taking off your shoes, rolling up your sleeves and turning out any pockets you may have in your dress?' The constable looked at Amelia. 'Both young ladies, please.'

'Not Amelia,' said the warden.

Amelia sighed. 'Sister, it's all right. I have nothin' to hide. Neither of us do.'

She set about rolling up her sleeves, unfastening and slipping off her shoes and smoothing her hands down the folds of her dress. 'No pockets,' she explained.

Nan followed her actions. Then she untied the linen pocket she carried at her waist and handed it to the constable. He put his hand inside it and felt around, then made a snorting sound and glared at Nan.

'What's this then?'

He took out a small box and opened it to reveal the silver cufflinks.

'She bought those, like I told you,' said Amelia. Nan could have kissed her for her indignance. 'She bought those for Ned for a wedding gift.'

'There's one more thing,' said Nan. She turned out the seam pocket in her dress. Coins spilled onto the carpet and she retrieved them. 'This is my money.'

'Where did you get it?' said Mrs Calver.

Nan turned to her. 'From Ned.' She offered no further explanation.

The constable sighed. 'We'll need to search the house,' he said.

Nan felt the warden's eyes on her and reluctantly met her gaze. Two spots of colour had appeared high on the woman's pale cheeks. Miss Barlow folded her lips and gave a tiny shake of her head. She blew air from her nose in a snort of derision and was about to speak when Mr Wallace held up the cape Nan had discarded on the back of the chair.

'Excuse me,' he said. 'Don't forget the young lady returned wearing this.'

The constable spoke defensively. 'I was getting to that.'

Mr Wallace nodded agreeably. 'It's fine material, but rather heavy,' he said, 'as if it could be weighted down, in the lining.'

Nan's shoulders sagged. The charade was over.

'Check her hair, an' all,' said Miss Barlow.

Amelia frowned. 'What do you mean?'

'Of course,' said the constable. 'Very clever.'

Nan smiled gently at Amelia as she reached up to unfasten the pins in her hair and tug at the thick coils of her braid. As her hair tumbled down, so did several rings and brooches.

'I'm sorry, my love.' She turned to the constable. 'Amelia is innocent. She didn't see a thing.'

–

Nan squeezed her eyes shut every time she heard footsteps echo along the corridor, her gut twisting with longing and, as the footsteps faded, a bitter relief.

The woman sharing the holding cell beneath the magistrates' court reached out from her supine position on one of the two iron-frame beds in the narrow space to tap Nan's foot. Her voice was raspy and faint and made Nan want to clear her throat.

'What are you afraid of?'

Nan opened her eyes and twisted her neck from side to side. She was sitting against the wall, her knees drawn up, a position she had remained in all through the long night, the damp seeping through her dress. She'd been unable to bring herself to lower her head onto the thin, stinking mattress. To do so would have been to admit defeat.

'Nothing,' she said. 'I'm all right.'

The woman blew air through her nose. 'Not if you're here, you're not.' She was a cowed-looking creature who repeatedly clawed with thin, dirty fingers at the bandage wrapped around her throat. 'I 'eard you tell the sergeant, no visitors, like you're the Queen of bleedin' England.' She snorted. 'No Ned. Who's Ned when he's at 'ome?'

When Nan didn't reply the woman sat up and examined her face. Nan didn't flinch when she reached out to touch her hair, which hung loose over her shoulders. 'Hmm. Reight enough. Brought off the street, were you? Yer pimp put you to the barracks? I'm 'ere because I were in love with a soldier.'

Nan smiled. 'I wasn't aware being in love was a criminal offence.'

'No, but trying to kill yerself is.'

Nan's eyes widened. 'You did that to yourself?'

'Aye.' She spoke matter-of-factly, as if she was talking about another woman who'd had her heart broken. 'Been in the infirmary for a bit. Got told I were lucky I missed the artery, but there were a lot o' blood. Anyhow.' She swallowed and winced. 'That man – what's he called – that solicitor's told me what's comin' to me, so long as I behave mesen.'

'And what's that?' Nan was genuinely interested. She, too, had been told what to expect. There would be an initial hearing before the magistrates, then because of the seriousness of her crimes, she would be sent to the York Assize for sentencing. Penal servitude was on the cards. Penal servitude. Hard labour. These were terrible phrases, whispers in her ear that made her shudder.

The woman's fingers fluttered again at the bandage. 'I'm to be handed back to me lovin' husband, on condition I never attempt owt like this again. Or it's the madhouse.'

'How long have you been married?'

'Couple o' years.' She croaked a laugh. 'I'll tell you summat else, he's movin' his mother in, to keep an eye on me. An' I'm to start producin' bairns, as soon as. That'll fix me, they reckon.'

'I'm sorry.'

'Aye. Me, an' all.'

'What about your soldier?'

'Weren't nowt, really, not on his part.' The woman's eyes were far away.

Nan pushed herself to the edge of her cot and stood up, flexing her stiffened shoulders and neck. She went to the bars that faced a small, unoccupied office and put her hand between them, feeling for the padlock and the keyhole, which of course was empty. She had harboured a fantasy, during the night, of the key being left in the lock – deliberately left for her by a sympathetic bobby – of her fingers twisting it, releasing the padlock, opening the barred door and walking out to breathe the night air, and to disappear.

There were cells to the left of theirs, stretching down the corridor, but it was impossible to see into any of them. In the night, someone – a man – had been hooting like an owl, a nonsense sound that came at regular intervals, so that she ended up waiting for each fresh call with an unbearable sense of dread. All was quiet now.

Nan walked to the back of the windowless cell. 'Do you want to hear my story?' she said.

'Why not? It'll pass the time.'

'I'm a thief, and a house-breaker.' She enjoyed the look of surprise on the woman's face. 'And I think I've lost the second man I ever loved.'

'Oh dear.'

'Hmm.' She drew out the word. 'Shall I tell you a better tale?'

She told the woman, whose name Nan realised later she had never learned, about her adventure at the House of Help, warming to her story, wanting to entertain. She created a new scenario, one in which she had taken baubles from a different jeweller's shop, and the police hadn't come knocking. Of course, she had left the house, just the same, just as she had always planned, walking past Cook in the kitchen, past Clara hanging out the sheets, walking out of the gennel and into the light, and all the way to the cottage by the river. There, she had buried in the hollow of a sycamore her magpie's hoard, all wrapped up in the green cape.

Amelia had remained none the wiser, nor did she connect the report of the burglary in the newspaper with their trip to Market Place. The woman laughed at this implausibility and Nan pouted. *It's my story. Listen.* She had bided her time, for a little while, but not too long as she wanted Ned to have the money before the Prescotts' fist closed on his life, on their lives. She was from the underworld and was not going to allow Ned to be dragged down. Packing a bag and secreting the cape inside it, she told Ned she was visiting family in Nottingham. No. Doncaster was better. Changing into black crepe at the railway station, she travelled to Rotherham and on to Doncaster. The young widow of a wealthy man who had secretly gambled their fortune away, she was left penniless and obliged to pawn her precious collection of jewellery.

She'd pick a few pockets, access a few mansions through the coal chute or an open door or window, and return triumphant, and ready to settle down with her man.

The woman was smiling. 'A fine tale. What do you say when Ned asks you where you got the money from?'

'Why, that I took from those that could afford it, that I did it all for him and am now a changed woman. Do you like my fairy tale?'

'Aye, very much. Now spin a tale for me. Make me forget about my ruin.'

Nan thought hard for a moment. 'Your soldier declares his love for another, and you see him for the vain, shallow man he really is.' She cocked her head to see how this version of events would be received. The woman nodded, then put her hand to her throat. A small amount of blood had seeped through the bandage at the side of her neck. 'But you are no longer in love with the man you married.' The woman's eyes began to fill with tears. 'And you despise his mother.' They both laughed. 'So you take his wallet and—'

The woman interrupted. 'There's always summat to steal with thee!'

'All right, all right. You have saved some money. Yes, you have put aside some of your wages, or your husband's if he keeps you, with the intention of giving it to your soldier to buy tickets to a new life. In America. But now you have a better plan. You will take your savings,' Nan paused, and glanced up. Footsteps were approaching. 'And go to the coast. Go where there are cliffs that fall into the sea. Stand on the very edge of the world. Live in a cottage, take in mending and keep for company a dog and a goat and a pig and a peacock.'

The sergeant stopped at their cell and gestured to Nan. 'You're up next,' he said.

When she stood, the woman grasped her hand. 'I'll get that peacock an' I'll name it after thee.'

Nan made a mock-curtsey. 'I'm Nan,' she said.

'Fancy Nancy.'

The sergeant shook his head. 'Did somebody smuggle the pair of you a bottle of brandy or summat?'

The exchange had, unexpectedly, given her a dose of courage, so that in the moment before the door to the courtroom opened, Nan knew she could face the magistrates with her head held high. She would focus on these men, these men who held the power over her life, and not risk a glance towards the public gallery. She would close her ears to any murmurs or sniffs or sighs. For that would undo her all over again.

Chapter 11

Ned recognised the butcher who emerged from the passageway of the Killing Shambles, his sleeves rolled up to his biceps, the long apron he wore streaked with blood and gore. He was rubbing his hands together gleefully.

' 'Ey up, lad.'

Ned stopped, glancing down the Shambles at the sheds that lined one side of the narrow street. There was nothing to see in the darkness between the wooden shutters but he could hear the lowing of cows and the shouts of the slaughtermen. ' 'Ow do, Davy.'

'Want to hear summat?'

The two men occasionally chewed the fat at the Castle Inn and Davy told a good tall story when he wasn't gossiping about his customers. Ned could use the distraction. 'Aye, go on then. I've a bit o' time to kill.'

The butcher laughed but Ned barely raised a smile. The pun had been accidental. Anxious about missing Nan's court appearance, he had arrived early that morning and found the court building still locked and bolted. He'd been too restless to stand and wait in the light drizzle that was falling, and was carrying some daft notion that he'd stay drier if he kept moving. His grandmother had probably planted that in his head, God rest her soul. He'd set off to walk down to Lady's Bridge and back. Hopefully, by the time he returned, the fortress would be open.

'Tha'll not believe this,' the butcher said, 'but I've just weighed me cow's neers – tha knows, the fat round the kidneys—'

'The suet,' said Ned.

The butcher reached out to slap his shoulder in approval and Ned resisted the temptation to check whether the man had wiped blood on his clean shirt and waistcoat. 'Aye! The suet. Guess the weight, go on. I can tell thee this, nob'dy's ever seen the like.'

Ned pretended to give it consideration. 'No idea, Davy.'

'Twelve stone.' The butcher smiled triumphantly. 'Twelve stone! That's heavier than our lass an' the bairn inside her. I'm not lyin' to thee. Come an' have a gander.' He backed away, towards the sheds. 'Come on, lad.'

'I can't, Davy.' Ned shook his head regretfully. He'd come out with an empty belly, unable to face breakfast, and the last thing he wanted to look upon was a giant slab of white fat. The smell rising from the man's clothes was bad enough. 'But mebbe I'll see thee later.'

The butcher called after him as Ned walked away. 'I'll 'av it on display, in't shop. Come an' have a look later. Tha needs to see it to believe it!'

Ned raised a hand in acknowledgement without turning around. Gradually, the smile faded from his face. Davy had taken his mind off his troubles for a moment, but now, as he walked down towards Lady's Bridge, his stomach resumed its churning and the taste of bile rose in his throat. He had no idea what happened in a courtroom, having never set foot in one before. Would he be allowed to approach Nan, to reassure her that he would never abandon her? Would he be allowed to embrace her? He'd been turned away when he went to the cells, the guard

114

telling him she wanted nothing to do with him. 'She's moved on, pal,' the man had said, his mouth twisted in spite, 'like her sort do.'

Ned had known this to be untrue. When he saw her, when their eyes met, the world would right itself on its axis. He walked onto the bridge and stopped halfway along to gaze down at the brown waters of the Don, the traffic rattling by behind his back. When a barefoot boy laden with pots and pans approached him, Ned dismissed him with a shake of his head and turned back towards the town.

–

The deputy warden of the House of Help was standing with another woman wearing a fur cape at the foot of the staircase Ned had been told led up to the court chambers. The clerk who pointed him in the right direction had confirmed that Miss Nancy Turpin was listed to appear before Mr Mappin and Alderman Clegg, and that these were the magistrates who dealt with petty offences. Hope introduced Ned to Mrs Calver, a House trustee who had come along to observe the proceedings.

'Petty offences,' Ned repeated to Hope as they ascended the stairs. 'He said petty. That dun't sound too serious. I reckon she'll get a suspended sentence.' He wasn't sure what this meant, but had heard the phrase used in relation to other cases of theft. It meant there was usually a fine to pay but no spell in jail. He'd get the coin from somewhere to pay off her fine, from Mr Prescott if need be.

Nerves were making him overly chatty. 'This is why we need to be 'ere, so's she can leave wi' us,' he said. 'I

115

know she won't be comin' back to thee, after what's gone on. I'll look after her.'

He'd take her to the cottage, tell her the tale of Davy's fat cow while Nan knocked up a meat pie for tomorrow's dinner, make those blue eyes light up.

Hope frowned and bit her lip. 'I'm not sure her case will be dealt with today. I think this is a preliminary appearance.'

Ned swallowed. He was out of his depth here, in this place. 'But she's on the list,' he said, hating the pleading note that had crept into his voice.

Mrs Calver spoke in a low whisper. 'Apparently, she's to be taken to the York Assize as the severity of her crime is out-with the jurisdiction of this court. She'll be put in the women's prison there and learn the error of her ways. House-breaking and theft are serious crimes.'

'House-breaking?' A chasm opened inside Ned, leaving him light-headed. He gripped the banister with one hand and with the other took the old woman by the arm, ignoring the little shriek she made. 'Who's got it in for her?'

'Nobody. She has created this situation through her own foolhardiness,' said Mrs Calver, quickly regaining her composure. Her eyes flicked to the police officer who was standing at the top of the stairs, looking down on them. 'Let's not make a scene, Mr Staniforth.'

'Come,' said Hope, gently. 'We ought to find our seats in the public gallery. There's little point in speculating, is there, Mrs Calver?'

Mrs Calver pursed her lips. 'That is correct, Hope. The wheels of justice are in motion.'

Ned took off his cap, ran a hand through his hair and replaced it. 'Let's hope them wheels don't run o'er our Nan,' he said.

The courtroom smelled of beeswax and was alive with the hum of whispered conversations. Ned and Hope found seats on the third tiered row of the public gallery, with Mrs Calver sitting in front of Ned on the tier beneath. His gaze kept returning to the small cluster of striped feathers in her hat. Some poor bird was going about with a bare arse. He looked away to the leaded windows that lined the opposite side of the room. It would be lovely if the sun was shining when he left this place with Nan's arm tucked in his. Ned observed the people around him. Hope and Mrs Calver were the only females in the room. Seated with them in the public gallery were a handful of men wearing bowlers or, like Ned, peaked caps. The chatter died away as two men wearing dark suits, silk cravats and stern expressions entered from a side door near a raised plinth. A police sergeant standing at one of the desks in the middle of the room gestured for everybody to rise. The two men took their seats, which was evidently the signal for everybody else to sit back down. A clerk rose from his desk beneath the plinth and handed up several sheets of paper, which one of the magistrates took with a nod of thanks.

There were a few seconds where the only sound in the room was the fierce patter of rain against the window panes. Hope rested her hand lightly on Ned's arm and he became aware he was breathing heavily through his nose. He grimaced and tried to breathe more quietly, but couldn't now seem to get enough air into his lungs. He looked around, restlessly, then back at the feathers in Mrs Calver's hat. The central feather, poking above the others, was purest white. The thought that it meant something, that it was a symbol of cowardice, or surrender, or a sign of good fortune, circled in his mind. He would take it as a sign of good fortune, regardless of whose head it adorned. Another door opened, and Ned sat to attention as a skinny young lad was led to a small, enclosed platform on the same side of the room as the public gallery and at right angles to the magistrates' bench. The lad entered the dock to stand beneath the men who would pass judgement.

Hoping to gain an understanding of what fate might befall Nan, Ned was keenly interested in the fates of the succession of men and boys who trooped into the room, some coming in from the side entrance with a guard, others walking in freely through the same door Ned had entered by, and, hearteningly, walking back out of it after the sentence was delivered. He would guide Nan through that door, once she had taken her turn in the dock and been freed. Every time the door leading from the cells opened, his heart raced in anticipation. Every time, his hopes of seeing Nan were dashed.

The parade of offenders continued. A pasty-faced sixteen-year-old youth was fined forty shillings for robbing children on the street. He'd been taking any coin they had on them, or the clothes off their back and shoes from their feet if they had no money. Nasty little piece, Ned decided. A thief who had stolen donations from a church box – not his first offence, the magistrates were told – was handed a sentence of twenty-eight days' hard labour, which he accepted with a gruff *Aye, well, fair enough* before being led away. An old man whose eyes were almost invisible within a network of deep wrinkles above a bushy white beard, and whose stomach was as round as any wealthy gentleman's, cheerfully denied stealing a bottle of whisky from a beer-off and downing its entire contents outside the premises. An empty bottle wasn't evidence, was it? Where was the whisky he was accused of stealing? *In that great belly o' thine*, called someone from the public gallery. Ned stifled a laugh. Hope was smiling. The member of the public who had called out was bundled out of the court for making a nuisance of himself and white-beard followed on his heels with a fine plus compensation to pay.

Ned watched the old man pause on his way out, turn and execute a deep bow to the room, so there was a wide grin on Ned's face when he turned back. It froze there.

Nan was walking into the room, preceded by a man in a constable's uniform who guided her towards the dock.

Ned opened his mouth and drew in a deep breath, and did not know whether he was calming himself or preparing to call out her name. Once again, Hope's hand on his arm acted as a restraint. He fought the urge to leap up and go to Nan, and, instead, willed her to turn towards where he sat. Surely, her eye would be drawn by the feathered hat that perched on the head of Mrs Calver, and thence to Ned sitting above it.

He drank her in. The thick auburn hair that hung loose to the small of her back burned all the other colours of the room to ashes. He wanted to gather that hair in his hands. He wanted to see her mouth curve in pleasure before he kissed her lips and enfolded her in his arms. Frustratingly, Nan had her profile to him as she walked towards the dock and all that was visible behind the vivid curtain of hair was the tip of her nose. Impatiently, he waited. Once in the dock, she would be facing the room, and then she would see him, and understand that he would never abandon her.

He barely registered the opening remarks of the prosecuting sergeant, so eager was he to catch her eye. Frustratingly, Nan kept her gaze focused mostly on the police officer, with one or two quick glances at the magistrates, but Ned knew she was aware of his presence, knew it from the set of her jaw, the deliberate angle of her head. She was avoiding his gaze and this hurt more than the guilt and shame he felt seeing her in the dock. When a short, bespectacled man entered the witness box to confirm this was the woman who had been in his shop and that the items found on her belonged to him, Nan gave every appearance of listening carefully, a trace of a polite smile on her face. Another witness, a pawnbroker from Gibraltar Street, further confirmed that a silver letter opener and snuff box belonging to a banker whose home had been burgled were brought to his shop by the woman in the dock. Several five-pound notes that she could give no reason for being in possession of, being as she was a destitute living at the House of Help, were found on her person. Five-pound notes were taken in the same burglary she was accused of, in addition to the jewellery theft.

Mrs Calver slowly shook her head from side to side when Nan's residence at the House of Help was brought up and it was all Ned could do not to stave in the woman's silly hat and the skull that lay beneath it. His squeezed his hands into fists to stop them shaking but his heart was trying to pound its way out of his chest. Any moment now, he would explode like a cracked crucible.

And still Nan refused to meet his gaze.

It seemed only moments had passed since she entered the room but already the guard was opening the small gate on the side of the dock and ushering her away. Now, surely, she would look over her shoulder and find him.

Ned stared at the door she disappeared through, and was still gazing at it when it opened again – she was returning, having been freed! – and another woman entered, a sick-looking creature. This woman's eyes immediately went to the public gallery, where a man raised his hand in greeting. She looked away and raised shaking fingers to touch the rag wrapped around her throat.

–

Ned leaned against the wet brick outside the court building, watching dirty spray being flung onto the pavement by passing carriage wheels, nodding occasionally as Hope explained the situation. The new clothes he had worn for Nan were soaked, his shirt-sleeves clinging to his skin, the cuffs of his trousers as wet as if he'd been wading down a stream. He'd rejected Hope's offer to share her umbrella. She stood beside him, water dripping all around her, and told him Mrs Calver was acquainted with the solicitor acting for the gentleman whose house had been burgled. She had collared him as he left court and made it clear that Nan Turpin would never again be allowed to set foot in the House of Help. The girl had abused the faith placed in her and should be banished from the town, if not the country. Mrs Calver was sorrowful that transportation was no longer practised.

Ned spoke the word softly. 'Stop.'

'I'm sorry,' said Hope. 'I was getting to the point.'

'She din't look at me once,' he said.

'But that's only because she was afraid to,' said Hope. 'She did not want to lose her composure.'

He looked up from his study of the pavement, into her eyes. 'D'you think so?'

'I'm certain of it.'

He knew she was only telling him what he wanted to hear.

Ned nodded wearily throughout Hope's explanation of what the solicitor had said would happen next, giving a small and bitter laugh when he learned that Nan would be transported to York to be sentenced, and would probably be put in the women's prison there, which was on the same estate as the men's jail but in a separate, secure building. If she was unlucky enough to receive a more severe sentence she would go elsewhere for a longer term of penal servitude. Ned could write to her, and after a time she might be allowed to write back. This all depended on her behaviour. Model convicts were granted certain freedoms while those who misbehaved were denied all privileges.

Nan would be locked up. It did not seem real to him.

'How long?' said Ned.

'We shall find out soon enough.'

'Aye.' He raised his head so that the rain fell onto his cheeks. He could not think beyond the fact that she had not wanted to see him when she was locked in the cells and she had refused to meet his gaze in the courtroom. It may have been pride, or the guilt and humiliation of committing a crime and being captured for it. It may have been disdain. He had failed to protect her.

What difference would a letter make?

Chapter 12

Hetty quelled the urge to intervene in Amelia's interrogation. In any event, the girl seemed unperturbed as she leaned against the side of the kitchen sink, arms folded, fielding questions from the residents who had come back for their dinner. Amelia rarely sat with the women, and Hetty had, that morning, expressed her surprise at how thick Amelia had been with Nan Turpin. It was Hetty's way of gauging Amelia's mood, although she despaired at herself for wondering whether a state of mind existed that could swallow the truth Hetty was going to have to reveal.

At least Nan's arrest had granted a stay of execution. The day Amelia had insisted they would go to Grimsby had come and gone, giving Hetty more time to consider how to broach the truth.

'She used me,' Amelia had said when Hetty asked her about Nan, simply and with no bitterness in her voice. 'Good riddance to her.'

There were few empty spaces at the kitchen table. Wednesday was meat-and-potato pie day so all those women who could return to the house halfway through the day were sure to do so. Naturally, all the talk was of the thief and house-breaker who had dwelt in their midst.

A young woman who was given half an hour at dinner time from her new job in a sweet shop on Norfolk Street spoke through a mouthful of food. 'Tha must have seen her, doin' the thievin'.'

'No,' said Amelia. 'I already told thee I had no idea. I found out when she did.'

She gestured to Hetty, who was sitting at her small table in the corner of the room, pencil in hand. Amelia had asked her to double-check the grocery bill before it was paid. Unfortunately, it tallied up as far as Hetty could see. The grocer had put up his prices and had also, without prior notice, added another shilling to the cost of the delivery service. That was a luxury that would have to go. Collecting the groceries from the shop would shave a small amount from the bill, and there were certainly enough females in the house to help with the task.

'By all accounts, she's thieved all her life,' said another girl, whose gaunt cheeks reflected the circumstances that had brought her to the house. Half-starved and dressed in little more than rags, she'd been picked up by the police for begging outside St Peter's Church. The girl's mother had remarried and thrown her out when she reached the age of fourteen, could not find work and became a burden. Hetty had furnished the girl with suitable clothes and was hoping to get her a place in the servants' school, or secure her a position that required little or no training. If nothing could be found, the girl would go to the workhouse. The House of Help was full to the rafters once again.

'I overheard her tellin' Hope that she ran away after reportin' her own mother for baby farmin',' said another woman, 'and has fended for herself for ten year or more, livin' off her wits.'

'Won't need to do that no more, will she?' said the sweet shop girl. 'Fend for herself, I mean. Wonder what you get fed in jail? It won't be owt like this.'

'Stir-about three times a day,' said another woman, to general laughter.

Cook, who had remained silent in the midst of all the chatter, slammed the door of the range and turned on the table of women. 'Tha wun't last five minutes in prison. None of tha would!' She marched out of the room.

'She has a soft spot for Nan,' said Hetty. 'Ladies, let's mind what we say at the table, shall we?'

The woman who had made the reference to prison gruel shook her head sombrely. 'I tell thee what, she'll need to keep her wits about her, an' all, in jail. Good lookin' lass like her'll have the guards on her like dogs on…'

'That's enough,' said Hetty. 'I won't have this talk under my roof. Dinner time is over.'

Getting to her feet, the woman shrugged. 'Where was Hope today?'

Hetty exchanged a glance with Amelia. Hope had not yet returned from the magistrates' court, and Hetty had a feeling this woman knew precisely where the deputy warden was.

'She's runnin' an errand,' said Amelia. She picked up the cloth Cook had discarded and used it to carry the pie dish to the sink in the scullery. 'Reight, then, before you all disappear, who's helping me clear up?'

Hetty was grateful for Amelia's intervention. The sooner the exploits of Nan Turpin were behind them the better it would be. Mrs Calver had insisted on accompanying Hope to court, and was no doubt mithering the deputy warden with her philosophy on how the house should be run. Hope, fortunately, was Hetty's staunchest ally. She was, Hetty considered, one of the house's greatest success stories, having entered pregnant and friendless, and fearing for her life, and was now deputy warden, albeit unpaid. Hers was an honorary position. Hope's wealthy father would never tolerate his daughter doing anything so demeaning as earning a wage. Mr Hyde would be mollified by the fact that Hope was now residing most nights at the mansion of the family's acquaintances on the outskirts of town. This was because the house needed the bed space. Hope would prefer to remain in the dormitory. But having her rubbing shoulders with the wealthy and influential was exactly what her father needed. Now the scandal was beginning to fade, he wanted to marry her off. Hetty smiled, imagining Hope's reaction if this proposal was put to her. She wondered whether Hope ever thought about her illegitimate child, now adopted by the owner of a steelworks and his childless wife. Of course she did. Hetty had thought about Amelia every single day since the day she was born.

In any event, she no longer had to worry about Hope. Mrs Calver, however, was another story. The woman was making a downright nuisance of herself. She had turned up the previous evening, immediately after tea time when the house was at its busiest, and requested privacy for *an important conversation*. Hetty had eventually shown her upstairs to the classroom, where Hope was cataloguing materials for the next reading and writing class. After Hope had left, quietly closing the door behind her, Hetty folded her hands before her and looked at the clock on the wall.

'I apologise for taking up your time,' Mrs Calver said, in a tone that conveyed the opposite. 'It is unfortunate that we harboured a thief who was allowed to continue to steal—'

Hetty interrupted her. 'Allowed?'

'—whilst under our roof,' Mrs Calver said. 'I must speak plainly, Miss Barlow, from my observations of the house.' She waited for Hetty to nod her assent. 'The regime here is far too slack. We need to implement a curfew on these women. I believe seven-thirty in the evening would be adequate. In addition, there should be a ban on visitors, unless authorised by the board of trustees. And every resident must report their daily comings and goings to you or to your deputy, so that you can veto activities deemed unsuitable.'

Hetty would have to appear to be taking the woman seriously. 'A curfew would be difficult,' she said, 'as we sometimes have women staying with us who work night shifts. An actress who is appearing at the Royal has returned to us for four nights. You've met her cat, Jenkins.'

'The black panther?' Mrs Calver smiled. 'He's a lovely creature. Is he a good ratter?'

'Aye, he does a good job,' said Hetty.

'Night shifts and actresses.' Mrs Calver waved her hand in the air. 'Of course, there are going to be exceptions to the rule.'

Hetty cleared her throat. 'But you do agree that our door should always remain open?'

'Yes?'

'Well, then you can see how impractical it would be to wait for the board to say aye to every individual visitor. As it is, we only admit those gentlemen who have doings with the house, the likes of our Mr Wallace and our beneficiaries who come for the Sunday Bible read.' Hetty took a breath. 'And, wi' respect, Mrs Calver, this isn't a workhouse. We can't tell our women what they can and cannot do with their time.' She recalled Mr Wallace's words when she was interviewed for the job of warden.

'This house exists to bridge the gap between circumstance and ambition.'

'Nan Turpin was certainly allowed to realise hers,' said Mrs Calver, triumph in her voice.

Hetty laughed. 'Nan is — what did you say, a minute ago – the exception that proves the rule? A misguided lass, our Nan.' Hetty could hardly believe she was defending the girl. 'Anyhow, she's payin' for her misdemeanours.'

She went to the door and opened it to show Mrs Calver out. 'Is that everything? It's just that Hope needs to get the room ready for her reading class.'

Mrs Calver nodded. 'As always, thank you for your time, Miss Barlow. I'll be seeking an urgent meeting of the trustees that you must attend. I hope you'll come around to my suggestions and that I can count on your support, as warden and in honour of the profession we share.'

Hetty smiled. 'I can only speak the truth to thee. I think we'll have to agree to differ.'

'We'll see,' said Mrs Calver. 'We'll see.'

–

Mercifully, Mrs Calver did not return to the house with Hope after their attendance at the magistrates' court. The kitchen was as crowded at tea time as it had been earlier in the day, the women hanging on Hope's account of Nan Turpin's appearance in the dock. After a while, Hetty noticed that Amelia was missing, that she had slipped from the room unnoticed. She knew where she would find her, and her breath caught in her throat when she contemplated what lay ahead. Nobody, not even Hope, entered the warden's private quarters without an invitation from within. Only Amelia had that right, as she was occasionally required to sleep with Hetty in her bed. Amelia had given up her dormitory bed for Hope on the night she arrived, being woken in the early hours with barely a grumble. The girl had a good heart. Hetty was counting on it.

If the front door knocker sounded, Hope would deal with it. If a knock came on Hetty's door, she would tell whoever it was that she was not to be disturbed. If Amelia was not in the warden's quarters, if she had taken herself off somewhere else, for a walk or even just to sit in the front room, then Hetty's confession would wait for another day. The idea that she might have to put off the inevitable gave Hetty the courage to go to her quarters and open the door.

The armchairs by the fireplace were empty, the coverlet on the bed stretched tight over the sheets. Amelia's pillow, from her dorm bed, lay next to Hetty's, undented. The door to the warden's office was closed. Hetty couldn't remember whether she'd closed it herself, earlier in the day. She approached it with trepidation in her heart.

As she pressed down on the handle, the sound of sobbing came from within.

Chapter 13

She was nineteen years old, the naïve product of a sheltered upbringing, the only child of doting parents, and in love.

The new vicar's congregation had inexplicably swelled, the pews filled with young women wearing their Sunday best and hanging on every word uttered by the handsome young man in the pulpit. But it was Hetty, quiet and reserved Hetty, who caught his eye, much to her surprise. It was common knowledge in the parish that the young vicar was in search of a wife with whom to share the pretty rectory across the road from St Augustine's Church and cemetery. During an afternoon tea party under the green canopy of the rectory garden, he found Hetty sitting alone on a bench and sat down beside her. They talked about books and he took her inside to show her his library. He loaned her a red cloth-bound copy of *Little Dorrit* on condition that she visited again, after the Sunday service, if her parents allowed it. He would ask their permission.

It became their habit to sit in the garden and discuss the latest borrowed book that she had diligently carried home to read. He begged her to call him by his given name, James, and praised her wit and intelligence. 'Don't be bashful,' he said. 'These are the qualities I shall be seeking in a wife, Henrietta. A woman whose conversation revolves around the housekeeping would bore me silly.'

She fell in love, blissfully unaware that she was not the only young woman he entertained in the rectory garden. Hetty discovered the truth when the day came that a female acquaintance took her to one side to tell her breathlessly that she believed James was going to propose to her, that he told her that she was demurely beautiful and would thrive in the domestic sphere, that she would know her place as a vicar's wife and he would be proud to have her by his side. She was entrusting Hetty with her secret. It was too late by then. Hetty had been seduced, had become swept up in romantic passion, and gone willingly with him up the stairs of the rectory, into the bedroom, where she had disrobed and slipped between the cool sheets, listening to the birdsong that filtered through the open window on a sunbeam, exhilarated by the feel of his skin against hers, and shivering with delight as he murmured words of love in her ear.

There was nothing romantic about what followed.

Her father's sister, Gertie, had come up with a solution that she said would save the family from being embroiled in scandal. By the time Hetty's condition was apparent, the vicar had gone, banished to a parish far away, but evidently not far away enough. Police inspectors were on his trail, investigating how he had come so quickly into possession of a large sum of money from a widowed parishioner. He had proved to be the ruin of one young lady, who according to Hetty's parents had been sent away to have her child. He had reneged on his engagement to another. Hetty learned about these women via a paragraph in a gossip column in the local newspaper.

'He's being sued by the father of the girl who's having his bastard. It will go to court,' said Gertie, her lip curling. 'Well, we're not getting dragged into this mess. You,' – she was talking to her brother – 'should move out of the area, go to another colliery, keep the girl out of sight and pass off the offspring as your own. A late baby. It's not unheard of.'

Hetty had no say in the matter.

When the pains came, she was attended by her mother, who prayed loudly by the bedside that neither midwife nor doctor would be required. Hetty's one rebellious act was to insist on naming the child herself.

'You ought to name her after me,' said Gertie. 'I was never blessed with children.'

'I'd be agreeable,' said Hetty's father. Her mother was holding the wailing baby in her arms, and Hetty's body ached with the urge to take the child and run. Her heart was heavy with the knowledge that there was nothing for her beyond the front doorstep of the house that had become her prison.

'No,' she said, snatching up the offending page of the newspaper and twisting and rolling it into a ball. 'I'm naming her. I'm naming her Amelia.' She threw the paper into the fireplace, struck a match and set it alight.

Her mother lifted the baby onto her shoulder, stroking the back of her head. 'Good morning, Amelia,' she said in a sing-song voice. 'Little Amelia.'

Gertie was staring at Hetty, her face set.

–

Amelia slouched in the chair at Hetty's desk, a handkerchief bunched in her fist. When Hetty entered the room, slowly, to give the girl time to compose herself, Amelia sat up straight, swiped at her eyes and commenced to loudly blow her nose.

Hetty grimaced sympathetically. 'Are you all right, love?' she said.

Amelia shook her head impatiently. 'Just needed a good cry, that were all.' She laughed shakily. 'There's no bleedin' privacy to be had in this house, is there?'

'I shouldn't have come lookin' for thee.' Hetty twisted her hands together, wondering whether she ought to further burden the girl, and recognising with grim certainty that there never would be a right time to impart the truth.

'What's up?' said Amelia. She looked at Hetty curiously. 'You comin' down wi' summat?' She caught her breath. 'Is it about what Nan did?'

'No, it's not that.' Hetty turned and went back into her bedroom, perching on the edge of the mattress. 'She won't be back to bother us.'

Amelia got up to follow. 'What, then?'

Hetty couldn't bear to have the girl looming over her. She went to sit in one of the armchairs by the fireplace, her fingernails scraping the fabric arms, her lips folded. She had no idea how or where to start but knew she must speak, must explain the reason for her agitation. Amelia would see through a lie.

Amelia sat facing her. 'Hetty, is summat up?'

She took a deep breath and released it on the word: 'Yes.' Amelia's eyes widened in alarm. 'It's all right,' said Hetty, quickly. 'You're not in any bother.' She put a hand over her mouth. 'But I might be.' She twisted her top lip between thumb and finger, her breathing growing ragged. 'Wi' thee.'

'Me?' Amelia's eyebrows shot up. 'Why?'

The truth lay fathoms deep behind a dam her words would burst. It might drown them both. It was too late to turn back.

'Hetty, what is it?'

It occurred to her that there was a way she could ease the torrent, by beginning with a lesser secret. Hetty clasped her hands in her lap. 'I need to tell you summat. It's about me, and it's about the past. I need thee to let me talk wi'out interruption.'

Amelia's tone was cautious. 'Aye,' she said. 'Go on then.'

'Aunt Gertie and me, well, we never got along with each other.'

'Aye, I'd never have guessed that.' Amelia clamped a hand over her mouth. 'Sorry.'

'You were barely walking when I went away, and wouldn't remember it, but she drove me out. Our Auntie Gertie wanted me gone.' Hetty gazed at the scoured grey of the empty grate, aware of Amelia's eyes on her. 'I found work at a hospital, scrubbing floors, and I got a room in a house and I got stuck there for a long time, a very long time. I was sad. I suppose I must have been very sad.' Hetty's eyes filled with tears but she shook her head when Amelia reached out to touch her. 'No, I need to finish. I was missing you and Mother and Father.'

'I miss Mother still,' Amelia said in a whisper.

Hetty wrapped her arms around herself. 'They told you I was doing well, a matron at this women's hospital I worked in, in Whitby, and I let them, and after Father died Gertie moved in, and said it was best if I stayed away. They told you I was too busy to come home for a visit.'

Amelia nodded. 'Aye, I remember it. But why would Gertie drive you out?'

Hetty sighed. 'I'm gettin' to that. The point is, I've got no fancy certificates, love. I never was a matron.'

'But…' Amelia gestured around the room, 'how would you get this job then?'

'Under false pretences,' Hetty said. 'When I came home for Mother's funeral and I saw how Gertie was treating you, I decided to come back and fetch you away from there. I wanted to look after you.' She rushed on, watching Amelia's face, which the girl was deliberately holding still, expressionless. 'It was time I did summat. It was beyond time, an' I'm sorry for that, for leavin' you with Gertie for so long. I had no plan, not really, so we ended up in a boarding house here, and I paid a neighbour to forge papers for me with the last bit of coin I had, and I got this job, and your job too, although I know you dislike it. Still, we landed on our feet, love.'

'All right,' said Amelia. She rubbed her forehead. 'So you took a gamble, an' it paid off. I could allus have gone back to Auntie Gertie if we got in dire straits. Why are you in trouble wi' me? No, wait. Wait. Who knows, who in this house? Does Hope?'

'No, just me, and now thee, and that's how I want it to stay.'

'Why would I tell?' Amelia laughed. 'Dark horse, eh? I'm not judgin' you, Hetty. I've seen enough in this place to know how hard things can get. I'm sorry, sister.' She rose to her feet and bent over Hetty, enveloping her in an embrace. Hetty clung to her. She closed her eyes, savouring her daughter's touch, her scent. After a moment, Amelia resumed her seat. 'An' I've been nowt but trouble,' she said.

'No,' said Hetty. 'Never say that, love.'

Amelia leaned her head against the back of the chair and looked at Hetty thoughtfully. Hetty met her gaze with difficulty. 'Why tell me now, though? An' why would I be upset with thee?' Her features were animated. It was the first time since Amelia had returned to the house that Hetty had seen anything other than moroseness in those brown eyes. 'Got any more secrets to tell?'

She could stop now, leave it at that, convince herself that Amelia needed time for this revelation to sink in. She could shake her head, reassure Amelia that there were no more secrets, and go on as before. She would disregard the words her aunt had flung at her at the end of their last encounter. *I'll tell her, do you hear me? Harlot!*

Gertie's sneer rose in her mind and the words fell from her lips. 'Amelia, I'm not your sister.'

–

The ripples from the scandal surrounding the vicar never reached the Barlow family. Hetty's mother, who had previously had a fractious relationship with her sister-in-law, was now beholden to Gertie and her fine idea for avoiding catastrophe. Hetty's mother doted on Amelia, and Gertie encouraged her in her motherly role, frequently commenting on how much Amelia resembled her and how calm the infant grew in Hetty's mother's arms.

Gertie had few kind words for her niece.

'If you can't find a decent man to marry, and I don't see any knocking on the door, then you need to get a job,' Gertie told Hetty. 'And find a place of your own. You're under everybody's feet here. Your mother is sick to death of you moping around.' She reminded Hetty of a little bird, constantly pecking with her sharp beak. 'I'm only saying this for your own good.'

When Hetty's father died in a mining accident, her mother used the compensation money to buy the cottage on the estuary and set up as a seamstress. Gertie was a constant presence in the house after Hetty's mother slipped on fish guts and broke her leg. She began bringing over her friends from her spiritualist church, although Hetty's mother resisted attempts by Gertie to host séances in the sitting room.

A little while before Hetty decided she could take no more, she brought a tea tray to Gertie and a female visitor, at her mother's request. She'd placed it down and had turned to leave the room when the visitor asked her whether she was going to pour. 'You won't get far with that sullen look on your face,' the visitor had said. 'Let's hope the wind doesn't change.' Gertie had laughed. Hetty had apologised and obeyed, realising as she poured that she'd been mistaken for a maid, and that her aunt wasn't going to correct her friend.

It was shortly after that Gertie insisted on moving into the cottage. She never left. Hetty did.

–

Now she had spoken the words she'd bottled up ever since her mother's funeral.

'Not sisters?' Amelia frowned. 'What are you on about?'

Hetty lowered her chin and pinched the bridge of her nose. She tried to keep her voice calm. 'I was pregnant, when I was the age you are now. Out of wedlock, to a man who… well, he was a bad sort. It was Gertie's idea.'

'What was?'

Hetty looked up finally, into Amelia's frightened eyes. The girl knew, but the truth would have to be spelled out.

'It was Gertie's idea,' Hetty repeated, 'for me to give up my baby, to prevent a scandal, and for her – for *you* – to be raised by my parents.' She paused. 'Your grandparents.'

'No, no, no.' Amelia laughed, a raw, harsh sound like metal against metal. 'If this is your way of tryin' to stop me going to see Auntie Gertie it's not goin' to work. You must've gone mad.' Her voice cracked. 'My mother is dead.'

'I'd no choice,' said Hetty. 'I'm sorry your father wasn't a better man.'

Amelia put her hands on the arms of her chair. 'I'm not listenin' to this.'

Hetty leapt up and rushed to the door with the intention of preventing Amelia from leaving. She had confessed, and did not want to have to chase her daughter through a houseful of women, pleading her case. Amelia, now on her feet, stared at Hetty, shaking her head in disbelief. She retreated to the window and stood with her back to the room, a dark and still figure against the light streaming in. Hetty began, falteringly, to tell her story to the back of her daughter's head.

Amelia didn't speak until Hetty had finished, then said quietly, without turning: 'You're worried Auntie Gertie will tell me the truth, aren't you?' She looked over her shoulder at Hetty. 'Or you'd 'av let me think we were sisters forever, wouldn't you?'

'I don't know. I had an idea I would tell you, one day.' Hetty tried to smile. 'I found you, and I got you away from her – you remember, that séance, where she tried to raise your grandmother—'

'Don't call her that!'

'—and you were terrified and I didn't want to lose you, not again.'

'If this is true, and I'm not sayin' I believe it, you left your own baby behind an' waited nineteen years to say owt.'

'It wasn't that simple, love.'

'You never raised me. You don't get to call yourself my mother.'

'I know that. I would have looked after you, if I could.' Amelia didn't respond. 'You're all I thought about.'

'Thought about but didn't do owt.' Amelia's voice was flat. 'Will you leave me alone?'

'What?'

'Can you just go, just leave me alone.'

'Amelia, I want to explain, about Gertie. You don't understand.'

'I lived wi' her for long enough! I know what Auntie Gertie's like. This has got nowt to do wi' her.' Amelia turned away again, to gaze out of the window.

'She drove me away. You don't know what it was like.'

'Aye, well, poor you,' said Amelia.

Hetty was glad she could not see her daughter's face. The contempt that dripped from her voice was difficult enough to bear.

'Go an' find summat else to do,' said Amelia. She finally faced Hetty but only to gesture to the door. 'Go on. You're allus complainin' about how busy you are. Don't hang about here on my account.'

Hetty swallowed. 'It's a shock. You need a bit o' time to take it in. I'm sorry. Amelia, I'm sorry.'

Amelia laughed, a cruel sound. 'Go away, Hetty. You'll only be doing summat you're good at.'

Chapter 14

Hailed by one of the drinkers standing outside the Q in the Corner in Paradise Square, Ned acknowledged the greeting with a terse nod and hurried by, his boots scuffing up dust from the cobbles. The warm early evening light that bathed his face and forearms served only as a painful reminder that Nan was locked up in the darkness of a prison cell.

He hated to think of her alone in the dark. He'd been comforting himself, in the days following her court appearance, by imagining the excursions they'd go on, once Nan was released, and surely that day would not be far off. They would trek up to Bole Hills in the Walkley countryside to breathe in the clear air and enjoy the panoramic view of the valleys. He'd take her on an expedition to Wharncliffe Crags with a picnic and they'd sit on the worn-smooth stone of the ancient cliffs, and dangle their legs over the sweeping valley below.

Nan was going to mend her ways, he was certain of it, and the two of them would soon be setting about raising a family. The girls would be red-haired and beautiful and the boys tall and strong. Ned flexed his shoulders as he reached the steps of the House of Help. There were only good things ahead. Frank had told him that Mr Prescott had, through one of his many contacts, secured a large order for anvils and vices from a shipbuilder in Belfast.

There was the promise of business from America too. What was good for Ned was good for the Prescott family, and Mr Prescott would be taking a generous commission for the business he generated, which was fair enough. Ned had explained all this to his cousin. It frustrated him that Jacob remained wary of Prescott's involvement.

Ned recognised the mousy-haired girl who opened the door to the House of Help in response to his knock. She'd been reclining on the doorstep with the housemaid the last time he'd visited, and had told him Nan was gone for good. It seemed an age ago. ' 'Ey up, look who's back.'

' 'Ow do, Molly.'

She stepped outside, closing the door behind her, so that only a hair's breadth separated their bodies, and tapped her fingers against her lips. 'I'm reight sorry to hear about your lass.'

'Aye.' He smiled at the girl and took a step back. 'But don't worry theesen. I knew a bloke got put away for theft. Two weeks later an' he were out.'

The girl smirked. 'Two weeks, eh? That's what tha heard?'

Ned shifted from foot to foot. 'Your deputy warden's expectin' me.'

'Aye. Best she gives thee the news. Wait here an' I'll fetch her.' Molly opened the door, then paused. She put a hand on Ned's arm. 'Listen, Ned.'

'What?'

Whatever she had been going to say she evidently changed her mind about. 'Nowt. Hope'll tell thee.'

She turned and disappeared into the depths of the house, leaving the door standing open and Ned entertaining the uneasy thought that perhaps, after all, he was the one who had been left in the dark.

Several minutes went by before Hope emerged. She did not look like the composed woman who had been a steadying influence on him in the magistrates' court. Her blonde hair hung down her back in a frayed plait, her face was flushed and the cuffs of her blouse unfastened. She put the palm of her hand against her forehead.

'I'm so sorry to have kept you waiting,' she said. 'Unfortunately, I'm caught up in a contretemps – oh!' She must have seen his expression. 'Not involving Nan. I'm sorry if I alarmed you.'

She took his arm and guided him down the steps. 'Shall we find a bench outside St Peter's to sit on?'

'Aye,' said Ned, warily. 'What's goin' on, then, at your place?'

Hope shook her head again. 'I'm not at liberty to say. It's a private matter, really, not a house concern. Goodness. Please excuse me.' She ran back into the house, returning with a bonnet that she tied on as they walked. 'How is your forge doing? It must be gratifying, running your own business?'

'We're doin' well and, aye, I'm enjoyin' it. Or I will be, tha knows, once Nan is at my side. Not long now, eh?'

'Let's sit,' said Hope.

The nearest bench was in the shadow of the tall spire of St Peter's. They sat, Ned hugging his elbows. It was cold out of the sun. 'I've waited long enough,' he said, 'an' I'm thinkin' it's not good news.'

'No. It's very far from what you want to hear. I'm sorry.'

All she had done since greeting him was apologise. He tipped his head back, despair clogging his throat. The outline of the spire was darkly vertiginous against the faded blue of the sky. The air smelled of smoke and there was a faint almond scent from a nearby clematis vine that choked a metal railing. Somewhere around the corner, a man sang drunkenly, harmonised by the whining of a dog. Ned noticed all these things but was removed from them, as if a sheet of steel had fallen between him and the outside world. 'Let's have it then,' he said.

Hope sat forward and waited for him to look down, to acknowledge that she had his full attention before she spoke. His gut churning, Ned met her eyes. 'Nan's been sentenced,' said Hope, 'and is being taken to Millbank.'

'Millbank?' said Ned. He'd never heard of the place. 'What's Millbank?'

'It's a prison. In London,' said Hope.

Ned's shoulders drooped. *Prison.* A prison halfway across the country. There was nothing he could do for Nan. He burned with the shame of it. 'Aye, all right,' he said. 'Go on. How long?'

'She's expected to be moved to serve out the majority of her sentence in Woking Female Prison,' said Hope.

Ned groaned. 'An' where the hell's that?'

'It's just south-west of London.'

'Why can't she be kept up here, closer by?'

'I'm sorry,' said Hope.

Ned grunted in exasperation and dropped his head, clenching his fists in his hair. 'How long?' he repeated. When Hope didn't respond Ned lifted his head and stared at her. 'Come on.'

'It is a long sentence,' said Hope, 'but if Nan is a model prisoner she'll be given an early ticket of release, and might serve only half of it.'

'Do I really have to ask thee again?'

Hope shook her head. 'Seven years' penal servitude.'

An icy coldness crept up Ned's body, paralysing his limbs. He cleared his throat. 'Me grandmother always said

I had cloth ears. For a minute, I thought tha said seven years.'

He searched her eyes, the sympathy in them telling him he had not misheard, then dropped his gaze to the ground. There was a scrim of black fungi on the edge of the flagstone beneath his feet, where the sun's rays did not reach. Ned rubbed at it with the toe of his boot. Nan would be spending the prime of her life – and his – locked up and far away.

'It's very harsh,' said Hope, 'but there was the house-breaking as well as the theft, and all premeditated, and a criminal record, before she arrived in town. We didn't know what trouble she'd been in before she came here and it seems her recklessness and, let's say, *laissez-faire* approach to life has finally caught up with her.'

But Ned was no longer listening. He lurched to his feet, the blood roaring in his ears, and strode away, glancing back once to see Hope still seated on the bench, staring helplessly after him. He was barely aware of making his way back to the Q but suddenly he was inside, and standing at the bar, being jostled on a tide of noise and bodies. He was served a pint of porter that he carried to a corner table behind the door, keeping his head down. Anybody who caught his eye was liable to get short shrift.

He returned to the bar for a second pint that went down as quickly as the first, then Frank appeared, pulling out a stool and plonking himself down. 'Tha's half an hour early, Ned. I've not completed me business yet.' He looked around and raised his voice. 'Any chance o' service round here?'

Ned lifted his glass to his mouth, swallowing down the bitter liquid. A serving maid put down a pint pot in front of Frank and a plate containing two slices of pork pie soaked in the local relish. She stepped back with alacrity when Frank's hand went out to pat her backside, but wasn't quick enough. He grabbed a fistful of her skirt and pulled her towards him, moving his hands to grip her waist. She pushed at his shoulders, ineffectually, a nervous smile on her face.

'Mr Prescott, you'll get me in bother.'

Frank pulled her closer. 'Come on, love. A kiss on the lips and I'll let thee go.'

'Give over,' said Ned quietly.

Frank relinquished the girl. 'Make yersen useful, then. Another ale for my mardy-arse pal here. On the house, aye?'

She scurried away.

'Got this landlord in tha pocket, an' all?' said Ned.

Frank leaned back and lifted his eyebrows. 'Bad news, then.'

'She's been put away for seven years.' He could not believe what he was saying. 'Seven years, Frank. What does tha have to say about that?'

'Nowt.' Frank ignored the serving maid when she returned with Ned's drink. He waited until she had walked away. 'There's nowt to say, except,' he held up a hand, 'an' hear me out, but this lass came out of nowhere an' has gone back there. I'd say tha's had a lucky escape. Sit down.'

Ned had got to his feet so abruptly that his stool overturned with a clatter. There was a momentary hush when all eyes turned in the direction of the two men, before the patrons of the Q decided it would suit them better to mind their own business. Ned righted the stool but remained standing. Frank smirked up at him.

'What will tha do, then? Bust her out?'

Ned shook his head. 'I'm waitin' for her.' Even in his own ears, the words sounded feeble.

Frank laughed. 'All right, then. Will tha do me a favour an' sit down? I'm gettin' a crick in me neck.'

Ned sat, reluctantly. 'I'll build up the business,' he said, 'an' when Nan gets out I'll be able to give her a good life.'

'What about me father?'

'What about 'im?'

'He's busy sellin' thee to all an' sundry, and tha wants to stick by a convicted house-breaker and Lord knows what else she's hidin' in her murky past. It's not the respectable look we're after, is it?'

'Well, excuse me, pal, but Mr Prescott's no stranger to a prison cell, is he? And nor are thee.'

Frank gave him a thoughtful look. 'I'll let that pass considerin' the shock tha's had. I don't think tha realises me father's investing in thee because tha's a respectable fella.' He threw up his hands. 'An' let's face it, Ned, tha knows it's different when it's a woman. If she's not gone in wi' a screw loose, she'll come out that way. Tha'll be a laughing stock. And tha needs to think about this.' He leaned towards Ned and dropped his voice to a whisper. 'Prison's not kind to females. She'll be in her thirties when she's let out, an' beat down by prison life. An' tha's wantin' kids, aren't tha?'

'Aye, wi' Nan.'

'Well, tha's not gettin' any younger.' Frank shrugged. 'I'm only tellin' thee the truth of it. Tha's had bad luck wi' women. If it were me, I'd be washin' me hands o' this one, an' all.'

'Good thing for Nan that I'm not thee,' said Ned. He forced a laugh, wanting to close the subject, aggrieved on

Nan's behalf, and his, but recognising that this would be the opinion of most of the folk he knew.

A few days later, Ned moved his meagre belongings from the lodging house in West Bar to the cottage at the forge. He sat in the garden as spring bled into summer, listening to birdsong, watching the morning mist dissipate into the air – and wondering what Nan was doing now, early on a Sunday. He'd been back to see Hope, to get the address of the prison from her so that he could write to Nan, make her understand that he would never abandon her, tell her that while he awaited her release he'd create a home for her, here on the riverbank, where they would live out the rest of their lives together.

SUMMER

Chapter 15

Nan's name was hissed from across the aisle of the chapel as the hymn ended. She risked a sideways glance, the corner of her mouth lifting into a smile, and put out her hand to accept what the woman across from her was concealing in her fist. Both dropped their arms back to their sides as the warder's eyes swept over the congregation.

Early Sunday morning Chapel was Nan's favourite time of the week. Along with the other inmates, she gave every impression of listening to sermonising on the repentance of sins and the desirability of conforming to the womanly ideal. Chapel served another purpose entirely. It was an opportunity for the women to exchange messages, either via notes scratched on scraps of paper, lip reading or tokens. It was in Chapel that the declaration – or destruction – of friendships and feuds could be easily delivered and went mostly undetected, or, Nan considered, were overlooked by warders who recognised the rituals were a means of letting off steam.

She looked down, opening her fist to reveal a thin lock of blonde hair. Closing her fist again, satisfied, Nan looked across the aisle and half a dozen pews forward, eyes sparkling. A woman wearing the grey striped flannel robe and muslin cap of a special-class prisoner locked eyes with Nan, her mouth curving into a smile. This woman's dress marked her out as a prisoner who was within nine months

151

of her release. The lock of hair came from her, passed from hand to hand and safely into Nan's. It was an expression of devotion. This woman had been in Woking for several years. She knew her way around and was able to offer protection and privileges to a favoured few. Nan was now one of those few, and her status in the eyes of the other inmates would improve accordingly.

When the warder looked elsewhere, she tucked the lock of hair into the band of the small linen bonnet she wore. Like all the probationers, Nan was dressed in the prison uniform for the summer months of a lilac cotton skirt and blouse-bodice with a checked blue and white apron. After the first nine months of her incarceration, she would be moved up to third-class and into a different uniform, a striped blue dress in summer and, so she'd been told, a brown serge dress for the winter months. Brown didn't suit Nan's colouring but that didn't matter. She wasn't planning on spending the winter at Woking jail.

It intrigued her that the period of time served between classes, and the duration of demotions for bad behaviour, was nine months, the exact term of a pregnancy. Was this deliberate, devised to remind the women of what they had lost? Many of her fellow inmates had children they might never see again. One woman's eight-year-old had been put in the workhouse when she was jailed for manslaughter, having killed her abusive husband. There she stood, just behind Nan's champion, her head bowed. She went about like a ghost after receiving notification her son had died, his body disposed of in the paupers' grave. Even if he'd had a funeral, a proper burial with a gravestone, she would not have been allowed to attend it.

Nan wished now that she had given Ned a sign, a signal of some kind, when she was taken from the magistrates' court. Naïvely, she had imagined she would be permitted to see him, or to write, but she had to serve half a year before she would be given the privilege of putting pen to paper. Once she reached third-class status she'd be able to write one letter every six months, and receive one letter in return. Ned would be permitted to visit her every six months for a period of twenty minutes. In those first weeks in isolation at Millbank, her whole body had ached with despair. On arrival at Woking, she told the doctor conducting her medical interview that Ned Staniforth was her next of kin simply to enjoy the pleasure of speaking his name, of seeing it written down, an acknowledgement that made a connection back to him, however tenuous it might be.

Filing out of Chapel, Nan stifled an exclamation when, from behind, a finger was jabbed between her ribs.

'What?' She whispered the word.

The voice that replied came from a woman named Rhoda. Her story was that she had been caught stealing bread from a bakery and returned to torch the place. Convicted of arson and jailed for fifteen years, she had the cell next to Nan's. Her raucous singing in the hours before dawn kept Nan awake. Inevitably, a guard would eventually come along and hammer on the door and threaten Rhoda with solitary.

Now, she grabbed at the back of Nan's blouse, jerking her backwards. Her breath was hot in Nan's ear. 'Think you're special now?' Nan shook her head. 'Good. You're not fit to lick my boots.'

She twisted the fist that was gripping Nan's uniform, kneading her knuckles into her back, relinquishing her grip only when a warder came forward to see why they'd stopped. 'Don't go snitchin'. I've matches from the kitchen, did I tell you that? Ever seen a lass on fire?'

She subsided when the warder stopped beside her. Nan walked on, keeping her gaze on the ground.

Rhoda had been a second-class prisoner, demoted back to third for smashing window panes and gouging the mortar around the door of her previous cell. Nan couldn't seem to shake her off. Rhoda was behind Nan in the exercise yard, scuffing up dust. She sat opposite Nan in the hall, shovelling down her meat and potatoes, and declaring – in a whisper, of course – that it was better to eat prison food than be free and starving. It was Rhoda who imparted the news that a baby farmer had been brought in, convicted of killing several of her infant charges, and put in solitary as she was expected to hang for it. This was too close to home for Nan. 'Why don't you shut up about it?' she'd said. The woman's lip had curled.

'Feel sorry for the old bitch, do you?'

That could not have been further from the truth but Rhoda started the rumour that Nan herself had farmed babies, had taken the mothers' money and drowned the infants. Nan went hungry when her food was spat on, and her refusal to eat might have resulted in force-feeding if her champion had not sat down beside her one day.

'What are you in for, dear?'

'Larceny,' said Nan.

Without seeming to care whether she was being observed, the woman took Nan's hand and guided it onto her lap, beneath the table. 'I'm Sarah. Do you want to know why I'm here?'

Nan's response – 'Not really, no.' – made Sarah laugh. She squeezed Nan's hand.

'You need somebody to look after you, don't you?'

Nan extracted her hand. She cupped Sarah's knee. 'I do.'

A few days before Sarah gave the token of a lock of her hair, Nan was allocated a job sewing burlap sacks for the Admiralty in a room supervised by two female guards. She was certain her champion had a hand in it.

—

Her mother had lain on a bed in a cell like this one, staring at the ceiling and contemplating her fate. Nan did not know what that fate had been, and did not want to know. At Woking, there were women who had their death sentences commuted to life. Her mother might still be alive, might be staring at the ceiling of a prison cell now. Mother and daughter in jail. Bad blood, Miss Barlow would say.

Swinging her legs to the ground, Nan sat on the edge of the iron cot and looked around, measuring the dimensions of her captivity. The whitewash on the walls had crumbled away in places to expose the red brick beneath. There were fourteen tiny panes of glass in the window beneath the arched ceiling. She counted them often. In the corner was a wooden table and chair. A Bible sat on the table, her only reading material until she had earned enough marks to be allowed to borrow a book from the prison library. It was the door to the cell that made her shudder every time she looked at it. There was no handle on the inside, and at any time of day or night an eye might be pressed to the spyhole.

Her nemesis was using her tin cup to bash the window, by the sounds of it. Nan prayed that Rhoda would be removed to solitary, where the walls were clad in coir and the window a thin, unreachable slit. It was all she deserved. Nan was afraid of the wild look in Rhoda's eyes, her unpredictability, her viciousness. It was the same fear she had always felt in her mother's presence, the same fear that had paralysed her until the day of her sixteenth birthday.

'What did you do?' Sarah had asked when Nan confided the truth of her childhood. Sarah was threading a needle, sitting close beside Nan in a room containing some two dozen women. Nan shuffled on the bench, a sack across her lap, waiting for a warder to lament her shoddy workmanship. Her hands were scratched to pieces.

'I reported her,' said Nan. 'She'd let most of the infants starve. I gave them food when I could but I would get a beating for it.'

'That's hard. There!' The needle was threaded. 'You went to the police?'

'And to the court to give evidence against her.'

'Your own mother.'

A guard walked past, stopping to observe the pair, and then continuing on. Nan spoke through lips that barely moved. 'She'd taken thirty shillings from a young mother, a servant who'd got herself knocked up by the master of the house, and promised she'd get the infant adopted. She never did.'

'What happened to the baby?'

Tears rose in Nan's eyes. She shook her head.

Sarah put her hand to her mouth.

'What's the noise over there?' called a warder from across the room. Sarah bent her head over her sewing. 'Keep your gobs shut. That goes for all of you.'

Nan kept her head down. 'She was put away. I went off after that.'

She recalled her first day in the House of Help, hearing a baby's cry and asking Hetty if she was running a baby farm on the quiet. She had felt the old terror inside her, a fear that she concealed beneath a friendly grin. Now she knew the truth about that baby's cry, about Hope giving away for adoption – a proper adoption – her illegitimate child. What a dark horse the deputy warden was. It was Hope that Nan had come closest to the truth with. Others she'd told she never knew her mother. She supposed both could be true, in their way.

Nan put her hand on Sarah's leg, concealed by the burlap. 'You're the only person I've ever told.'

Sarah glanced around and kissed Nan on the cheek, a quick peck. The white lie had served its purpose but Nan was surprised to find a lump rising in her throat. She was a poor enough sewer as it was. Being blinded by tears was the last thing she needed.

It was during the long nights that her helplessness almost got the better of her. What if there was a fire and she was left here, forgotten, to choke to death? What if the male guard who patrolled the corridor at night, and who had openly given her lascivious looks, took it upon himself to unlock the door she had no control over and have his way with her? Nan tried to escape into her imagination, to invent a better story. She returned to Ned and took him away with her. In one scenario, they went north and Ned got work at a shipbuilder's to maintain respectability while Nan liberated wealthy gentlemen of their purses and watches. In another, the two of them worked their passage across the ocean.

In all her dreams, Ned had no qualms about discarding his old life to run away with Nan.

Chapter 16

It was a relief, besieged as Hetty was by her duties as warden and Amelia's sustained campaign of silence, to open the door to Mr Wallace's delighted smile. Rainwater dripped from the brim of his hat while his mackintosh coat was speckled with droplets. Hetty ushered him inside.

'I walked from my office,' he said. 'As you can see, I've been caught in a downpour.' He tipped his hat and shook moisture from his fingers. 'I am overjoyed to see you, Miss Barlow.'

'Overjoyed?' Hetty said faintly. Had anybody ever been overjoyed to see her? Not since the vicar claimed to be, and he had been leading her by the nose. Amelia could not be said to be overjoyed by the revelation that Hetty was her mother. Nor was Mrs Calver overjoyed by Hetty's management of the house. Hetty gave herself a ticking-off. She'd never been one for self-pity. It wouldn't do to start feeling sorry for herself now.

'Yes, yes, I hoped to find you here and not in Grimsby,' said Mr Wallace. 'When is your excursion, by the way?'

'We haven't yet set a date,' said Hetty. The more time that passed the more she could dare to believe that Amelia had given up on her hare-brained scheme.

'Not,' said Mr Wallace, in the same hurried, nervous tone, 'that I'm trying to interfere in warden's business or monitor your movements. Heaven forbid. I have a piece of art I wish to show to you, a gift, for you and for the house.'

He stopped talking for long enough to draw a flat, paper-wrapped package about twice the size and shape of Hetty's ledger from inside his coat, looking at Hetty expectantly from the corner of his eye as if he was a magician about to release a lovebird. 'This was my idea and I have to say that Flora embraced it wholeheartedly and has worked upon it night and day. I think you'll be impressed, if I may be so presumptuous.'

His enthusiasm was infectious. Hetty smiled. 'Aye, I'm sure I will be,' she said. 'Let me take your coat.'

The awkwardness of divesting Mr Wallace of his slickly wet Mackintosh as he juggled the package, transferring it from one hand to the other, made them both smile. She finally had the coat in her hands and hung it on a hook, where it commenced dripping onto the tile. Mr Wallace looked at the floor mournfully.

'Summer downpours can be intense,' he said, handing her the package and executing a little bow. 'All the more so for their unexpectedness.'

'Thank you, Mr Wallace.' Hetty held the package in both hands. 'Shall I open it in the parlour?'

She was curious about the painting. The previous year, when Hetty had attended Mr Wallace's office on house business, she had seen on the wall one of Flora's studies of the glasshouse at the botanical gardens, and had admired it. That was the afternoon she met Mrs Calver, who had been already ensconced in Mr Wallace's office. Hetty's prediction that she'd have dealings with that woman was coming true. She recalled, also, that she'd gone to Mr Wallace's office because of his reluctance to visit the house to discuss a resident's infection by smallpox. But who could blame him? The shadow of the disease still hung over the town, and had claimed Amelia's fiancé and countless others.

Mr Wallace removed his hat and placed it on the table in the hallway.

'It might look splendid hanging here,' he said, making a frame of his hands against the wall beside the door to the parlour. 'We have not nearly enough art,' he paused and looked around, 'on the walls of this house. Not that my daughter is a great artist, no, not by any means. You mustn't feel obliged to display her work.'

He wiped his hand over his beard, a nervous gesture that provoked in Hetty a wave of affection for this kindly man. He opened the door to the parlour and Hetty nodded her thanks and went in ahead of him. The largest uncluttered flat surface in the room, apart from the floor, was the old chaise longue. Hetty could feel the indent of the frame beneath the paper and laid the package face up on the faded fabric. She was aware, as she bent to untie the string, of Mr Wallace's presence at her side, so close she could hear the tick of his pocket watch. He was wearing cologne, a light pleasant scent that almost masked the stale aroma of pipe smoke that clung to his clothes. If she was his wife, she'd see to it that the suit he was wearing got cleaned and mended on a regular basis. Mr Wallace looked like the widower he was, frayed around the edges, and oblivious to it. It was disconcerting, having him loom over her – they were the same height when both were standing – and she felt her cheeks colour, aware of his gaze on her fingers as she separated the sheets of paper to reveal a watercolour painting.

'Oh, that's lovely.'

Forgetting her self-consciousness, Hetty lifted the frame and held it before her, arms outstretched. The foreground was dominated by the cobbles of Paradise Square and a sliver of black iron lamp-post in one corner. Vibrant shades softened the façade of the three-storey houses at the top of the square – dusky pink for the brick, a pale blue sky, soft grey rooftiles and stone-coloured chimney pots. Hetty's eyes were drawn first to a flower cart blocking the gennel by the gable end of the House of Help, multiple-coloured blossoms in miniature tumbling down to the pavement, and then to a small figure standing on the doorstep of the house, hands clasped before her. There was little more detail than a blob of pale lemon for her apron, a swirl of dark brown hair, a simple brushstroke for a smile and tiny blobs of blue for the eyes.

Hetty turned to Mr Wallace and raised an eyebrow. 'Who's this then?'

Mr Wallace rested his hand, very lightly and for only the briefest of moments, on her shoulder as he leaned forward to peer at the picture. 'Why, it's our very own Miss Barlow, welcoming to the house all young ladies in need.'

Hetty's breath caught in her throat. She was glad to have her back to Mr Wallace as she walked over to the mantelpiece and propped the painting on it. It gave her a few moments to compose herself. She made a show of examining the painting more closely. 'I remember now,' she said. 'I came outside to see off young Olive Wright.' That girl had landed on her feet, picked up from the doorstep by the driver of her new employer, no less, to go to a scullery maid's position at a country estate. 'And afterwards I saw there was a young lady sitting at the foot of the square with an easel. Miss Wallace painted me in, didn't she?'

'Ha!' said Mr Wallace. 'When I saw the painting and decided that ought to be our warden Flora thought it a fine idea. And it turns out it *was* you.' He beamed. 'Perfection. You must decide where it should hang.'

'Miss Wallace is very talented.'

'She likes the impressionists. I prefer something a little more true to life myself. The girl's a dreamer, head always in the clouds. I despair of her.' The pride in his voice belied his words. 'She is missing her mother's guidance, of course.'

'Well,' said Hetty, 'please pass on the house's thanks, and mine. Can I offer you a cup of tea?'

This unexpectedly turned into a tea party. As was her wont, Mrs Calver made an unexpected visit to the house, this time with Mrs Shaw, the secretary to the trustees, in tow. Hope joined them. Clara, aided by one of the residents, fetched and carried, and Hetty was content to sit in silence and listen to the others talk about art and the galleries they had visited, in the town and further abroad. Inevitably, her thoughts turned to Amelia. Hetty was leaving her be, her instinct telling her to give Amelia the room she needed to absorb the truth. One encouraging outcome was that the girl had become wary of Gertie, the woman she now knew to be her great-aunt and the architect of the great lie, although she considered Hetty weak for going along with Gertie's plan. Hetty had not had this from the horse's mouth but learned of it through Hope, who said Amelia had sought her out. Still, the girl remained determined to visit Gertie, and Hope had extracted a promise that Amelia would go to Grimsby in the company of her mother.

Hope had smiled grimly, recounting this. 'I ought to tell you that she told me not to call you that. You know how she can be.'

Impetuous, foolhardy and grudging. Was Hetty these things too? Like mother, like daughter? Amelia was also generous to a fault and soft-hearted, qualities Hetty didn't believe she herself possessed in any great quantity.

She suppressed a sigh and returned her attention to the room. Parlour talk had turned to the forthcoming funeral of one of the agents of the house, a volunteer who until the end had displayed a vitality that belied her great age. She had helped many young women find their way to Paradise Square, and had even employed one of them as a cook's assistant in her own home.

'There'll be a good turnout, standing room only at the church,' said Mrs Shaw.

'The wake is to be held…' said Mr Wallace, the words dying on his lips as Amelia entered the room, nodded to the assembled company and sat down beside Hope. She smoothed her hands over the lap of her black dress.

'Who's gone an' died now?'

Mrs Shaw gasped. 'Young lady, you must show some respect.'

Hetty's heart lurched. Amelia had been close to the agent, and Hetty hadn't yet given her the news. She didn't want to add to the girl's burden, but now regretted it. It would be another black mark against her. 'Amelia is grieving the loss of her fiancé,' she said. 'I apologise on her behalf.'

Amelia snorted. 'I can say sorry for mesen. I don't need thee to speak for me.'

'Oh my goodness,' said Mrs Calver. 'We can all see you're in distress, my dear. Perhaps, Hope…?'

Hope got to her feet. 'Will you come and keep me company, Amelia? I am developing a headache and could use some fresh air.'

Mr Wallace stood too. 'I should take my leave too. I'd forgotten I have a meeting to attend.'

Amelia clasped her hands demurely in her lap. 'Don't all leave on my account.' She caught Mrs Calver's eye. 'Nob'dy in this house is capable o' tellin' the truth, are they?'

Mrs Calver frowned. 'What do you mean by that?'

'Amelia,' said Hetty, quietly. Her heart was hammering in her chest. Surely, the girl wouldn't act on the malice in her eyes, and spew forth Hetty's secrets. There was too much at stake. 'Please go with Hope to get some fresh air and I shall speak to you later.'

Amelia laughed wildly. 'What shall we speak about? How about my mother passin' herself off as my sister?' She looked around the room. 'That's right. What does that make me, eh? Shall I tell you?'

Hope took hold of Amelia's wrist. 'You go too far.'

Amelia shook her off. 'All right, then. Here's another one. How about the warden o' this house gettin' her job under false pretences? Shall we speak about that, Hetty?'

'What do you…'

Amelia turned on Mrs Calver. 'Stop askin' *me* what *I* mean.' She pointed at Hetty, whose still expression belied the fear that choked her. 'Ask this one. Ask her about abandonin' a baby.' She took a deep breath, and Hetty saw fright in her eyes, but still she did not stop. 'Ask her about scrubbin' hospital floors. Ask your precious warden how she got this job.'

It was Mr Wallace who persuaded Mrs Calver and Mrs Shaw from the room. 'Let's give these ladies some privacy,' he said. 'We should not be privy to words spoken in anger.'

For once, Mrs Calver had nothing to say. She stopped for a moment on her way from the room, in front of Hetty, who kept her head bowed, then continued out of the room without speaking. Mrs Shaw's skirt swished past followed by the stiff-legged gait of Mr Wallace, who closed the door gently behind him.

Hope came to sit beside her. 'Miss Barlow, can I do anything?'

Hetty raised her eyes to Amelia, who glared back. 'No, love.' She got up slowly, not trusting her legs to carry her out of the room. But they did, all the way to the warden's quarters, where she collapsed into the chair at her desk and stared at its cluttered surface. There was her weekly report to write, and updates to be recorded in the ledger. The actress Anneliese Titterton had given a substantial donation of two guineas following her second stay at the house and Hetty had wanted to personally write the letter of thanks. A runaway girl of fourteen had fetched up at the house and had finally, encouraged by Hope, revealed her address in Leeds. The parents would be contacted and, all being well, would come to collect the girl, or she could always be returned home on the train. There was much else to do. There always was.

She realised the House of Help had been her haven, too, an oasis she had stumbled on after years of drudgery and unhappiness. Her good fortune, turned bad.

Hetty opened her ledger, then closed it and got to her feet. She went to the window to look out over the square, where everybody went about their business as usual. Resting her forehead against the cold glass, she contemplated her ruin.

Chapter 17

Dear Nan, I hope they are treating you right. I am all right.

Ned lay down the dip pen he had liberated along with a bottle of black ink from the clerk's office at the forge. He leaned back in his chair and flexed his fingers. The problem had nothing to do with spelling and grammar. He was handy with a pen, having been educated at school until the age of eleven, and on top of that home-taught by his grandmother. She liked to tell him a man who could read and write fluently would never be deceived in matters of business. Matters of the heart were another affair.

No, his dilemma was that he had no idea how to go about writing a letter to Nan and after these first two sentences he was, as usual, stuck. They were terrible sentences at that, stilted and insincere for being untrue. He had a feeling he'd used exactly the same opening phrases in every previous letter, but what was the alternative? *I can't bear to think of you locked away. My heart is breaking.* Ned lifted his gaze to the whispering leaves of the trees beside the path. He was sitting, as he did every evening at half past six if the weather allowed it, in his shirt-sleeves at the patio table in the garden of the cottage. This evening, a breeze cooled by the river played with his hair and with the edge of the writing paper, as if it would whisk it away and save him the embarrassment of others reading his prose. He raked his fingers over his scalp. Nan liked to put her fingers in his hair, to gather the thickness at the back of his skull in her fist when they kissed. If he closed his eyes he could feel her slender waist in his hands, her lips parting against his.

He sighed and picked up the pen.

The business is going well. He hesitated over the next sentence. It felt like a betrayal. *I am living in the cottage now.*

Ned had got into a daily routine. He rose with the light at six in the morning and worked until six in the evening, overseeing production, making sure the foremen were happy and managing the workforce from the stoker to the furnacekeeper, and the patternmaker to the puddler. Like the men, he took half an hour for dinner. Unlike them, he returned to the cottage for a hot meal that a woman from Malin Bridge came in and cooked for him, and occasionally for his cousin, if Jacob was around. Jacob took care of the paperwork, including stock-taking, sales and new business.

If Ned timed it wrong, if hunger had driven him home early and his food wasn't yet on the table, he was forced to listen to the latest mishap to have befallen the woman's daughter, who was an all-round darling lass, but unlucky in love and therefore still single at twenty-eight, but desperate for babies. Ned nodded along. He knew that in this woman's eyes he was an eligible prospect. He wasn't sure who knew about Nan, and wasn't going to broadcast it to all and sundry. Enduring Frank telling him on a regular basis what a fool he was being was enough.

On Sundays, he worked in the garden and later walked into town to meet pals in the Castle Inn or the Swan. Sometimes he'd be summoned to join Frank and Mr Prescott at the coffee house in Pond Street to talk business. Occasionally, his cousin would invite him to his house in

Hillsborough for tea but it hurt Ned's heart to see children running about, knowing he might never have any of his own. Waiting for Nan meant taking that risk, and he didn't want to be reminded of that.

Ned shivered. It had grown chilly and the light was waning. He picked up the fish paste sandwich the woman who did for him had left for his tea. What would Nan be doing at this hour? He wondered what she was given to eat and drink, and when. She'd eat when she was told to, and the same went for everything she did, as if she was a helpless infant instead of a woman in the prime of her life. He still could not picture her caged.

Ned's stomach turned and he put the sandwich back on his plate, uneaten.

I have visited the house and Hope told me she is writing to you, which is kind. Molly is still there and asked after you.

He'd confided in Molly that it was a lonely existence, waiting for Nan. She'd been sympathetic. Best not to write about that, though. Ned dipped the pen in the ink, shaking his head in exasperation. This was his umpteenth letter to Nan – he'd lost count – and the worst yet. He wondered what her first letter to him would contain. Hope had warned him that letter-writing privileges had to be earned. Was Nan behaving herself? The thought made him smile.

I'm waiting for your letter.

Now he was repeating himself.

With all my love. Ned.

–

'Thing is,' said Frank, 'a leopard doesn't change its spots. An' the fox an' the hen will never be bedfellows.'

Ned laughed. 'She's not an animal, tha does know that, reight? Hang on, I suppose I'm the chuffin' hen in this picture?'

'Aye.' Frank nodded sagely. 'Nan's the fox. An' you're a cluckin' fool.'

He hunched over his pint of ale and cackled with glee. The side of his face was livid with bruises. Ned didn't understand why Frank continued to allow his father to beat him. Frank was bigger than his old man now, and stronger, but still took his licks. And now Ned was in with Frank's father, and owed him commission on the recent business Mr Prescott had brought to the door of the forge. The swelling on Frank's face served as a useful reminder to be prompt with the payment.

They had the snug of the Blue Pig to themselves. The landlord, whose face showed he felt as sorry for Frank as Ned did, although he was careful not to pass comment, had barred the room to other customers. He was serving them himself, keeping post at the end of the bar that opened into the snug, washing pots, wiping down the varnished surface and whistling under his breath in the vain hope that Frank wouldn't suspect he was listening in on their conversation.

Frank downed his whisky chaser and lifted the glass without looking up. The landlord came around with the bottle and refilled it. Ned put his hand over his own glass and shook his head. 'I've a busy day tomorra.'

'Me an' all,' said Frank. He touched his jaw and winced. 'Got a mess to clean up regardin' a couple of missin' firearms.' After Ned's initial enquiry – 'Did tha fall down the stairs again?' – and Frank's wry smile of acknowledgement, nothing had been said about what had led him to the receiving end of his father's fists.

'Tha'll be reight,' said Ned.

'Aye.' Frank clapped his hands together. 'Anyway, to get back to thee and tha woes wi' women. So the point I were makin' is, she were askin' after Charlie Peace because she thinks she's his daughter, and now she's locked up. Like father, like daughter, eh? Bad blood.'

'Nah,' said Ned. 'Nan looks nowt like him, an' she never killed anybody.'

'She'll have her mother's looks then,' said Frank. 'We all know Charlie were a charmer who scattered his seed all o'er the place.'

Ned curled his hand around his pint pot. 'What's it matter, though? He were hanged a while back an' he's no family, at least none that'll admit to it. He had a son but he died.'

'She came 'ere lookin' for her roots.'

Ned sighed impatiently. 'Aye, and there's none to be found, an' now she has me.' He leaned forward to drive home his point. 'She found me, instead.'

Frank opened his mouth to speak.

'Don't say it,' said Ned.

'How about…'

'Don't say it.'

'…if tha got out of tha head a bit? Take our Ellie to the music hall. As a friend.'

Ned snorted. 'Are tha comin' an' all?'

'I can't be doin' wi' it. Ellie would love it, though, get her out the house, away from him. He trusts thee to chaperone her about town.'

'It wouldn't be reight,' said Ned. He was sorry for Frank, and for his sister. It wasn't easy, being a Prescott, but he'd be giving Ellie the wrong idea, and how could he even contemplate gadding about town when Nan was locked up? All he wanted to do was to run the forge and write his terrible letters.

Frank sat back and looked at him through his one good eye. The other was swollen shut, and that side of his face a puffy purple and red mess. What had Mr Prescott hit him with, a hammer?

'Tha wants to stay on me father's right side,' Frank said. 'He likes thee, that's why he's makin' such an effort wi' thee. An' if tha wants a family, tha needs to be gettin' on wi' it.'

Ned laughed. 'You want me as a brother-in-law?'

'Why not?' Frank looked away, hiding his bruises. 'One for the road?'

'This road's gettin' longer an' longer.'

Frank nodded briskly to the landlord. 'Eat, drink an' be merry, Ned, for tomorra tha could be dead.'

—

They were down two men in the puddling room and Ned was mucking in. He was draining the furnace, sleeves rolled up and peaked cap pulled low, when Mr Prescott found him. The man had a favour to ask. Ned directed him to the clerk's office and said he'd be along as soon as he'd finished. It turned out Frank's father wanted Frank kept busy. Ned ought to send him to Europe to drum up some business for the forge.

'An' who's payin' his way?' said Jacob, when Ned relayed the request.

Ned grimaced. 'We are.'

Running the forge kept him occupied in body and mind, but every now and again, Ned's feet turned in the direction of Paradise Square. Another week went by and he found himself back on the doorstep of the House of Help, knowing it was hopeless, that there would be no news of Nan, but obeying the urge to be near the last place she'd laid her head. Hope was running an errand, Molly told him, and neither the warden nor Amelia were at home. Reluctant still to leave, Ned sat on a bench on the edge of the square and watched the townspeople go about their business.

When drops of rain began to fall, he rose and gave the house one last look. As he did, the door opened and Molly emerged, carrying a small cloth bag. Ned lifted a hand in greeting and began to walk away, embarrassed to be caught lingering after she had so recently sent him on his way.

She fell into step beside him. 'Goin' my way?'

'Depends where you're goin'.'

'I've been found a job at a cutlery works down Shalesmoor. Fresh start. Another one.' She held up the bag she was carrying. 'Got me uniform in 'ere and it's straight on wi' me first night shift. An' nobody to wish me luck an' wave me off, except Clara.'

'Well, good for thee, Molly.' He was pleased for her and grateful to hear a bit of good news. 'I can walk down wi' thee. I'll carry tha bag.'

'Grand,' said Molly, handing it over. 'All me worldly possessions.' The bag weighed next to nothing. She took Ned's arm. 'Let's pretend we're promenadin' through the botanical gardens.'

Ned laughed. 'Aye, why not?'

After they had parted ways, Ned walked back to the forge with a spring in his step. He felt certain there would be a letter from Nan waiting for him. He could even picture it, a small white square on the woven rush doormat, brought over from the clerk's office where all the mail went, and pushed through the letterbox. He took a deep breath as he opened the door to the cottage, his heart racing in anticipation.

The doormat was a blank rectangle, mocking him.

Chapter 18

Two days before Ned knocked on the door of the House of Help, Hetty came out of her quarters, head bowed, and almost collided with Clara, who was striding through the hallway with an armful of bedding.

'Up an' down, up an' down like a fiddler's elbow.' The maid directed these words over her shoulder at a girl who was polishing the banister. 'I don't know why I can't just chuck 'em over. It's not bricks I'd be flingin' at thee, is it? But no, up an' down I must trot.'

The girl shook her head. 'You're not throwin' filthy sheets on my bonce.' She'd had the misfortune to arrive the night before the bi-annual deep clean of the house and hadn't taken well to Amelia's dishing out of tasks at breakfast time. 'I weren't expectin' to be slave labour.'

Clara snorted. 'Tha wants to try the workhouse for size.'

'Where's the nearest one? I'm off!'

It would free up a bed, Hetty thought as she continued down the hall towards the kitchen, leaving the bickering behind. She glanced into the water closet where another resident was scrubbing the tile. All the women who did not go out to work, and were strong enough, joined in the cleaning. Two malnourished girls of twelve, twins, remained in bed in the attic space. A distant relative from Manchester would be collecting the poor mites the day after tomorrow. Would she still be warden then? Hetty had gone up herself with porridge and honey first thing that morning, reflecting that if this house had taught her one thing it was there was always somebody worse off than you.

Amelia wasn't in the kitchen or the scullery or the back yard. Hetty retraced her steps through the house. Clara said she hadn't seen Amelia in any of the upstairs rooms and hadn't seen her leave the house. 'Not that I've been payin' attention wi' all this lot to herd about.'

Clara's exasperated tone told Hetty that she wasn't yet privy to the truth, and if Clara didn't know about Hetty's deception nor did anybody else in the house. Amelia had been icily polite to Hetty after her outburst before the trustees. It was wearing.

'Miss Barlow, are you all right?' said Clara. 'D'you want me to give Amelia a message if I see her?'

'No,' said Hetty. 'It's all right.'

She went back into her quarters and through to the anteroom, where she stood at her desk, touching its wooden lip with the tips of her fingers. She wanted to warn Amelia that she had been summoned to a meeting of the trustees, taking place that evening in a side-room at Cutlers' Hall. The building was a minute's walk from the house so she had the whole day before her to fret. The situation wasn't dire. She had money saved from her wages, having always had this eventuality in mind. It was enough to accommodate them both in lodgings while she searched for a job. Maybe they would go to the coast, to Cleethorpes or Scarborough, and find work in a guesthouse. She could clean. Amelia had housekeeping experience.

She jerked her head up when the door knocker sounded. This might be the last time she admitted a girl or woman in need into the house. Would she be allowed to work out a notice period, or did the trustees already have a new warden in mind, a woman who could start immediately? Perhaps the reason they had waited until now to call her before them was that they'd been busy interviewing her replacement. Hetty's mouth curved into a bitter smile. Perhaps the new warden was a protégé of Mrs Calver's who would be sure to enforce her silly ideas about how the house should be run.

There was a knock on the door of her quarters. Hetty straightened up and took a deep breath. 'I'm comin'.'

Clara put her head round the door. 'Our Mr Wallace has come calling,' she said.

Hetty emerged to find the house treasurer standing in the hall, an apologetic expression on his face. 'I hope I'm not disturbing you, Miss Barlow.'

'No, you're not.' She mustered a smile. 'I was about to make myself a cup of tea. Would you like one?'

He followed her to the kitchen where a young woman knelt on spread-out newspaper pages, blackening the range with a cloth. A shoe brush that had seen better days was on the floor beside her. 'Mornin',' she said.

'Don't forget you need to leave it a bit, Polly, before you buff it up,' said Hetty.

'Aye, I know.'

'Good morning,' said Mr Wallace. He patted his cheek. 'You have some on your face.'

'Do I?' The girl swiped at the wrong cheek, adding another smear.

Hetty smiled. 'I think we'll leave you in peace, Polly.' She ushered Mr Wallace from the room. 'You've caught us doing our big clean.'

Mr Wallace stepped nervously around a woman yielding a sweeping brush as if he expected her to bundle him out of the house with it. 'A busy day indeed.'

'We never have any other variety,' said Hetty.

Mr Wallace rubbed his hand over his beard. 'I wonder, if you can spare five minutes, whether we might take a short stroll?'

Hetty's gut churned. Was she about to get her marching orders? Had it been decided she would not be paraded before the board of trustees? Was Constable Goodlad waiting in the square to arrest her for fraud? As they left the house she saw the constable, standing tall in his blue cape, waiting on the edge of the square, and her heart began to pound. Where was Amelia? What if Hetty was locked up, and Amelia decided to wash her hands of her? She faltered, and Mr Wallace put his hand on her arm and gave her a concerned look. Then she saw that the tall figure wasn't Constable Goodlad after all, wasn't even a police officer, just a gentleman standing beside the coffee stall, cup in hand.

'Can we sit?' she said weakly, hoping her legs would carry her to the nearest bench.

'Of course, of course.' Mr Wallace took her arm and led her to the bench, and lowered her onto the wooden slats by her elbows as if she was a feeble old woman. 'You must be in a terrible state of mind. I'm so sorry.'

Hetty shook her head. 'I'm the one should be sayin' sorry. I deceived you all. I'll be sorry to leave.'

'It might not come to that,' said Mr Wallace. 'Miss Barlow, you've proved yourself to be the gem in our crown.'

Hetty stared at him. 'I don't think Mrs Calver would agree.'

'Admittedly, she has some opinions on how the house ought to be run, in the wake of the misfortunes of Miss Turpin. And,' he stopped speaking to sigh, 'she took it upon herself to check your credentials and has confirmed to the board that the women's hospital in Whitby has no record of your working there as matron. Rather, you...'

'Scrubbed floors. I scrubbed floors.' She felt the blush of shame rise in her cheeks. 'Amelia told the truth about me. I never thought she would betray me, but she did. I understand why, an' all.'

'Here.' Mr Wallace produced a handkerchief and Hetty wiped her eyes.

'Thank you.' She clasped her hands in her lap and looked up at the house, where rugs hung from the sash windows like spiteful tongues. It was no longer her house. She had ruined everything. 'I need to find Amelia,' she said, 'and we will leave as soon as is practicable.'

Mr Wallace coughed gently. 'Miss Barlow, tonight's meeting of the trustees is to give you an opportunity to make your case for staying on as warden.' He put his hand over hers. 'I want you to know that I am your most fervent friend and champion.'

'You want me to stay on?' Hetty examined Mr Wallace's smiling face, his greying beard, his kind eyes. 'I forged my papers. I wasn't a matron. I've never managed owt, in my life, until I came here.'

'And look how you have taken to it, like a duck to water.' He patted her hand. 'I believe I can persuade the other trustees to overlook this, um, economy with the truth. We will not find a better warden, and I'm sure none of us wish to expend the effort trying. All you have to do, Miss Barlow, is give a good account of yourself this evening.'

Mr Wallace got to his feet and Hetty took the hand he offered. 'Please don't fret, Miss Barlow. All will be well.'

She hoped he was right.

–

Clara was on her way back up the stairs with a folded pile of clean bedding. 'Oh!' she said when Hetty and Mr Wallace entered the house. 'There's a note for you. Must've got knocked off the side. Polly found it on the floor under Amelia's bed.'

'You saw her?' said Hetty. 'Amelia, I mean?'

'No. Not since breakfast time when she was dishin' out the orders.' Clara trotted upstairs. 'I left it on the kitchen table for you.'

The last note Amelia had written to Hetty had contained the news that she was off to catch a train to track down her errant fiancé. Fearing the worst, Hetty hurried into the kitchen, Mr Wallace following behind. She nodded to the woman now using the shoe brush to buff up the range, and snatched up the note. She was aware of Mr Wallace's eyes on her as she unfolded the paper. Written on it in pencil were the words that confirmed her fears.

'What is it?' said Mr Wallace.

'She's gone to Grimsby.' Hetty swallowed, determined not to burst into tears and lose her final shred of dignity. 'Without me. She's gone to see Gertie an'…' She crumpled the note in her fist. 'We were supposed to go together. I can't have that old woman getting her claws into her.'

The imperative to act was overwhelming, yet she remained frozen to the spot.

'She might still be at the station,' said Mr Wallace. 'I'll drive you. My dear, I'll take you all the way to Grimsby if need be.'

His words, spoken calmly, had a soothing effect. 'Thank you,' Hetty said. 'Thank you so much.'

In her quarters, she threw a few items of clothing and toiletries into a valise, instructed Clara to let Hope know what had happened and ran down to the foot of the square where Mr Wallace helped her into his cabriolet, and they were away. It only occurred to her during the journey that, unless she could persuade Amelia to come home, she would have to follow her to Grimsby. When Hetty failed to show up to plead her case at tonight's meeting of the trustees, they would naturally reach the conclusion that she was not committed to the job of warden. It was too easy to imagine Mrs Calver's scorn.

'Don't concern yourself with the meeting,' said Mr Wallace. Hetty looked at him. He kept his eyes on the road. 'This is more important.'

Mr Wallace insisted on accompanying Hetty into the station. He persuaded her to sit on a bench under the awning of the station master's office, the cold seeping through her clothes, a chill in the breeze making her shiver, while he went to investigate the timetable. There was a service to Grimsby, via Lincoln. The train had departed three hours earlier. The next service was at eleven o'clock the following morning.

Hetty wrapped her arms around herself. 'P'raps there's a coach,' she said. 'I need to go to her. If that old woman harms a hair on her head with her witchcraft…' Her voice faded. 'She's my daughter.'

Mr Wallace nodded calmly. 'I'll take you. We'll go today. You have a bag already packed.'

He didn't seem to require any further explanation, and Hetty loved him for it.

Chapter 19

The inmate walking behind Nan was mumbling to herself as they entered the exercise yard in single file.

Nan risked a glance behind her and met the woman's eye. She was sallow-complexioned, somewhere in her fifties or sixties, and was complaining, to an audience comprised only of herself, about her weak heart and her good-for-nothing soldier son. She paused her monologue to raise an eyebrow at Nan – *Mind your own business* – then resumed her muttering as soon as Nan's back was turned. Her son was the real culprit. If he'd looked after her properly as a good boy should, she wouldn't have to melt spoons for counterfeit coins. She'd die here in jail rather than be returned to him. Anyhow, he'd washed his hands of her. Her heart would give out, you just wait and see. Been getting away with it for years, she had.

Nan wasn't sure whether the *getting away with it* related to the counterfeiting or cheating death. She was more concerned that upon turning she had seen Rhoda, previously three inmates back, exchange places with the woman behind the counterfeiter. It was a quick sashay that went unnoticed. With a sick feeling, Nan accepted that Rhoda was working her way towards her favourite victim. She flinched in anticipation of a finger in the ribs. It was Rhoda's speciality, delivered swiftly and leaving the recipient gasping in pain while the guards remained oblivious.

Nan had begun counting her steps as soon as the inmates started their circumnavigation but the sight of Rhoda worming her way towards Nan had alarmed her, and she'd lost her place. She'd only once completed the count in the enforced hour of exercise, clocking up four thousand, seven hundred and thirty-eight steps. She began to count again, from scratch. It calmed her to mentally box away every five hundred steps completed. It helped pass the time. *One, two, three, four.* The counterfeiter's mumbling had faded and Nan knew without looking that Rhoda now walked behind her. Nausea twisted her gut.

Two guards: one male, one female, stood side by side on the inside of the parade of women. They had wandered to the south-facing section of the exercise yard, where the light fell, and were chatting to each other, their eyes roaming the yard. Nan passed behind them, the warmth of the sun briefly caressing the side of her face. She turned the corner into the shadow of the high wall. *Fifty-nine. Sixty. Sixty-one.* Next, she walked against the back wall. This one and the next were lower, but still unscalable, being some fifteen feet in height. These were the prison's boundary walls. Sometimes she could hear sheep bleating and rooks cawing in the fields, and occasionally she imagined these bricks she walked by did not face into the yard but onto the surrounding countryside. At any moment, she could turn and run across the open land, free as a bird.

Nan was now furthest away from the guards. The attack came on step number *one hundred and eight.*

She was braced for a poke in the ribs and a hiss of satisfaction. The remainder of the walk would be spent anticipating the next, and the next. Instead, a heavy blow on the side of her face sent her head ricocheting off the wall.

Nan went down on her hands and knees, stunned, and too shocked to cry out. More blows rained down, against the back of her head, her neck, her shoulders. Where were the guards? She raked her fingers in the dirt of the yard, overcome by a sudden fury, and reared up, throwing her arms around the skirt of her attacker, her face pressed against Rhoda's midriff. Nan brought them both down with a thud she felt in every bone of her body. She scrambled up the woman's body. Rhoda now lay pinned beneath her, on her back, her mouth making a perfect circle of shock. Nan made a fist and punched the gaping maw. She was vaguely aware of shouts and pounding feet as they rolled into the wall, Rhoda screaming through blood-covered teeth, her hands snatching at Nan's hair. Nan managed to free her arm, pulling it back again to deliver another punch. Then she was suddenly weightless, her legs dangling above the dirt.

The two guards deposited her on her feet, the male gripping her arm while the female guard bent to shake Rhoda, who had curled, sluglike, into a ball. Panting heavily, Nan tried to explain that she had been attacked first but the words wouldn't come. The guard shook her so violently by the arm he was gripping that her teeth chattered. 'Wild animals, the lot of you,' he said. Nan's vision swam. She felt a trickle on her forehead and raised her free hand to her temple. The skin was wet. Her finger-tips came away with red mixed in with the grey dust of the yard. It was the last thing Nan saw before she lost consciousness.

The chief matron of Woking jail glided into the infirmary, her chimney-pot shaped bonnet tied under her chin by a wide black ribbon, the fringes of her shawl spread across her substantial frame. There was an implacability on her heavyset face that told Nan no amount of pleading would help her. A guard had already warned her what the consequences were likely to be.

Rhoda had not been brought to the infirmary. Nan had punched out two of her teeth but that was the extent of Rhoda's injury, according to the guard. 'Of all the people to smack,' he'd said, shaking his head. 'You'll be glad to know she's in solitary for the next six months.'

'And then what?' said Nan.

The guard had shrugged. 'Watch yer back.'

It turned out Rhoda had smuggled her tin pint out of her cell and used that as a weapon to batter Nan. The tin was dented, Nan's skull was not. But the impact of her head hitting the wall was enough for her to sustain a concussion, the doctor said. It had not been a comfort to be told she would be right as rain in no time. Right as rain for what? To continue her miserable existence here?

Now, the matron pulled up a chair and sat by her bed.

'How are you feeling, my dear?'

Nan touched the gauze at her temple, gingerly. 'I have a headache.'

'It might have been worse,' said the matron. 'The governor and I are in agreement that you did not instigate the scuffle.'

'Please may I speak, Miss Jameson?'

The matron nodded.

'This wasn't a scuffle. I was attacked, from behind. That woman's got it in for me.'

The matron continued as if Nan hadn't spoken. 'However, the incident cannot go unpunished. We considered placing you in the silent system but have decided you may continue to work and mingle with the other inmates. Your punishment will be an extension of your probationary period for a further nine months.'

'But I didn't do anything,' said Nan, as loudly as she dared.

The matron compressed her lips then continued speaking. 'No privileges will be extended to you during this period.'

She tilted her head, waiting for Nan's acknowledgement. 'Miss Turpin?'

'Thank you,' said Nan, through numb lips. She closed her eyes. It would be over a year before she would be allowed to write to Ned, or to receive a letter from him.

The matron stood. 'I'll leave you to recover and to reflect on your behaviour and your future in this institution. Don't let us down, Miss Turpin. I should hate to see further penalties laid upon you.'

The following day, Nan was returned to her cell and the daily monotony of serving time resumed. At Sunday morning Chapel she was offered smiles, discreet pats on the hand, small gestures that were all the inmates were able to give. She was to be pitied, then. When Sarah took her hand under the table in the hall, Nan snatched it away. 'Don't lose heart,' Sarah whispered. 'Help is coming.'

Nan hissed back. 'Is it coming before Rhoda does?'

A week went by. Nan was returning to her cell when she was stopped by a female warder who slipped a scrap of paper into her hand. Her heart raced as the door clanged shut behind her. Lowering herself onto the bed, she unfolded the piece of paper. It was a flyleaf from a library book, and pencilled on it was Sarah's address in the Highlands of Scotland. There was a date, too. January 11, 1889. A sob rose in her throat.

Sarah would be freed about the same time that Rhoda came out of solitary confinement. Nan had no doubt Rhoda would campaign to destroy Nan's chances of early release. It was a game to the other woman, one that Nan did not want to play. She'd have no choice in the matter.

Help was coming. Sarah had promised. The sympathetic warder would play a role, Nan was convinced. Was that freedom she could taste? She read the address over and over, memorising it, then tore the paper into tiny fragments that she would sweep out with her brush the next morning. It had to be a sign she would soon escape.

If she remained trapped here, she knew that she would go insane.

Chapter 20

Hetty wondered whether she had taken leave of her senses. How else could she account for where she now sat, staring into Gertie Barlow's gimlet eye?

The folds of a heavy tablecloth brushed the toes of Hetty's shoes. She was sitting at a small round table between Mr Wallace and Amelia, and directly opposite Gertie. The old woman's features wavered in the light from the candle flame between the two adversaries. Gertie's hair was loose around her shoulders, like the fragile seeds of a dandelion clock, the high collar of her black gown tight around her scrawny neck. In the flickering light, her head appeared to be floating, disembodied. It was one of her tricks.

Amelia's grip on Hetty's left hand was tight, while Mr Wallace held the fingers of her right hand lightly in his, as if he was about to lead her somewhere. After they had been summoned to Gertie's cottage just before midnight, Mr Wallace had shown a professional interest in the old woman's assertion that she could communicate with the spirits. He asked polite questions about her church. He flattered her. 'The uncanny is all around us, isn't it?' he said. 'What is the new science of telephony but one disembodied voice speaking to another?'

Gertie had suggested he subscribe to the news-sheets that advertised séances in his area. Attendance was charged at a very reasonable rate and the séances attracted many fine ladies as well as gentlemen such as himself. Mr Wallace had taken out his wallet but Gertie gracefully declined his offer of a donation, patting Amelia's hand and declaring that she would waive her charge in lieu of the fact she was helping her great-niece to find peace. Amelia was so wrapped up in the idea of communicating with Linus that she appeared not to take in Gertie's sly *great-niece* reference, which anyway had been intended for Hetty's ears.

'I am a spirit medium, acting as an intermediary between the living and the departed souls,' she had told Mr Wallace. *Acting* was right. And up the garden path was where Hetty was now being led. Amelia and Mr Wallace too, like trusting children.

Gertie had chosen which seats each of them should take at the little table by the window of the sitting room. The only illumination came from a single candle in its tall silver stick in the middle of the cloth. The spirits, she explained, preferred the semi-darkness and there was, she assured Mr Wallace, a scientific reason for this. Gaslight produced concentric circles of heat – like ripples on a pond – that interfered with the manifestation of the spirits, making them reluctant to emerge.

She had instructed them to join hands. Never in a month of Sundays would Hetty have imagined herself here, holding the hand of the treasurer of the House of Help so that they might close the circle of a séance. She risked a glance at his profile. Mr Wallace turned his head towards her and dropped one eye shut before returning his attention to Gertie. Had he just winked at her? Hetty's lips twitched. She switched her attention to her daughter, whose eyes were wide with wonder and fear. Hetty reflected, once again, that her decision to rescue Amelia from this house after Hetty's mother's funeral had been the correct one. If she hadn't taken Amelia with her, the poor child would by now be this woman's apprentice. Nevertheless, here they sat. It seemed all roads led back to Gertie.

The old woman's hands were linked to those of Amelia and Mr Wallace. She stared into Amelia's eyes, then Hetty's and finally turned her gaze on Mr Wallace before slowly lowering her chin to her chest. Outside, an owl hooted.

'I require complete silence from everyone around this table,' Gertie said. Her voice had deepened. A shiver ran up Hetty's spine. There was no denying it, the mad old bat could conjure an atmosphere.

Finally, Gertie lifted her gaze to the candle flame. Hetty could see its light reflected in the old woman's eyes like cataracts. Gertie slid her gaze to Hetty, the slightest of smiles on her thin lips, then away again. She spoke in the same ponderously deep tones. 'Are you with us, my dear? Knock once for yes.'

There was silence. The owl hooted again. Hetty realised she was holding her breath in anticipation.

'Knock once for yes,' Gertie repeated. She looked at Hetty. 'Knock twice if you are inhibited by this company and do not wish to come forth.'

Amelia smothered a groan. Hetty squeezed her hand.

'Knock once if you are with us and wish to make yourself known.'

This time, a single heavy rap resounded around the darkened room. Amelia gasped. Mr Wallace leaned forward, eager, his eyebrows raised. Hetty was tempted to remark that there must be somebody at the door, but she'd had words with herself about going along with the charade, for Amelia's sake, and held her tongue.

'Then please find your way to me,' said Gertie. 'I welcome you in.' She repeated the words in a whisper. 'I welcome you in.'

She threw back her head in a sudden, forceful movement, startling them all, and stared at the ceiling for long enough for Mr Wallace to begin shifting in his seat. Finally, Gertie lowered her head and narrowed her eyes to look beyond Hetty at a point over Hetty's right shoulder. The old woman was staring at the door that opened onto the garden path. Hetty suppressed a shudder. Along with the others, she could not resist the urge to follow Gertie's gaze.

The door was barely visible in the gloom. Another shiver ran up Hetty's spine when it creaked open, even though she had already predicted this might happen. The night air rushed in, carrying the tang from the estuary of fish and salt air. What if she had been wrong all along? What if Gertie really could conjure the spirits? Hetty could not tear her eyes away from the empty threshold. She drew in a sharp breath when a puff of air caressed her cheek. In the same instant, the candle flame was snuffed out and the door slammed shut.

Amelia screamed. Her grip on Hetty's hand loosened as she scraped back her chair.

Gertie's growl raised the hairs on the back of Hetty's neck. 'Quiet, girl. Do not break the circle. Do not speak.'

Hetty squeezed Amelia's hand. The darkness was not total. A sliver of moonlight bled into the room between curtains that had not been fully drawn. But there was not enough light for Hetty to make out the expression on Amelia's face. Like everyone around the table, she was a dark bulk. The light was behind Gertie and fell like a rapier into her skull. She remained as still as the rest of them.

Mr Wallace cleared his throat. As Hetty's eyes adjusted to the gloom she saw him raise the arm furthest from her into the air. It appeared as though he had released Gertie's hand, had broken the circle in defiance of the old woman's direct instruction. His other hand still rested in Hetty's. 'Mr Wallace?' she whispered, her gut contracting in fear. Then Amelia let go of Gertie's hand too, raising her arm in the same eerie manner, a moan rising from deep within her throat. It took Hetty a second to grasp that it was Gertie who was manipulating the pair, raising her arms up and down, up and down, as if she was trying to scale a wall before her that did not exist. The others' hands were still linked to Gertie's so that they were forced to join in this macabre dance. Hetty was torn between letting the scene unfold or decrying it as nonsense. She strained her eyes. Now, both Gertie's arms were raised, along with Amelia's right arm and Mr Wallace's left. An effortful grunting sound came from Gertie's mouth. In a sudden, jerking movement, she pulled on the hands of Amelia and Mr Wallace so that they landed again on the table.

Amelia moaned and was hushed by the old woman.

'Will you help us?' Gertie said. She replied to herself immediately, in the sing-song cadence of a child. 'If I can, I will, Miss Barlow.'

Hetty sat up, ramrod straight, before realising that of course there were three Miss Barlows present in the room, and that one of them belonged in the madhouse.

'It's so crowded in here,' said Gertie, a note of whining creeping into her impersonation of a child's voice. 'So many souls.'

The people sitting around the table were obviously meant to believe they were surrounded by a roomful of spirits. Hetty wished she could make out Gertie's features. The old woman's body was outlined by the sliver of light behind her but her face was invisible. There was something wrong, something different about the shape of her shadowed bulk, but Hetty couldn't say what it was. The rest of the room was cloaked in darkness as black as coal. What lurked in its farthest corners? Hetty realised she was being infected by Gertie's act, by Amelia's belief, by her own exhaustion, and shook herself. She had to credit the old woman. This was a fine performance.

'Tra la la, tra la la,' said Gertie, a young girl, singing a nursery rhyme. 'Who would like to sing with me?'

Were they now to suppose Gertie was possessed? She had told them earlier that her guide in the spirit world was a servant girl from the last century who had drowned in a well. When she was called to a séance, the girl used the dank walls of the well to climb into the realm of the living. Hetty realised, suddenly, what it was that had been bothering her about Gertie. She could see the top two rungs of the ladderback chair that the old woman sat on. She had shrivelled, shrunk down to the size of a child. Hetty was glad that she couldn't see Gertie's face. She quashed the vision that swam into her mind of the old woman's wrinkled visage replaced by a child's smoothly rounded cheeks and eyes that were as devoid of life as those of a china doll. Hetty shook her head again, as if she could dislodge the image, and forced herself to focus instead on the solidly reassuring bulk beside her of Mr Wallace. She moved the fingers of the hand he loosely held and received a brief squeeze in return.

Amelia was breathing heavily, almost panting. Hetty returned her attention to her daughter, pushing her knee into the side of Amelia's thigh, trying without words to tell her not to fear, to recognise this for the sham that it surely was, or at least to find reassurance in her mother's touch. The girl didn't acknowledge Hetty. Her ragged breathing continued.

'We can sing, my darling,' Gertie said, using her own voice, 'but first, do you have with you this young lady's fiancé, so recently passed over? I am certain he remains close by Amelia's side, so soon after passing.'

'Linus?' said Amelia. 'Is he here? Linus, can you hear me?'

'I told you to be silent,' said Gertie, irritably. She took a deep breath. 'My darling girl, is Linus here?'

They all cried out when the table lifted, tilting up where Gertie sat, before thudding back down onto the rug. Gertie slumped sideways, then righted herself. Hetty laughed shakily. 'Gertie,' she said, a warning note in her voice.

Gertie laughed along with her, a girlish chuckle. 'Don't be afraid,' she said in the sing-song child's voice. 'He's here, standing behind the young lady. Can you feel his hand on your shoulder?'

'Yes, yes, I can feel it,' said Amelia. She was sobbing, making deep wrenching noises that tore apart her mother's heart. 'I have to see you, Linus.' She twisted, this way and that, restrained by the hands holding hers. 'I need to see him. Auntie Gertie, can I?'

'No-one in this realm can look upon the spirits,' said Gertie, still assuming the high-pitched voice. 'The human heart is too frail to bear it. But you do feel his touch, don't you?'

'Yes, I feel his hand, on my shoulder. Is that you, Linus?' Hetty could feel, transmitted through Amelia's hand, the deep shudder that ran through the girl's body. 'Are you really there? Please say something. Please.'

'Tra la la. Can you hear that echo when I sing?' said Gertie in the same eerie voice. 'Can you hear it?'

'Yes,' said Amelia uncertainly. 'Is Linus still here? I thought I felt him.'

'I couldn't get out.' The voice was petulant now. 'I shouted but nobody came.'

Gertie switched to the voice that was hers, only deeper. 'Does Linus have a message for the fiancée he left on this plane?' She giggled. The child was back. 'Yes. He's with his mother and his father. They liked you very much, did you know that?'

'His parents?' said Amelia. 'But Linus's parents are still alive.'

Gertie giggled again. 'You ran to the doctor, do you remember? You were quicker on your feet than the old people.'

'I did,' Amelia said excitedly. 'I fetched the doctor, but it was too late.'

'Linus has a request.'

'Anything,' said Amelia. 'Linus, I'll do anything.'

'You'll have children. Linus can see them. A boy and two girls. Will you name your first-born son for him and your first daughter for my dearest friend, Gertrude?'

Unseen in the dark, Hetty rolled her eyes.

'Yes, yes,' sobbed Amelia. 'I will, I will. What is it like, where you are? Linus, can you hear me? I love you.'

'He loves you too. He's watching over you. Shall we sing a song now?' Gertie's voice deepened in pitch. 'Not now, dear.'

The table rocked and bucked. 'But I want to sing a song with you!' Gertie snapped into her own voice. 'Leave me now,' she said, and rose up in her seat. Hetty realised, with more relief than she would care to admit, that Gertie had slid down earlier, to give the impression of being smaller, the size of a child, and that had been the cause of Hetty's unease. It was an obvious trick but, caught in the moment, Hetty could not deny she had felt a frisson of fear.

Amelia's sobs punctuated the silence that followed. Mr Wallace cleared his throat.

'She's gone,' said Gertie flatly. 'You may break the circle.' She reached behind her to pick up a box of matches from the window ledge and relit the candle. The faces of everyone around the table wavered back into focus, and the shadows lengthened in the room behind them.

Amelia was staring at Gertie, who had leaned back in her chair and was smoothing her hair away from her forehead as if she'd just woken from a nap. Amelia's eyes next searched the face of Mr Wallace, who smiled kindly at her, before coming to rest on Hetty.

'He was here,' said Amelia. She crossed an arm across her body, clutching at her shoulder. 'I felt him. I felt him touch me here.'

'I'm sure you did,' said Hetty, as reassuringly as she could.

'Where's he gone, Auntie Gertie?'

Gertie gave her a withering look. 'Can you still feel his touch?'

'No.' Amelia looked crestfallen. She turned her tear-streaked face to Hetty. 'He was here,' she repeated. 'I felt him. He was here.'

Hetty nodded. 'I believe you,' she said. What else could she say? Gertie had set the scene to elicit hysteria. There would be a system of wires, attached to the front door, and a box under the table for Gertie to tap her foot on and recreate the knock that had startled them all. She would use it to lever herself up and down in her chair. But Hetty wasn't inclined to investigate. The séance had been for Amelia's sake and exposing Gertie's tricks would make a lie of the connection she believed she'd made with her Linus.

'Might we be offered a cup of tea?' said Mr Wallace.

Gertie nodded and jerked her head towards the kitchen. Hetty knew what was coming next. This endless night wasn't over yet.

—

'Amelia, there is something else that I am privy to, that the spirits insist I reveal to you now. The time is right.'

Gertie stood in front of the dresser in her kitchen, her arms folded. The room was lit by the golden glow of two gas lamps on the kitchen table and the crackling fire, and scented by the sprigs of holly hanging from the doorframe. It would be a cosy scene in other circumstances. The old woman had made a pot of the foul-tasting tea Hetty recalled all too well. Mr Wallace was endeavouring to sip at it. Her heart went out to him.

'What do you have to tell me, Auntie?' Amelia said eagerly. 'Is it another message from Linus?'

Hetty leaned back in her chair and folded her arms. 'I know what's comin', love. I'd save your breath, Gertie, if I was you.'

But the performance was not to be interrupted. Gertie pointed an arthritic finger at Hetty, keeping her eyes on Amelia. 'The woman you call sister has been keeping a secret from you. This fallen woman – this harlot here – is your mother.' She nodded triumphantly. 'Your mother, d'you hear?'

Hetty and Amelia exchanged a look.

'What do you think about that then?' said Gertie, a little uncertainly.

'She told me, a while back,' said Amelia. Gertie's mouth soured in surprise and Hetty allowed herself a small measure of satisfaction. But Amelia's next words cut her to the core. 'But I don't care about that. Hetty can go whistle. I came here to speak to Linus, an' I have.' She frowned. 'Haven't I?'

'Oh aye,' said Gertie. 'You have that. Can't bring yourself to call her *Mother*?' She curled her lip and turned her attention to Hetty. 'Din't she fall into your arms, then, like you were expectin'? Did you tell her you ran off, abandoned her?'

'Your malice knows no end,' said Hetty.

'Auntie Gertie,' said Amelia. 'Was it real? I felt his hand. I felt Linus's hand on my shoulder, I'd swear to it. But his parents aren't dead.'

'My guide says they are,' said Gertie, shortly. Her face was creased with disappointment. She'd been denied the thrill of revealing Hetty's true identity. For Hetty, it was a bittersweet victory. She would rather have Amelia's regard.

Amelia nodded thoughtfully. 'I should go to Tamworth, to see if that's true. Aye, I'll go there.' She looked around the room, her eyes full of tears. 'They were kind to me.' When she pushed back her chair and got to her feet, Hetty rose to embrace her. It was a mistake. 'Don't,' said Amelia. 'You're not my mother. My mother's dead.'

A sly grin spread across Gertie's face. 'And turnin' in her grave. She'd be heartbroke, seein' this.'

'Shut up, Gertie,' said Hetty. 'Don't you think you've upset her enough?'

'I gave her what she wanted,' said Gertie. 'What have you ever done for her?'

Amelia looked from one to the other. 'I'm sick o' this,' she said, 'an' I'm bone tired. I'm goin' to bed.'

She went to the door and looked back at Hetty, who stood helplessly in the middle of the room. 'He was 'ere, sister. I mean, oh, I don't know what I mean.' She went out, closing the door behind her.

Hetty sat back down and put her head in her hands. Perhaps after a night's sleep Amelia would reconsider embarking on the journey to Tamworth. Perhaps Hetty ought eventually to explain to her how Gertie managed the tricks she played on the gullible and the heartsick. She sighed and looked up at the old woman.

'We'll need to stay 'til morning,' she said. 'We have rooms at the guesthouse down the road but it'll be locked up this time o' night.'

'The gentleman can have the armchair in the sitting room. There's nowhere for you to sleep,' said Gertie. 'You're not comin' in wi' me, and I don't think Amelia will want to see thee.'

'Then I'll sit up,' Hetty said.

'In my house? Tha'll have to ask nicely.'

'My mother's house,' said Hetty.

She was weary of treading over well-worn ground but being here had sown the seed of an idea that was blossoming in her mind. She might have burned her bridges by snubbing the meeting of the trustees but, after she and Amelia were inevitably sacked from their jobs at the

House of Help, they could return here. Would Gertie be able to stop them? Could Hetty contemplate living under the same roof? No, she could not. Gertie would have to go. Hetty was certain one of the members of her church would take her in.

'My mother's house,' Hetty repeated. 'I dread to think how you convinced her to put it in your name. It should, by rights, be mine, and then Amelia's. You might despise me but surely you have a shred of feeling for her?'

'You'll lose,' said Gertie. 'I've willed it to the church to atone for your sins.'

Hetty laughed. 'The Royal Mint hasn't enough coin to pay for your sins.'

Gertie threw up her hands. 'Haven't I done enough for you? I helped raise her.' She pointed at the ceiling. 'An' now she's had the séance she wanted, though every single one I do drains more of the essential life force from me.'

'You can spout as much gobbledegook as you like,' said Hetty. 'I'll be makin' a claim. My mother wasn't of sound mind when she died.'

'How would you know? *You* weren't here.' Gertie marched to the door. 'I'm going to bed, an' all. You'll leave tomorrow, you and her and your fancy man, and I don't want to see hide nor hair of you ever again, you hear me?' She stood on the threshold, her arms folded. 'You have no claim to stake here.'

Mr Wallace coughed gently into his hand and spoke for the first time since he had taken a seat at the kitchen table. 'That's not quite true,' he said, 'if indeed the property was purchased by Miss Barlow's mother and the will is in dispute.' Hetty gave him a grateful look and met Gertie's scowl. 'I'll certainly help look into it,' Mr Wallace continued, 'once we have returned to Sheffield. Would you be agreeable, Hetty?'

'Aye, I would.' Hetty smiled. This was the first time he had called her by her given name. 'I like the sound of that very much.'

Chapter 21

Hetty pinned on her cap, frowning at her reflection in the rosewood-framed mirror that hung on the wall in the hallway of the House of Help. This might be the last time she wore the dark blue dress of warden of the house, the last time she fastened the tiny mother-of-pearl buttons of the round white collar under her chin.

Her humiliation would be complete when she appeared before the trustees wearing a uniform she had come about by false means, displaying an authority she was not entitled to. A sham.

The cap was askew. Hetty sighed, and began pulling out the pins.

'Is everything all right?'

The voice belonged to Hope, who was walking towards her from the back of the house. Would this composed young woman be given the job of warden? She was competent enough.

'Let me,' said Hope.

Hetty turned to face her. 'I don't know what's wrong wi' me. I can't get it straight.'

Hope set about fixing and re-pinning the cap on Hetty's head. 'What time is your interview?'

'Half past one.' Hetty sighed again. 'I hope they tell me straight away, one way or the other. I never really knew—' She stopped herself, afraid she might break down in tears, standing here, facing her deputy as if she was a child being dressed by her mother. It would be another humiliation piled on the rest.

'What?' said Hope, gently.

Hetty took a breath. 'How much this job means to me.'

Hope put her hands on Hetty's shoulders and turned her to face the mirror. 'There. Presenting Miss Barlow, warden of the House of Help, a friend to friendless girls like me.'

Hetty tilted her head. 'You're doing very well for yourself, I'd say.'

'Thanks to you, Miss Barlow.'

'An' I have to thank you, Hope, for fulfilling your role as deputy so well.'

Hope smiled. 'Without a single qualification to my name.'

A smatter of laughter floated up from the kitchen.

'Will you come and say goodbye to Lottie before you go?' said Hope.

Hetty took a shaky breath and sniffed. 'Aye, I've a few minutes.'

In the kitchen, Lottie Henshaw was slicing a knife into a three-layer carrot and cream cake, one of Cook's confections. The house had been filled all morning with the delicious smell of baking and the cake was Lottie's leaving gift, although judging by the number of women crowded round the table, including Amelia in her black, there would be none left for Lottie to take with her to the railway station. For the past month, this woman had been one of the House of Help's easier residents. She was a good needlewoman, was around the same age as Hetty and acted as a calming influence on the younger women in the house. She had arrived on the doorstep after discovering the man she was living with was married, bringing only the clothes she could carry and a photograph of her late husband. Lottie had been found a permanent servant's position at a house in the village of Grasmere, on the edge of the lake of the same name. One of the women was asking where exactly Grasmere was when Hetty entered the room.

'I've heard of it,' said another. 'It's in the west, all lakes an' hills. Rains a lot.'

'Sounds borin',' the first woman replied.

Hetty accepted a small slice of cake on a saucer. 'The lakes are beautiful,' she said. 'Wordsworth died in Grasmere.' All eyes turned on her, even Amelia's. Hetty coughed self-consciously. 'I wandered lonely as a cloud that floats on high o'er vales and hills.'

'What're you on about?' said Amelia.

'I learned it, at school,' said Hetty.

'Oh yes, it's lovely,' said Hope. She recited the next line of the poem. 'When all at once I saw a crowd, a host, of golden daffodils.'

Hetty took it up again. 'Beside the lake, beneath the trees, fluttering and dancing in the breeze.' She trailed away when she caught sight of the mocking expression on Amelia's face.

'Well, I do like daffs,' said Lottie.

Hetty cleared her throat. 'Ladies,' she said. All the women turned to her expectantly, except for Amelia, who was busy brushing crumbs from her dress. Hetty wondered whether Amelia felt remorse about blurting out a truth that had led to Hetty's summoning before the trustees. She wanted to tell her that it was of no account, that Amelia was her first and last and only concern, even when her daughter demonstrated only contempt towards her.

She pasted on a smile. 'Let's all wish Mrs Henshaw the best of luck, and safe travels.'

'Safe travels!'

'Good luck wi' all the daffodils, love!'

'Come back and visit. I'll bake thee another one of me cakes!'

Hetty glanced at Amelia, who had begun an animated conversation with the woman sitting next to her, put on the table her untouched piece of cake and slipped from the room.

The trustees had agreed to re-schedule their meeting regarding Hetty's employment. The venue had changed too, from the Cutlers' Hall that was only a few hundred yards from the house to the Royal Victoria Hotel on the far side of the town's main thoroughfare. Her future would be decided in a meeting room there, her presence required at half past one in the afternoon. Mr Wallace had offered to drive Hetty to the hotel but she had demurred. It seemed appropriate to arrive under her own steam, and she would use the walk towards the railway station to compose her thoughts with a focus the busy house – and Mr Wallace's driving – did not allow. She fastened her cape and took an umbrella from the stand in the porch. A fine drizzle was falling on the square and there was a cold nip in the air that sharpened the ever-present smell of coalsmoke. Hetty sidestepped a shallow puddle of water on the pavement and turned right in the direction of the railway station and the fanciest hotel in town.

If the sight of the trustees ranged before her on the other side of a large mahogany table failed to make her quail, then the grandeur of the meeting room inside the

Royal Victoria was certainly up to the job. Hetty stood beneath an enormous chandelier she hoped was securely bound to the high, frescoed ceiling. The biggest mirror she had ever seen, resting in an ornate gilt frame, dominated the wall at one side of the room, the wall facing it taken up almost entirely by the marble surround of a fireplace, unlit. Hetty shivered.

'Please sit, Miss Barlow,' said the chairman of the trustees. Dr Bartolome spoke in a hoarse and evidently painful whisper. He was an elderly gentleman who had been deep in conversation with Mrs Calver, who was sitting on his right, when Hetty had cautiously entered the room. The former matron acknowledged Hetty's presence with a curt nod.

Hetty sat in one of the empty chairs on the other side of the table, opposite Mr Walmsley from the School Board. He sat on the left of Dr Bartolome. She liked Mr Walmsley. Previously, he'd always tried to put her at her ease when it was time for her to report the doings of the house. Beside Mr Walmsley sat the vicar of St Philip's in the district of Upperthorpe, who looked at her curiously. Mr Wallace sat on the other side of Mrs Calver, an encouraging smile on his kindly face. Beside Mr Wallace sat purse-lipped Mrs Shaw, the secretary, with blotting paper, ink, pens, a book for taking notes and a pair of spectacles laid out before her. Her gaze was disapproving.

Hetty declined Mr Walmsley's offer of a drink of water, folded her hands in her lap and focused her attention on Mrs Calver, who had begun to speak.

'...so in light of our chairman's throat infection I shall be the conduit for today's meeting.' She looked exceptionally pleased with herself. The woman was in her element.

'Madam deputy chairman,' said Mr Wallace. Mrs Calver inclined her head towards him, politely. 'Might we convey to Miss Barlow that this is an informal meeting, that we have gathered to allow her to explain why she... um...'

'Deceived us?' said Mrs Shaw, icily.

'Please, Mrs Shaw,' said Mrs Calver.

'Hetty – Miss Barlow – is doing a grand job as warden,' said Mr Wallace. 'Whatever qualifications she may or may not possess, she has proved herself to be a fine asset to the House of Help.'

'But does deceit and dishonesty set the right example?' said Mrs Shaw.

Mr Walmsley raised his hand. 'Mrs deputy chairman, perhaps the best thing to do is to allow Miss Barlow to explain herself.'

Mr Bartolome nodded solemnly and lifted a hand. *Proceed.*

Hetty's gut tightened. She would tell them the truth, warts and all. It was all she could do.

–

The drizzle had become a downpour. Muddy streams raced along the gutters and the pavements were greasy under a crowded canopy of umbrellas. By the time Hetty reached the steps to the House of Help the hem of her skirt was soaked and her feet wet and cold. She let herself in, leaving the umbrella open on the floor of the porch, hanging up her cape and going quickly to her quarters, her vision as blurred as if the rain had filled her eyes as well as her boots. Thankfully, the hallway was empty.

Closing the door to her quarters behind her, Hetty unlaced her boots, kicked them off and walked into the middle of the room where she stopped and put her hands over her face. She tried to control her breathing and thence, she hoped, the painful knocking of her heart. The trustees had dismissed her from the room after listening to her story. First, they had sought her opinion on the choices she had made, and had gone on to question her about her commitment to the role of warden. Mrs Shaw had raised the issue of Amelia's parentage and been silenced, via the deputy chairman, by Mr Walmsley from the School Board who insisted the trustees had gathered to consider only the matter of Miss Barlow's deceit in relation to her job. *Deceit. Forged papers. Lies.* Her past was engulfing her and there was nobody to save her from drowning. There was only Gertie's scowl of hatred. *Harlot.* Only Amelia's lament. *You're not my mother. My mother's dead.*

Breathe. *You'll manage. You always have. Things could always be worse.*

Slowly, Hetty regained her composure, enough so that she was startled by a gentle knock on the door.

'I'll be out in a minute,' she called, aiming for a light-hearted tone, certain her voice would betray the hollowness inside her, the same hollowness that had attached itself to her during all her long years in exile. 'I need to get out o' these wet clothes.'

Whoever had tapped on the door went away without comment. Hetty heard feet ascending the stairs and let out a breath. It was no use dwelling on her situation. She would change her clothes, put on the slippers that had been warming by the grate and ensure that the bed and bureau latterly occupied by Lottie Henshaw were ready for the house's next admission. There was plenty of paperwork to keep her busy. The last thing she had been told by the trustees was that she would be notified of their decision that same day. She would maintain the illusion of normality. A thought occurred, and she bowed her head, praying it would not be Mr Wallace who came calling. She didn't think she could bear to see the sorrow in his eyes when he told her she was no longer warden, and would have to leave the house. The irony of the warden being ejected from a house that had a policy of never turning anybody away was not lost on her.

At tea time, she found Hope and two of the residents making sandwiches and preparing pots of tea in the kitchen. All that remained of Lottie's leaving gift were a few crumbs on the cake stand. Hetty got a cloth and wiped the cake stand clean and put it back in the cupboard.

'Were you looking for me, earlier?' she said to Hope.

'No,' said Hope, enquiry in her voice. She would not ask about the meeting in front of the other women, although Hetty was certain word had got around. How could it not, in a houseful of women?

'Can you tell everyone to please keep out of the parlour?' said Hetty. 'I'm expecting company.'

'Would you like summat to eat now, Miss Barlow?' said one of the residents assisting Hope.

Before Hetty could reply in the negative, Clara put her head into the room. 'Miss Barlow, you've got a visitor. I've stuck her in the parlour.'

Her. It was a small mercy that the bad tidings would not be delivered by Mr Wallace. The decision had been made quickly. Hetty wondered whether that signified good news or bad. She opened her mouth to ask Clara who she had stuck in the parlour – it might not be a trustee at all. It could be an agent for the house, or a woman needing help – but Amelia hurried into the kitchen from the scullery, already talking.

'There you are. I've been lookin' for you everywhere. Can I have a word?' Amelia swept her gaze over the room. 'In private?'

'I've got someone waitin' to see me,' said Hetty.

Amelia scowled. 'Oh well, reight then, that's more important.'

'It might be quite important,' said Hope, quietly.

Amelia ignored this. 'I'm allus at the bottom of the list,' she said.

This was so far from the truth that Hetty couldn't help laughing, which infuriated Amelia all the more.

'All reight, I'll say it in front of everybody. I'm goin' to see Linus's folks. I'm goin' tomorra mornin'. I thought you should know, that's all.' She lifted her chin. 'I thought you might come wi' me.'

The vulnerability in her eyes wrung Hetty's heart. 'Aye,' she said, carefully. 'I would, a'course I would, but you know I'm waiting on a decision that might affect us both, an' we can't go gallivanting off again. We're not long back from Gertie's.'

'I wouldn't call it gallivantin', when I'm wantin' to check they're not dead!'

The women helping Hope with the sandwiches stopped buttering bread and slicing ham to stare open-mouthed at Amelia.

'This isn't the place to be discussin' Linus's parents or what went on at the—' Hetty had been about to say séance '—at Gertie's.'

'I *know*.' Amelia threw up her hands. 'Why'd you think I asked for a word in private?'

Hope signalled to the women to get back to the sand-wiches and said to Clara. 'Who is waiting in the parlour?'

'That Mrs Calver,' said Clara.

So it was bad news, for Hetty, and Mrs Calver had jumped at the opportunity to deliver it. She clenched her jaw. 'Amelia, I might be out of a job tomorra.' There was a sharp inhalation of breath from Clara. Otherwise, the silence in the room was as deep and absolute as the grave. 'So let me deal wi' one thing at a time, all right?'

She left the kitchen without waiting for a response.

The door to the parlour was closed. Hetty stood for a moment, twisting her hands together. There might be nothing to stop her accompanying Amelia to Tamworth the next day. The girl needed her mother, but could not admit it to herself. She had returned from Grimsby in a mood Hetty could only describe as hysterical. One moment she was gabbling to Hope about Linus's revela-tion that she would marry and have children, and how wonderful that would be, although no-one could ever replace him, that went without saying, then the next moment she'd be weeping uncontrollably in Clara's arms over the touch she insisted she had felt on her shoulder. *His* touch. And how could she be expected to live without him?

A cough came from inside the parlour. Hetty wondered whether Mrs Calver knew she was standing on the other side of the door, prevaricating. She took a deep breath and grasped the door handle. Let the guillotine fall. She hoped it would be quick.

Mrs Calver was sitting on the chaise longue. She smiled politely when Hetty entered the room. 'Good afternoon, Miss Barlow. Please do sit down.'

Hetty sat in one of the two Queen Anne chairs that had been recently donated in a house clearance. She gripped the arms. 'Well then, what's the verdict?'

'Goodness,' said Mrs Calver. 'You do come to the point. May I say, first, that I am personally disappointed in the extreme that you lied to me. You were never a matron, yet led me to believe you were, and allowed me to think that we had a bond in common. I am wounded by that.'

'I apologise,' said Hetty. She could not keep the abruptness from her voice. 'What have you decided?'

'Well, there was some little dissent amongst the trustees,' said Mrs Calver. 'Our dear Mr Wallace, as you are aware, is enamoured of your work here.' She paused. 'I must admit, I prevailed upon him to clarify that his interest in you, Miss Barlow, is purely professional. It could not be otherwise, could it, bearing in mind the obvious, ah, divides in social standing?'

Hetty felt her cheeks begin to burn. Part of her – and not a small part – wanted to remind this woman she wasn't the Queen of England but a former hospital matron who'd made a good marriage, but instead she nodded.

Mrs Calver continued. 'I, too, think you have been a quite marvellous warden.'

Hetty managed a weak *thank you*. Mrs Calver had spoken of her role in the past tense. The woman was a malicious cat, and Hetty the mouse being toyed with.

'In addition,' said Mrs Calver, 'you are trying your hardest to make amends for abandoning your poor child. Amelia is a troubled soul.'

Anger flared in Hetty's belly. 'That is a private matter,' she said.

Mrs Calver's smile was frosty. 'And private matters can impinge on professional life. Mr Wallace did confide in me that he is helping you with regard to the property your aunt claims belongs to her.'

Hetty drew in a breath. 'That's also private business,' she said.

'Please don't be cross, Miss Barlow.' Mrs Calver gave her a coy look. 'I should tell you that Mr Wallace confides in me a great deal. We have much in common.' She seesawed her hands to imitate scales achieving perfect balance. 'A widow, a widower, a desire to see this house succeed, a common interest in the arts, an equal footing in society. I noticed you have hung one of Flora's works in the hallway. I've had the pleasure of meeting her. A delightful young woman.'

Hetty was glad she had the arms of the chair to hold onto or she might by now be gripping this woman by the neck. She bared her teeth in the closest approximation she could to a smile. 'Aye, well, that's nice. I'd like to hear the decision of the trustees.'

'Oh, I do apologise. I digress.' Mrs Calver sighed. 'The decision goes in your favour, Miss Barlow. You may keep your job, although your performance will be subject to rather more scrutiny than you have been accustomed to, and I'm certain you will now take on board the suggestions I have made for the running of the house.'

Hetty gasped. She spoke through lips numbed by shock. 'I am to remain as warden?'

Mrs Calver got to her feet. 'Yes.' She walked over and patted Hetty on the shoulder. 'You are quite white, my dear. Do remain seated. I'll let myself out.'

Hetty folded her lips. She would not burst into tears of relief in front of this woman.

Mrs Calver stopped at the door. 'You do remember, don't you, my suggestions? I believe they are more pertinent than ever. Let us make a fresh start, Miss Barlow. Why don't I return tomorrow? Perhaps I'll bring dear Mr Wallace along with me, and the house cook can prepare a brunch?'

'Aye, I'll tell her,' said Hetty. She waited for the sound of the door snicking shut then slumped in her chair, overcome by a sudden exhaustion. After a while, she sat up straight and tucked stray strands of hair behind her ears. There was much to do, but uppermost in her mind was Amelia, the girl's desire to visit Linus's parents and her seeming hatred of her mother.

Chapter 22

Ned came into the yard of the forge, raking back his hair with his fingers before replacing his cap. He glanced at the belly of the blackly bulging cloud that had been hanging like an ill portent above the hill across the valley all morning, then strolled over towards the men standing outside the clerk's office. His cousin and Mr Prescott, along with another man Ned didn't recognise, all watched him approach. Jacob, arms folded, was frowning mightily. Mr Prescott smiled and waved.

' 'Ey up,' Ned said to Jacob. ' 'Ow do, Mr Prescott. To what do we owe the honour?'

'Thought I'd bring tha new clerk for a look round,' said Mr Prescott. 'He can start today, if tha likes.' He shrugged. 'Or tomorra.'

Jacob's mouth twisted but he didn't speak. Words had obviously been had. The young man standing beside Mr Prescott stuck out his hand, cocksure.

' 'Ow do, Mr Staniforth. I'm Alfie Prescott.'

Ned shook his hand. 'Related, are tha?'

Mr Prescott spoke for the youth. 'Alfie's me nephew. He's smarter than the lot o' us put together. I reckon he's just the man tha needs.'

'Oh aye?' said Ned.

'I were explainin' to 'em,' said Jacob, 'that we've already got a wages clerk.'

'An' now tha's got another one,' said Mr Prescott. 'Easy as that.'

Jacob laughed. 'We can't afford two, tha knows.' He turned to Ned. 'Who's runnin' this business, me and thee or,' – jerking his thumb at Mr Prescott – 'him?'

Thunder rumbled overhead.

'Storm comin',' said Mr Prescott. He seemed unperturbed by Jacob's show of disrespect. Ned knew better.

'I think we can work summat out,' Ned said. 'Come back tomorra, lad. All right?'

'Bright an' early,' the boy said.

Mr Prescott jerked his head once in assent. Then he turned on Jacob, stabbing his finger into Jacob's chest. Ned's cousin was twice the old man's size but had enough sense to remain still and endure the prodding. Mr Prescott glared up at him. 'I won't be talked to like that,' he said. 'I bring a lot o' business tha way.' He pointed at Ned. 'For starters, this one wun't be standin' here if it weren't for me. Does tha understand what I'm sayin'?'

The man's nephew looked from Mr Prescott to Jacob and back, agog. It was clear to Ned that Alfie Prescott would like nothing better than a front-row seat at a bout of fisticuffs.

Ned laid his hand on Jacob's arm. 'Aye, he does,' he said. Sheet lightening flashed in the darkened yard, followed immediately by a sustained rumble of thunder. 'Come o'er to the cottage, Mr Prescott. Have a drink wi' me. Tha nephew too. I think tha's right about that storm.'

The older man stood his ground. 'I want to 'ear him say he gets it,' he said.

Jacob spoke through clenched teeth. 'I do,' he said. 'I know which way me bread's buttered. But like I've told thee, we've no need for two clerks.'

'Not yet,' said Mr Prescott. He snapped his fingers in Jacob's face. 'But business is boomin' and tha'll be thankin' me for it soon enough.' He clapped his hands. The discussion was over. Mr Prescott walked towards the entrance to the yard, his nephew in tow. Ned gave Jacob a sympathetic grimace and strode after them.

'Well, Ned,' said Mr Prescott, throwing an amused look over his shoulder, 'a little bird tells me tha's out tomorra neet at Tommy's? About time, an' all.'

'That little bird your Frank, by any chance?' said Ned. He wondered whether Frank had also told his father who Ned was taking out on the town. Nan was the woman he wanted on his arm, but Nan wasn't there, and hadn't written, and Ned had finally agreed it would do no harm to be out and about. He told himself this, as guilt ate away at him.

'Keepin' thee counsel?' Mr Prescott thumped his nephew on the back. 'A gentleman, is our Ned. Watch an' learn, Alfie. Watch an' learn.'

Later that evening, Ned ate a lonely supper at his kitchen table, listening to the rain rattling against the window. There was a nip in the air, a portent of the approaching winter. He wondered, as he often did at quiet times, what Nan was doing, and whether she was as lonely as he, or had found some sort of companionship to help her through. It saddened him, the idea that she had washed her hands of him. He had posted several letters he might as well have chucked in the Don. Gradually, he'd come round to Frank's way of thinking. It would be years before Nan was released. She would be a changed person. And Ned wanted to start a family.

He would bury his feelings for Nan, find other ways to occupy these quiet times. It was time to get on with it, starting tomorrow.

–

Ned began the following day by introducing the new wages clerk to the existing incumbent. He made a point of explaining that Alfie was to be apprenticed to the clerk, although it went without saying Mr Prescott was angling to put one of his own in charge of the books, no doubt with a view to cooking them. Ned frequently wondered what he had got himself into, and then would decide that he'd deal with any Prescott family-related issues as they arose. He had his dinner ready for him at the cottage, followed by a labour meeting with his cousin and the works foreman, then got changed into his best bib and tucker and took a bus into town to buy two tickets for that evening's entertainment, a four-act drama entitled *The Fugitive*.

The place Mr Prescott had called Tommy's, that also went by the moniker The Alex, was the Alexandra music hall, owned by popular impresario Thomas Youdan until his death over a decade earlier but still fondly named for him by the older townsfolk. The imposing building that housed the Alexandra fronted onto Blonk Street, while the back of the structure rested on iron girders sunk into the riverbed of the Sheaf. The extension over the river had helped Youdan lay claim to the boast that this was the largest stage in the whole of Yorkshire and the biggest and best music hall in the provinces. Under new management, the Alex remained one of the most impressive entertainment venues in the town.

Ned hoped it would suffice.

Coming out of the box office, he stopped by the low wall that gave a view down to the brown sludge of the Sheaf and the heaps of rubbish that lined the banks. He tucked the tickets into the inside pocket of his jacket. The last time he'd worn his black three-piece had been to his grandmother's funeral. Time is precious, she'd told him, worth more than all the riches in the world. Don't fritter it away. Ned flexed his shoulders and set off towards the middle of town. According to the clock tower above the town hall, it would be curtain up on *The Fugitive* in two hours. He had plenty of time for a minor detour.

The Q in the Corner on Paradise Square was filling up with men who had gone straight to the pub after clocking off work. Ned stepped inside, self-conscious in his suit. He jostled his way to the bar, got the maid's attention and carried his jar of ale to the open front door to sip at it, nodding a greeting to a couple of acquaintances, acknowledging with a smile a wink from a former work-mate. Finally alone on the threshold of the pub, he looked along the terrace of houses to the place where he had last seen Nan, last held her hand and kissed her chastely on the cheek, promising to return the following day, to bring her to live in the cottage. The door to the House of Help was closed, and there were no lights in the windows that faced onto the square.

Ned shuddered. The air was cooler now, summer taking its leave. That must be what had made him shiver. It couldn't be the thought that tonight he'd have another girl on his arm, when all he wanted was to see Nan's face again, have her smile at him in that secretive way. He gazed at the closed door of the house, praying for time to turn back, for Nan to emerge, to see him and wave and run towards him. He would catch her in his arms. Ned smiled at the thought, a smile that faded as he turned and went back into the noisy pub. Two pints and some idle conversation later, he emerged onto the cobblestones of Paradise Square and strode along towards the House of Help.

He passed the premises without looking up and left the square, heading towards West Street, and the house that was his destination.

Ned was lifting the knocker when the door opened and a girl in a maid's uniform ushered him inside. He laughed. 'Were tha waitin' behind the door?' The girl frowned and shook her head. She led him along a short hallway into the sitting room and bustled about straightening antimacassars, turning up the gas lamps on either side of a cluttered mantelpiece and lifting the lid on an upright piano to reveal its keys, which she wiped with the duster in her hand, producing a discordant jangle. She exited without a word, leaving Ned standing awkwardly in the middle of the room.

A few moments passed, then the door opened and Mrs Prescott bustled in. She gestured for Ned to sit in an armchair. 'Make yersen at home, lad. I told Felicia, I said to get hersen downstairs, that you'd be here an' she should be ready to greet thee, an' where is she?'

' 'Ow do, Mrs Prescott.'

She shook her head in exasperation, went to the door and shouted down the corridor. 'Lydia, Lydia, get 'ere! The fire's not lit.'

Ned half-rose. 'Shall I do it?'

'No, no. Stay put!'

He lowered himself back down. The same girl who had let him into the house rushed into the room. She dropped to her knees in front of the fireplace and struck a match to light the newspaper and kindling under the coals, being admonished by Mrs Prescott throughout. Ned had forgotten how shrill the woman could be. As the maid left the room, Mr Prescott entered with Felicia. She was her father's daughter, the same small frame, narrow face and watchful eyes. She had on a white gown and a tailored, sky-blue jacket with gloves to match.

Ned jumped to his feet. ''Ow do, Ellie. You look lovely.'

She looked down, demurely. Ned suppressed a grin. Once upon a time, he'd climbed trees and grubbed in the dirt with this girl. Now they were both playing at being grown-ups.

Mr Prescott beamed as if the compliment had been directed at him. 'Steady now, lad,' he said. 'I only found out today it's Felicia tha's takin' to Tommy's. Hope you've got good seats.'

'I already told him,' said Ellie. 'Middle of the dress circle. I won't be seen dead in the gods or the pits.'

Mrs Prescott nodded approvingly.

'That's right where we are, love,' said Ned. He had forked out two shillings and sixpence apiece for the dress circle tickets. He could afford it now, he supposed. Business was booming.

'Whatever Felicia wants, Felicia gets,' said Mr Prescott. Ellie simpered.

'Is Frank in?' said Ned.

'Nope,' said Mr Prescott. He didn't elaborate.

'Will you have a cup of tea?' said Mrs Prescott. 'Looks like Ellie's been practising.' She gestured to the upright piano. 'Like to hear her play summat?'

Ned made a show of looking at the clock on the mantelpiece. 'Think we'd best get a move on,' he said.

'Take care o' my girl, lad.'

'I will.'

Ned had never been to the Alex. The décor was a sight to behold. He shuffled awkwardly along the front row of the dress circle and took his crimson-cushioned seat next to Ellie. She immediately found his hand, clutching it with her hot little paw. Ned took in his surroundings. He imagined this was how it would feel to sit inside an over-stuffed jewellery box. The walls and high ceiling of the auditorium were painted in pastel shades of pink and grey, the better to show off the bronze and marble columns and cornices. Every nook and cranny and balcony featured extravagant carvings. High above was a sunlight made up of at least a hundred gas burners, as far as Ned could make out.

'What are you doin'?' said Ellie.

He'd been counting the jets. Ned dropped his gaze to the stage, where an enormous set of red curtains in a green and gold surround were being lifted into folded pleats. A hush descended.

'Let the show begin,' said Ned. Ellie squeezed his hand.

Ned was dozing when the alarm was raised. He'd lost interest in the drama within the first few minutes of the second act, having persevered gamely up to that point. On the stage, the actors were retreating from tendrils of smoke that were rising from the gaps between the boards. Ned's first thought was that this must be part of the show and he leaned forward with renewed interest. Then, looking down, he realised the patrons of the stalls were getting to their feet. In the same moment, an usher appeared at the end of the dress circle and called for everybody to make their way to the exit in an orderly manner. *No running, please.*

Ned stood up and turned to Ellie. She huddled close, her eyes wide with fright. 'Come on, love,' said Ned. 'We'll be reight.'

They filtered down the narrow corridor with the rest. Outside, filling the pavements of Blonk Street, people milled about, some chattering excitedly about the last theatre that went up in flames, others muttering about obtaining a full refund. Hardly anybody left the vicinity. There might be a better show than the one they had paid for, one that featured a fire cart or two.

'Well, this is a fine state o' affairs,' said Ellie. She pressed herself against Ned's side and he put his arm around her, looking over her head towards the side entrance where three youths wearing overalls had just emerged. They were scowling, and scuffing their boots against the steps.

'Ellie, wait here,' said Ned.

He wandered over to them. 'What's goin' on, lads?'

Ned returned a few moments later, a wide grin on his face.

Ellie pouted. 'What's so funny?'

Ned laughed. 'That lot, they were havin' a reight old time of it smoking pipes under the stage, up until they heard us all pounding out. Poor blokes.'

'Why poor?' said Ellie.

'Stagehands for the travellin' company, just bein' lads. Tha knows. Out on their ear, though.' Ned looked around. People were trickling back into the building. 'Shall we go back in then, wi' the rest o' them?'

Ellie sighed. 'Might as well. They should be chucked in jail, though. Where's the police? That's what I'd like to know. I could've been trampled in the rush to get out.'

'It were quite orderly, I thought,' said Ned.

Ellie stopped and planted her hands on her hips.

'What?' said Ned.

'Look at your face. You think it's all a big joke. Well, I were terrified.'

Ned bit his lip. 'Sorry, love. Come on.' He took her hand and she allowed him to pull her towards the entrance. 'Let's not waste the best seats in the 'ouse. I'm dyin' to find out what happens next.'

He couldn't help thinking, as they filed back inside, that Nan would have found the whole episode as amusing as he did.

AUTUMN

Chapter 23

Nan lay on her bed, gazing at the faint stain of moonlight on the whitewashed wall. Sleep eluded her. It was unsettling, both knowing and not knowing what the following day held in store. The warning Sarah had promised Nan she would receive had been delivered in the exercise yard that morning – it was probably yesterday morning, by now. The messenger had been the male guard who had rattled her jaw when he separated her from Rhoda four months earlier. Nan had become aware of him staring at her as she walked around in single file, counting her steps. *One thousand! And one, two, three, four.* When her circuit of the yard brought her near to the guard, she lifted her eyes to meet his. He cupped his hand against the side of his mouth and spoke one word to her. Then he had snorted and hoicked up phlegm onto the dirt yard to cover the communication. The misdirection was successful. The female guard with him had clicked her tongue and told him he was a disgusting creature.

Nan had not broken her stride. She walked on, her mind racing, knowing she had heard him correctly but desperately wanting to hear that word again, to be certain. On the next circuit, and the next, and throughout the rest of the hour, he had ignored her entirely, his message delivered.

Tomorrow.

What mighty proportions that single, simple word had. It meant freedom, or punishment. It meant the beginning of her journey back to Ned, or the dashing of her hopes. There was no early release for failed escapees and Nan would be under constant scrutiny or, worse, moved to a different prison. Fresh meat.

She shivered and turned on her side, pillowing her head with her hands, searching her memory, looking for Ned. She recalled the scratchiness of the fabric of his coat against her cheek when they had last embraced on the doorstep of the House of Help. That had been the evening before her ill-fated trip to the jeweller's shop, and their last moment together. Miss Barlow had come outside to tell them off. 'Stop makin' a show of yourselves,' the warden had said, 'on my doorstep.'

She recalled Ned's sheepish grin. As she stepped into the house, he had grabbed her hand. 'Tomorra,' he had said. She hadn't known it then but this was the last word she'd hear him utter, the same word growled by the guard – *Tomorrow* – before he'd turned away and spat on the ground. She recalled the warm glow of happiness inside her chest as Miss Barlow closed the door on Ned's smiling face. It was still there, buried deep, the spark that would ignite when she next saw him.

Nan turned onto her back, restless. It was pointless to wonder about what might transpire tomorrow, or how many were involved in the plan, other than Sarah and the two guards, or why they were helping her. Sarah had hinted she had money, on the outside. No doubt, she had greased a few palms. Nan was told that she didn't need to know the details. She knew, and the thought was terrifying, that this was because if she was caught she could not have the truth squeezed from her. Sarah had kissed her, with lips that were softer than Ned's and brushed Nan's mouth like butterfly wings. 'Come and find me,' Sarah had said. 'Stay hidden through the winter, then come to me and I will keep you safe.'

She thought about Ned's mouth, his generous lips. Their last proper kiss had been in the sitting room of his cottage, standing by the window that looked over the garden. Jacob had come in from the kitchen. ' 'Ey up,' he'd said. 'Watch theesens. I've got five kids an' it all started wi' messin' like this.' Reliving the memory in her narrow prison cot, Nan smiled, her breath hitching in a sigh that fell somewhere between a laugh and a sob. That kiss had been hungry, one of Ned's hands cradling the back of her skull, the other moving up her body to caress the swell of her breast through the fabric of her blouse. It was the furthest they had gone, their passion barely controlled.

Recalling that moment, Nan moaned, deep in her throat, as she had then. This was how she kept Ned alive in her mind. One of her greatest terrors was forgetting him, forgetting the sound of his voice, forgetting how a loving look could set her heart tripping, a touch, however light, transmit warmth to all parts of her body. She had never been in his bed but imagined, now, how it might be in the early morning, after lovemaking. She would lay propped up on pillows, listening to birdsong. The air would smell of honeysuckle and the bacon and bread Ned was frying for their breakfast. Sunlight would stream through the window and, whenever she felt like it, she could rise and go down to find him, and wander outside, down to the riverbank, wrapped in a shawl. Or she could remain in bed, under sheets warmed by their bodies. It would be her choice.

She had never been with a man. She had admitted as much to Sarah, who had at first been sceptical that Nan could share a bed with a boy for three years and not be violated. 'It wasn't like that,' said Nan. 'We were as brother and sister.'

Nan had no siblings, as far as she knew, but there had always been babies and infants to console in her mother's house. She shoved the thought aside and closed her eyes. Ned would be sleeping now. He had probably moved into the cottage, there being no reason for him to stay in his lodgings, in her absence. Was he thinking of her now, as she was thinking of him? She imagined his bed. The pillows would be firm, the blanket soft and the sheets fresh-smelling.

Nan's eyes closed and she felt herself slip away, and had time to be grateful that sleep was finally coming. She would need all her wits about her the next morning.

Her rest was short-lived. A key rattled in the door and her mother glided into her cell and held out a small, filthy bundle, tied with a knot in the top. Nan got up, her fingers closing obediently around the greasy knot. 'Put this in the river,' her mother said. 'You're old enough to help me now. We're in it together.' A baby's blanket was draped over her mother's shoulder and she was clutching a pouch that Nan somehow knew contained exactly thirty shillings. She knew, too, that this was the price the infant's mother had paid to have her newborn adopted into a loving family. The girl was a maid, impregnated by the gentleman of the house, with no means of looking after a baby. Nan's mother had promised to take care of the infant. 'Go on,' she said, and gave Nan a shove so that she stumbled from her cell and onto a stone bridge. Nan peered over the side at the black water. 'Do it,' her mother hissed in her ear. Nan dropped the bundle in and watched it sink. It made barely a splash.

She woke, sobbing. She would never escape the horror of what her mother had done, nor her own guilt. In this recurring nightmare, she always did as she was told. In the world outside dreams, when her mother had given her the filthy bundle and her instructions, Nan had stumbled towards the river and over the bridge, ending up at the police station, knowing the cost of the evidence she carried would be another life.

Her mother's.

—

In the strengthening light of dawn, she swung her feet to the ground. *Tomorrow* had become *today*. On the floor of the cell, directly beneath where her head had rested, lay a folded sheet, a small oblong five or six inches thick. Curious, Nan reached down, intending to lift it up, then stopped and pressed both hands against her mouth, nauseated by the knowledge that somebody had entered while she slept, while she lay helpless, and had crouched close by her head to leave the folded sheet for her to find. Had they observed her sleeping? Was it the male guard who was in on Sarah's plan, creeping in? Nan shuddered and wrapped her arms around her body. There was a plan, she reminded herself, and she wasn't privy to it, but this sheet might be the first clue to her escape.

Sarah had told her how brave she was, how she would be spared Rhoda's wrath and how a reunion with Sarah would come about in a matter of months, on the outside. A route to freedom had been offered before, to others Sarah wouldn't name, and rejected, either out of hand or when the moment came. Be ready for anything. Nan was.

She bent again to pick up the folded sheet – it hung limply in her hands – and laid it on the mattress. She opened its folds, gingerly, and gasped when she saw the contents. Inside lay her clothes, her own blue skirt and bodice, her own underclothes. Only the shoes were missing. Nan felt inside the seam pocket and brought out two five-pound notes. She stuffed them back in, her hands shaking.

Knowing what she needed to do, Nan took a deep breath to calm her racing heart and set about getting ready.

–

Sitting with the makings of another sack draped over her lap, she stabbed ineffectually at the material. 'What if they can tell? I must look like an overstuffed settee.'

'They'd have pounced on you by now,' whispered Sarah. 'We're nearly there. You know what to do if the worst happens. Keep your mouth shut. Take your lumps, and don't lose heart. There'll be other chances.'

'You know I would never betray you,' said Nan. Her breathing was laboured but she couldn't seem to control it at all. 'Thank you so much. I owe you my life. I'll repay you.'

'I know,' said Sarah. 'Calm down. And don't thank me yet. You might be locked up in solitary tonight and be calling me all the names under the sun.'

The thought was terrifying. 'Don't!' said Nan.

The female warder standing under one of the room's large arched windows clapped her hands. 'Quiet over there!'

Nan let a few moments pass. 'Sorry,' she whispered.

Sarah coughed so that her mouth was covered when she replied. 'You will be if you keep drawing attention to yourself.'

They worked on. Nan couldn't help glancing repeatedly at the three-quarters-filled pallet of completed sacks at the far end of the room, near the door that opened into the prison courtyard. Sarah had told her what she needed to do, when the time was right. Nan had asked when that would be, and received no reply. What if the terror she felt prevented her from acting when she needed to? What would be the point of no return? She wasn't brave enough. It was time to tell Sarah she wouldn't – couldn't – go through with it.

Two prisoners approached, lugging between them a basket of sacks.

'Now,' hissed Sarah.

'What?'

'It's now.'

As Sarah spoke, the women carrying the basket slowed. One of them gestured to Nan to stand, thrust her handle of the basket forward, swiped the sack Nan had been sewing, and sat down in her place. The exchange of roles was completed in an instant. Now Nan was helping carry the basket across the room. She managed to resist the tremendous urge to look back at Sarah. The prisoner holding the opposite handle of the basket didn't acknowledge her but instead kept her eyes forward. Nan did the same.

The same command that had come from Sarah's lips now came from this prisoner as they placed the basket on the ground by the pallet.

'Now.'

'What?'

The woman gestured with her head towards the sacks already stacked on the pallet.

Nan's limbs moved seemingly of their own accord. She was aware of a high, keening sound in her ears. She lay face down on top of the sacks, resting her forehead on her forearms to create a space in which – she hoped – she would be able to breathe. Darkness descended as sacks were placed on top of her. Now there would be shouts of alarm, hands grabbing at her, heavy blows raining down. It was inevitable. Sarah couldn't save her now. Nan was on her own.

She braced herself.

Nothing happened. Sweat broke out all over Nan's body. How could she withstand the weight of the sacks? What if another pallet was placed on top of hers, when they were loaded onto the wagon? She would be crushed like an ant. No, the driver had to be in on it. Nan clenched her teeth against the urge to cry out, to plead for rescue. This was torture. She longed for the simplicity of solitary confinement. Months alone with only her thoughts to keep her company. No, *that* was torture. This was freedom, almost within her grasp.

A spasm of fear paralysed her muscles when the pallet moved. The bags shifted around her body. She clenched her teeth against another surge of panic. She might slide out. She was helpless to steady herself. There were muffled voices – Nan couldn't hear the words being spoken – and then the clacking of wheels over cobbles, and the snorts of cart horses. Was she now outside the building, outside the prison walls? Her heart thrummed in her chest. The movement went on, the darkness absolute, her breath coming in short gasps. Then a command to the horse – or horses, she couldn't say how many were pulling the wagon – to stop. More voices, indistinct. Then they were moving again.

Time lost all meaning. Nan might have been concealed between the sacks for minutes, or hours. When would her absence be noted? How quickly would it be before a search party was mobilised? A search would be made beyond the prison walls, but how far might it extend? The police would be notified and the photograph taken on her admission to Millbank plastered in the newspapers. She had never seen it, the image captured. Her hair had been scraped back into a loose bun by unseen hands. She had been required to sit and gaze into the lens of the camera for several minutes, and then to turn her head to the side to have her profile photographed. Other than those commands, nobody had spoken to her.

She was a fugitive now. The word sounded romantic but it was anything but. There was only this naked fear, this terrible vulnerability.

A tickling sensation crawled down her cheek. Nan shrieked – she couldn't help it – and rubbed her face against her forearm. Her skin was wet, the crawling sensation created by tears she hadn't even known she was shedding. The journey went on. Once or twice, she was moved so violently she thought the wagon must be overturning, then a gentler rocking would resume.

Cocooned in the stiff fabric, Nan tried to control the terror of not knowing what awaited her, at the end.

Chapter 24

Ada Cooper, age thirteen, gave address as 54 Crookesmoor Road, has come alone. Filthy and hungry.

Returning from a meeting with the trustees, Hetty scanned the note Hope had left on her desk and went in search of the newest arrival. She was already thinking ahead. St Joseph's reformatory might take the girl. She was the right age. The house was full to bursting, all the beds taken and the girl who arrived yesterday sleeping on a makeshift bed by the range in the kitchen, always the warmest spot in the house so there was that consolation, although the girl had to be up and the bedding tidied away before the rest of the house awoke. Amelia was in with Hetty again, while Hope grumbled about travelling backwards and forwards from Tylecote. Ada Cooper would be reassured the House of Help never turned away a needy soul. A solution would be found.

Hetty pushed open the kitchen door. At the table sat a small child, surely no older than eight or nine, her bare feet black with dirt. She was wrapped in a blanket, eating toast. Cook placed a mug of steaming tea in front of the girl and gave Hetty a meaningful look.

'Found this lovely lass on the doorstep,' she said.

Hope was standing by the range. 'This is Ada,' she said.

The girl looked at Hetty with large solemn eyes. She was all angles, not a bit of rounded softness on her pinched face. She was petite for thirteen and Hetty wondered how much of her lack of growth was due to malnutrition.

Hetty pulled out a chair. 'Nice to meet you, Ada. I'm Miss Barlow and I'm the warden of this house. Can you tell me why you came here?'

'Aye.' Her voice was surprisingly strong. 'There's never owt to eat an' she turns me out at night. Sometimes them next door take me in, but they've no food goin' spare neither. Winter's comin' an' we've no coal.' She shrugged. 'I'm famished.'

'Well,' said Cook, 'finish thee toast an' I'll warm up a bit o' porridge next.' Her voice faded as she disappeared into the pantry. 'I've some biscuits if I can remember where I've hid 'em.'

'Does your mother know where you are?' said Hetty.

The girl nodded, her mouth full. She chewed and swallowed. 'I telt her.'

'What did she say?' said Hetty.

'Sling thee hook, then.'

'Oh dear,' said Hope. 'Do you have a father at home, any brothers and sisters?'

'Nah.' Ada looked uncertain. 'There's men, but none's me da. That I know of. I had a sister.' She shrugged. 'That were ages ago, though.'

The two women exchanged glances.

'Oh,' said Ada. 'She din't die. She went to her da in Leeds.'

'Do you have any family, apart from your mother?' said Hetty.

'Not as I know of.'

The girl took another large bite from her slice of toast and began to chew enthusiastically.

Hetty and Hope left her with Cook and conferred by the foot of the main staircase.

'She turned up first thing, after you'd left, wearing only a shift,' said Hope. 'She'd walked all the way from Crookesmoor.'

Hetty rubbed the bridge of her nose. 'Will you fetch her summat to wear from the clothes box? See if we've any shoes her size. If needs be, she can bunk in with one of the younger lasses tonight. I'll see whether St Joseph's will have her.'

'Poor mite,' said Hope.

'Aye. She's a tiny thing.'

As Hope turned to go upstairs, the door knocker sounded.

'You go on,' said Hetty. 'I'll get it. At this rate, we'll be stackin' them in the coal cellar.'

A well-dressed woman stood on the doorstep, a cape draped over one arm. 'Is my daughter here?' she said. 'Ada? Ada Cooper?'

On closer inspection, Hetty saw that her clothes, though they'd been fine in their day, were frayed at the cuffs, the material patchily faded. She wore powder on her face that had clumped around her top lip and in the lines at the corners of her eyes, which were bloodshot.

'Come in,' said Hetty.

The reunion of mother and daughter took place in the parlour. Ada, now dressed in donated clothes, submitted to an embrace from her mother, her face a careful blank.

Hetty explained, as tactfully as she could, that Ada could spend the night at the house and would probably be sent to the reformatory school if she could not be looked after at home. 'She might do well there,' said Hetty. 'She'd be discharged once she got to sixteen and put into domestic service. There'd be no shame in that. What do you think, Mrs Cooper?'

The woman sat close beside Ada, clutching the girl's hand. 'I don't know. We've been strugglin' but I don't know how it come to this. She belongs at 'ome wi' me.' She cupped the girl's chin in her hand. 'What's tha want to do, Ada? Come 'ome now or stay 'ere? I'll let thee decide.'

Ada batted her hand away. 'Come 'ome,' she said. 'I'm not goin' somewhere they lock thee up.'

'And you won't run away again?' said Hetty.

Ada pulled a face. 'No.'

'It's been hard, makin' ends meet,' said the girl's mother.

Hetty nodded sympathetically. 'We're not here to judge. I still have to make a report.'

'Reight enough,' said Mrs Cooper.

'And our door is always open,' said Hetty.

The woman nodded.

'Then it's settled?' said Hetty, looking for a response from Ada.

The girl scowled. 'So long as she stops puttin' me out like a cat.'

'Ada Cooper! It's thee that takes theesen off, in thee nightgown an' all!'

Hetty suppressed a smile. 'Will you wait here for a bit? I won't be long.' She shook her head when she saw the look of alarm on Mrs Cooper's face. 'No, no, I'm just going to get some provisions for the pair of you to take home with you.'

'We don't take charity,' the woman said.

'It's not,' said Hetty, mildly. 'Ada came here for help so we'll give you a bit. That's all there is to it.'

She left them alone. In the kitchen, Amelia sat at the table, peeling potatoes. She had returned from Tamworth in a calmer state of mind, and informed Hetty that Linus's parents had indeed passed away soon after his death. A neighbour had seen them walking by the river and their bodies were fished from a weir a few days later. 'He was their only child,' she explained, her eyes full of tears. *As you are mine*, Hetty had wanted to reply. She had braced herself for Amelia to declare that Gertie's powers to summon the dead were real and not manufactured, but she had said nothing more about it, seemingly content to let the matter drop.

Now, Hetty thought of Ada and her mother sitting in the parlour. She wondered what they would be saying to one another. 'Amelia?'

The girl looked up. 'Aye?'

'I never asked, when I took you from Gertie's, what you wanted, did I?'

Amelia laid down the potato peeler and regarded Hetty. 'No, you never did.'

'I'm sorry.'

'All right then.'

Amelia carried on peeling. Hetty went to a drawer, shook out a cloth bag and walked into the pantry. She took down from the shelves two freshly baked loaves of bread – Cook would complain but she would make more – along with a block of cheese, three tins of sardines, a bunch of carrots and a packet of peas, and packed them into the bag. Amelia appeared in the doorway. 'What're you up to?'

'Donatin' a bit of food,' said Hetty.

'Are we a grocer's as well, now?'

'Aye.' Hetty smiled. 'Don't tell anybody, especially not Mrs Calver.'

Amelia gave a mock-shudder. 'Don't worry, I wun't ever tell that one owt.'

Their eyes met. Hetty knew they were thinking the same thing. Amelia had told Mrs Calver – had told a roomful of people – the truth about them, a truth that might have destroyed Hetty's life. But the storm had passed, and had left Hetty with nothing to hide. She was only now coming to the realisation that her conscience was clear, that the weight of her burden was lifted. It had been a heavy load to bear.

Amelia came forward and took the bag from Hetty's hands. 'Who is it then?'

'A mother, an' her daughter,' said Hetty.

'Oh aye? Are they walkin' far wi' this? It's heavy. I don't mind helpin', if you want.'

'That'd be grand.' Hetty was taken aback. 'They're in the parlour. It's a Mrs Cooper and her girl, Ada.'

Amelia leaned forward to kiss Hetty on the cheek. 'See thee later then.' She walked out and through the kitchen, humming a tune under her breath.

Hetty remained where she stood. She was wise enough to know there would be run-ins to come, and plenty of them, but for now she could bask in the moment, the absolute joy of the first physical display of affection her grown-up child had ever shown her.

–

Everywhere she looked was a riot of colour, the trees aflame and the ground carpeted in the same vibrant shades of orange, red and yellow.

Hetty sat on a bench in the botanical gardens, her back to the glass pavilion that housed exotically named plants under a row of domed roofs. She preferred it here, away from the heady scents of the hothouses. Here, she could watch squirrels dart about, listen to the liquid notes of birdsong and feel the residual warmth of the autumnal sun on her face. These few minutes of peace and quiet were worth the rackety discomfort of the omnibus ride to Ecclesall Road with eight residents of the house in tow. They had trekked up the hill to the gardens, meeting Mr Wallace and Mrs Calver at the turnstile. The two trustees had travelled separately in Mr Wallace's gig. This irked Hetty, although she couldn't exactly pinpoint why. After all, she had insisted on accompanying the women and girls.

'May I sit?'

Hetty looked up, startled. Mr Wallace was smiling down at her. 'Aye,' she said, 'a'course. I've got to admit, this jaunt was a good idea o' yours.'

'I'm glad you're enjoying yourself,' said Mr Wallace, sitting beside her. 'Oh, look!'

A squirrel was carving a zig-zag path over the leaf-strewn grass towards Hetty. It sat on its hindquarters at the hem of her skirt, making a noise like a chamois cloth against glass, a furious squeaking that made Hetty smile.

'The little chap's hungry,' said Mr Wallace.

'I'm afraid I don't have owt to give him,' said Hetty.

They watched the squirrel dart away and sat in companionable silence for a while.

'Isn't this lovely?' said Hetty, gesturing to the trees and shrubs.

Mr Wallace smiled. 'It is splendid, isn't it. Nature's gift to us before winter sets in.' He nudged her elbow and lowered his voice so that she was forced to lean towards him. 'If you ventured over there, Miss Barlow,' – he pointed towards a pile of leaves blown against a nearby wall – 'you would be camouflaged amongst those colours.'

Acutely aware of his shoulder pressing against hers, and suddenly self-conscious, Hetty sat upright. She had been persuaded by Hope to cast aside her warden's dress and cap for this outing. She wore a russet-coloured skirt and bodice with black piping and buttons. The ribbon on the boater she wore – borrowed from Amelia, Hetty had remarked that she would soon need a separate room for all her hats – matched her dress, and Hope had loaned her a blue cape.

'The blue would give me away,' she said, 'if I was trying to hide.'

'Would it be inappropriate for me to say the colour suits you?' said Mr Wallace. He cleared his throat. 'I mean to say, the blue is a good match for your eyes.'

'There you are!' Mrs Calver appeared from around the back of the bench, the bobbing white plumage of her hat preceding her. She sat down on the other side of Mr Wallace and leaned forward to address Hetty. 'Miss Barlow, your ladies are having a fine time. I have spied them at the old bear pit and at the pond looking at those marvellous water lilies. And have you seen the delightful new bandstand and the tennis courts? Oh, and you must have visited the topiaries at the Italianate flower garden?'

'To be truthful,' said Hetty. 'I've been enjoying the peace and quiet.'

Mrs Calver reclined back against the bench. 'Well, walking up and down all these winding paths has quite exhausted me,' she said. 'I shall be ready to leave when you are, Bertrand.'

Bertrand? Hetty glanced at Mr Wallace. He was staring into the distance.

Mrs Calver leaned forward again, a small smile playing on her lips, and said: 'No Hope?'

Hetty shook her head. 'She volunteered to stay behind, in case anybody calls, and Amelia has gone into town, to buy herself another hat, probably, and we have four women who are workin' so couldn't come.'

'Do you have a houseful?' said Mrs Calver.

'Aye,' said Hetty. 'No beds to spare.'

'And so it goes,' said Mrs Calver, as world-wearily as if she was the one constantly juggling the available space. 'I must say, you are doing such a wonderful job. Our decision to permit you to remain as warden was the right one, wasn't it, Bertrand?'

Mr Wallace shifted uncomfortably in his seat. 'Let's allow Miss Barlow to enjoy some time away from the house,' he said. He smiled at Hetty. 'Although, if you'll indulge me for a moment with house business, well, not business as such, a gift, rather.'

Mrs Calver clicked her tongue. 'Spit it out, my dear.'

'It's only that my Flora would like to donate another of her watercolours,' said Mr Wallace. 'She's painted the wonderful view from Wharncliffe Edge. I've been driving her up there. It's rather breathtaking, the view, I mean. Have you ever visited, Miss Barlow?'

'I don't believe so.' Hetty was thinking about Mr Wallace's hit-or-miss approach to oncoming traffic, particularly when applied to vertiginous roads.

'Oh!' Mrs Calver exclaimed. 'Flora has shown me the sketches. You know, she really ought to start exhibiting her work.'

'I'll bring it to you tomorrow, if you are at home,' said Mr Wallace.

'I should be in all day tomorrow,' said Hetty. 'Paperwork.'

Mr Wallace grimaced sympathetically.

Mrs Calver stood and looked at the sky. 'Those clouds have a threatening aspect. Shall we go?'

'Thank you, Mr Wallace, for the excursion,' said Hetty.

'You are more than welcome,' he replied, and bowed and offered Mrs Calver his arm.

She watched them walk away then sighed and got to her feet. It was time to round up her charges and begin the lengthy process of herding them all back to the middle of the town.

–

Hetty was in her quarters, reading by lamplight a novel called *Far from the Madding Crowd* that she'd picked out of a box of donated books and couldn't seem to put down, when the knock came. Amelia rolled over in bed, looked at the clock and moaned.

'It's nearly eleven,' she said.

'We've had later arrivals than this,' said Hetty, laying down her book. She tightened the belt of her dressing gown and wrapped a woollen shawl around her shoulders.

Amelia moaned again and turned away, pulling the bedsheets over her head.

Hetty took the lamp into the corridor and stood by the door. There were two more gentle taps. 'Who's there?' she called.

Sometimes no answer would be forthcoming and Hetty would have to unbolt and open the door braced for whatever might greet her. But she recognised the voice that identified itself and quickly opened the door.

'What on earth's the matter, Mr Wallace?'

She beckoned him in but he shook his head. 'I'm dreadfully sorry for this late hour,' he said. 'I occasionally go for a drive at night. I don't sleep well. I saw your light.'

Hetty frowned. 'Is everything all right?'

'Yes, yes.' His eyes roamed over her face and the hair that fell over her shoulder to rest against her shawl. Hetty wondered whether he'd been on the brandy, although he didn't smell of intoxicants. 'I only wanted to check that you and all the ladies returned home safely.'

'Aye,' said Hetty. 'We did.'

'Good, good.'

'Would you like to come inside for a moment? I promise you aren't disturbing me.'

'Oh no! No.' He smiled weakly. 'I am glad you all returned safely.'

'As you can see, we did,' said Hetty.

Mr Wallace breathed in, and held it. Then, on a quick outbreath: 'Good night, then.'

'Good night.'

Amelia sat up in bed when Hetty returned to her quarters. 'That were quick. Who was it?'

'Mr Wallace,' said Hetty. She slowly removed her shawl and draped it over the chair she'd been sitting in.

'What? At this time o' night? What did he want?'

'I don't know,' said Hetty. She turned down the lamp. 'He was acting strangely. He didn't seem to want anything. I'm goin' to bed.'

Amelia snickered. 'I know what he wants.' She rested her cheek on the bolster that separated the mattress into two halves, as Hetty got under the covers on the other side. 'An' she's just climbed in this bed.'

'Amelia, stop it.'

'I've allus said so, haven't I?'

'I'm goin' to sleep now.'

'G'night, sis… oops. I mean, g'night.' Amelia patted her arm and retreated to her half of the bed.

Hetty smiled in the dark. Amelia might never call her mother but that was all right. Actions spoke louder, she'd always believed that.

'G'night, Amelia.'

Chapter 25

Ned knew Ellie didn't feel at home in the little cottage by the forge. She'd told him as much, curled naked on her side, the crumpled sheets of his bed between her thighs. She was sipping the tea Ned had brewed and brought up for her. He stood at the window, looking down at the garden and river beyond. Cold air penetrated the cracks in the window frame, chilling the skin on his bare chest and arms. In the distance, church bells pealed, calling parishioners to Sunday morning worship. He wondered whether Ellie had heard them and been reminded of their forthcoming nuptials. Once they were married, she was saying, they should live in a townhouse with proper plumbing, four bedrooms, a stable for a gig and attic space for a live-in maid.

'What are you thinkin', Ned?'

'The leaves need raking.'

'Barmpot.'

Her tone was affectionate so he went over to the bed and lay beside her, stroking her hip then moving his hand lower to caress her buttock. It was small and pert, like the rest of her. 'I like livin' here,' he said.

Ellie pouted, moving away from his touch to place her cup on the rug, and remaining there, leaving a narrow chasm of cold air between their bodies. 'Too noisy. An'

I'm sick o' listenin' to that hammer. And tha brought *her* 'ere.'

Whatever Frank had told his sister about Nan was enough for Ellie to be able to deliver the occasional jab to the heart.

'It does for a bachelor,' she continued, her back still turned. 'If that's what tha wants to remain.'

Ned already knew he would lose this battle. He played his last card. 'It's handy for work,' he said.

Ellie glanced over her shoulder at him, eyebrows raised. 'Why not let Alfie live 'ere, then? A little bird tells me cousin Alfie's gettin' a promotion.'

This was, unfortunately, true. The wages clerk to whom Alfie had been apprenticed was leaving. The man had found another job, effective immediately. It meant that now a Prescott – namely Mr Prescott's nephew Alfie – was ensconced in the role, news that Jacob received with a stony silence. And another Prescott – namely, Mr Prescott's daughter Felicia – lay on Ned's bed, talking about married life in a house filled with modern conveniences. She wanted steam radiators and had laughed when Ned said he could make one for her, for a wedding present. No, they'd be purchasing a ready-made model with built-in plate warmers from an associate of her father's. Ned just hoped he'd have the means to furnish Ellie with the lifestyle she desired. How, he wondered, his eyes roving over the contours of her body under the thin sheet, had all this come to pass? *Don't kid theesen. Tha let it happen.*

He had never formally proposed to Ellie, but nor had he corrected her parents – or Frank – when they began to make assumptions. Ned readily agreed with Mrs Prescott when she talked about how pretty Felicia would look in the wedding gown that had been passed down two genera-tions. He went along with Mr Prescott's assertion that Ned would never find a finer woman to be his wife, although a recollection of Nan's low, husky laugh caught him like a blade to the stomach. When Frank ribbed him about how long it had taken for Ned to see the girl for him had always been right under his nose, he smiled along. Somehow, without even a firm proposal having been made, Mrs Prescott and her daughter were discussing winter nuptials in a church that would be already aglow with Christmas decorations, organising the banns and finding a venue for the wedding breakfast. This would, Frank had assured Ned, be a suitably raucous party. *Us Prescotts know how to entertain*.

Ellie stretched, arching her back and then rolling back into a ball, like a contented cat. 'Where's the covers?' she said. Ned retrieved the blanket from the floor at the foot of the bed and tucked it around her. He put on his vest and shirt and waistcoat. It was cold out but some physical exertion would soon warm him.

'Goin' back to sleep?' he said. 'I'll go an' get them leaves raked. Sweet dreams, Ellie.'

'That's another thing,' she said.

'Aye?' Ned, who had been almost out of the room, turned and leaned against the doorframe. *What now*, he wondered.

Ellie rolled over, pillowing her cheek with her hands. 'When we're a respectable married couple, I want thee to introduce me as Felicia. Makes me feel like we're still penniless kids when tha calls me Ellie.'

He laughed. 'It's tha name. It's what I've allus called thee.'

'We're too old for nicknames, Edwin.'

'It's Ned.'

Irritation had hardened his voice. Ellie's eyes were sparkling as she lifted the blanket. 'Come 'ere. You warm me better than owt else.'

Ned shook his head. 'I'm up now.' But he was already walking towards the bed, unbuttoning his waistcoat and pulling free his shirt. Ellie waited until their bodies were wrapped tight.

'Ned?'

'Hmm?'

'Tha does love me, dun't tha? Ned?'

'Don't be soft, lass.'

'Kiss me.'

He did.

Later that afternoon, Ned walked Ellie home and continued down to Pond Street. He stopped at the entrance to the coffee house, took off his cap, smoothed his hair back, replaced his cap and looked around the crowded interior, finally spying Mr Prescott sitting with Frank in the far corner of the room. The older man was jabbing his finger on the tabletop, talking intently to Frank, who had a surly look on his face. When he saw Ned, Frank's eyes widened in relief. He gestured him over.

' 'Ey up,' said Frank. 'I thought tha were never comin'.'

'Here's the man himself,' said Mr Prescott. 'How's my Felicia? Treating her well? I never see owt of her now tha's on the scene.'

'She's grand,' said Ned.

'Young love, eh?' said Mr Prescott.

'I wun't say *young*,' said Frank. Ned gave him a playful punch on the shoulder and took a seat opposite the two men, who were sitting with their backs to the wall.

'What's tha havin'?' said Mr Prescott.

'Nowt for me, thanks,' said Ned. 'Tha wanted me to call in, Mr Prescott. What can I do for thee?'

Mr Prescott looked at Frank. 'See, what I like about this fella is he dun't mess about. Allus gets right to the point. Tell him, son.'

'All reight,' said Frank. He leaned towards Ned, dropping his voice to a conspiratorial whisper. 'Your clerk is bringin' summat wi' him when he comes to work in the mornin'. We need thee to store it for us, tuck it away, like.'

'There'll be plenty o' cubby holes in that cottage,' said Mr Prescott. 'An' it won't be for long.'

Ned looked from father to son and back again, his growing disquiet tempered by the knowledge he would need to tread carefully. He was in the Prescotts' debt. 'What is it?' he said.

'Why does tha need to know?' said Mr Prescott. He smiled at Ned, a closed-lip smile that was a warning.

'I'd like to,' said Ned.

Mr Prescott sat back in his chair and sighed. Ned turned his attention to Frank, lifting one eyebrow.

'All reight,' said Frank. 'Don't get thee knickers in a twist. It's nowt much, a bit o' tobacco.' He tapped the side of his nose. 'Come off a liner at Hull.'

'Why me?' said Ned, relieved he wasn't being asked to keep firearms. Smuggled tobacco might be a lesser evil but he'd refuse just the same. 'Surely, tha's got all the space tha needs for this sort o' thing.'

Mr Prescott parroted him. 'Why me? This sort o' thing?' He folded his arms and looked up towards the ceiling before turning eyes that could freeze molten iron on Ned. 'Think tha's above it, does tha? I can tell thee, tha little bastard, tha's not. So don't go all high an' mighty on me or tha'll know about it.'

Ned's senses sharpened, his ears whining with the hum of muted conversations in the room behind him, his nostrils clogged by the pall of smoke that hung below the ceiling and his eyes fixed helplessly on the penknife Mr Prescott had taken out of his jacket pocket. The man opened the blade and began cleaning dirt from under his fingernails. Frank was looking away, to his left, as if his attention had been caught elsewhere. He kicked Ned on the shin.

'I'll do it,' said Ned, 'but I'm not 'appy about it.'

Frank sighed.

'Listen,' said Mr Prescott, folding up and putting away the knife. 'I'm not askin' much o' thee. Sixty pounds o' tobacco is worth a fair amount. Tha'll get a cut o' the profit.' He smiled. 'All reight, lad?'

'I'm still not comfy wi' it,' said Ned.

'But tha'll do it,' said Mr Prescott.

'What if it gets found?'

'Well, tha says it's for tha own personal use,' said Mr Prescott.

'I don't smoke.'

'Develop a habit, lad.'

Frank laughed.

His father ignored him. 'Tha'll do it,' he repeated.

'Aye,' said Ned.

'Good lad.' He tapped his hands on the table in a timpani of satisfaction. 'What did I tell thee, Frank? He's a good lad, this one. Our Felicia's a lucky lass.'

—

He needed a drink, a proper one.

Frank accompanied him to the Blue Pig, where Ned sat with his head in his hands. Frank put a pint in front of him and Ned lifted it up and took a long swallow, feeling the liquid run down his gullet.

'He's just testin' tha loyalty,' said Frank. 'Tha should be flattered, if owt. It's a little bit o' baccy.'

'Stolen goods is what it is.' He would have to make sure Jacob never found out.

'Don't think o' it that way. Tha's in the family now, or nearly. Once a Prescott, allus a Prescott, eh?'

Ned shook his head. 'Ellie'll be a Staniforth.'

'Tha knows full well what I mean,' said Frank. He got to his feet and adopted a more conciliatory tone. 'Why don't I get 'em in again? That lass behind the counter's givin' me the eye. Wish me luck and try an' get that glum look off thee face while I'm gone, reight?'

Ned laughed. 'Cheeky bugger.'

'That's more like it,' said Frank. He ambled away.

The smile faded from Ned's face. He and Frank would be brothers-in-law, and outlaws together, under the control of Mr Prescott. It might be bearable if he loved Ellie. The cold hollow in the pit of his stomach whenever he thought about their impending wedding reminded him that he didn't. Perhaps the affection he felt for her would grow, perhaps seeing Ellie raise the children they would have might make him forget that he had ever loved Nan, had loved her from the moment he first saw her, and loved her still.

For months, he had yearned to hear from Nan, to find a letter waiting for him at the end of his working day, full of words of love. He had written and posted a dozen letters to the prison near London, before admitting defeat. She could not have made it any clearer, from the moment she refused to meet his gaze in the courtroom, that she had cut their bond as neatly as snipping a thread. And now he was betrothed, and had come to dread any contact Nan might make. How would he explain himself? Still, he could not love Ellie. Ned's heart belonged to Nan Turpin. He had a feeling it always would.

Chapter 26

Tucking loose strands of hair into her maid's cap, the woman who went by the name of Ann picked up two pints of ale and carried them through the crowded tap room, depositing them on the mahogany table in the corner. A group of men in caps and waistcoats, shirt-sleeves turned up, were hunched around it, playing cards.

'Where's the rest?' one of them asked around the pipe clenched in his teeth. He tilted his chair onto its back legs, removing the pipe from his mouth. 'Oy! Ronnie! Where'd you get her from, this new maid of thine that can't carry owt?'

From his position behind the counter at the far end of the room, the landlord flapped his hand and turned away.

Ann made a moue of mock sorrow. 'Why, I'm a butterfingers, that's all. I wouldn't want to spill a drop, would I?'

'I don't mind waitin',' one of the other men said. 'Not when I'm gettin' served by a lass as pretty as this one. Are they all like thee back home? Need a man to show you 'round town?'

She smiled at him. 'I'm spoken for.'

'A'course you are, looker like you.'

'I'll fetch the rest now,' she said.

'Make sure you do, me dear. See, lads? That's how to treat 'em. Wi' respect.'

'I know what you want to treat her wi' but I've never heard it called that before.'

She went back to the counter with their laughter ringing in her ears.

'Pay 'em no heed,' said the landlord.

'Oh, I don't.' She smoothed her hands down the bib and skirt of her apron before picking up the remaining pints. 'I've had dealings with far worse than that.'

Ann's feet were aching. She'd been on them for eight hours, with half an hour off to sit and eat a meal. There were still three hours to go before the landlord would ring the bell for chucking-out time. Then there would be the stragglers to coax out and the clearing away to do. She wouldn't be able to fall into her bed until half past twelve at the earliest. But there were compensations, blessings to count. There was a handle on the inside of the door in the room where she laid her head and, if she felt so inclined, she could open the door, creep down the back staircase and step outside to stand in the velvety silence of the night. If the sky wasn't obscured by smoke or cloud she could gaze up at the same moon that shone on the little cottage by the forge.

Would Ned be sleeping inside it, or might he be standing on his doorstep, looking up too, and thinking of her?

–

A month earlier, she had lain cocooned between scratchy layers of burlap and been fearful for her life. The journey had seemed interminable, the motion of the wagon rocking her from side to side, sometimes slowing, occasionally stopping, and then jerking forward again. Every time the wagon stopped, her body vibrated with the hammering of her heart. Any moment now, hands would reach in and clamp around her ankles and drag her from her hiding place, as easily as pulling a piece of thread through a needle-hole. As a recaptured convict, she would be the lowest of the low, kept separate from the other prisoners for months on end, with nothing to think about except her failure and humiliation. She would be caged in a different prison or put back into Woking, where Rhoda would be waiting to exact her revenge.

Then the wagon would set off again, leaving her gasping with relief.

On what would be the final time the wagon stopped, Nan once again braced herself to be handled roughly. For a while, nothing happened and the only sound she could hear was her own harsh breathing. Then the load on her began to lighten. A whistle blew, loud and shrill. Blind terror drove Nan to twist her body and fling away the last sack, the muscles in her arms and torso protesting. She sat up on the pallet, screwing her eyes closed against the light. She put out her hands in what she knew was a pitiful and futile attempt to defend herself.

'All right, lass.' Strong hands clamped around her upper arms and she was swung to the ground, and held upright, her back against the wooden side panel of the wagon. Panting with fear, her head hanging, she couldn't bring herself to fully open her eyes. Any moment now she would feel the weight of cuffs being attached to her wrists. Instead, she was gently shaken by the arm.

'We've no time to lose.' The same voice as before. 'Can you stand? You'll need your wits about you.'

No time to lose. Your wits about you. Daring to hope, Nan looked up and focused on the face of the man standing before her. He had a grizzled beard and rheumy eyes set in a ruddy complexion. Where she had expected to see the shiny buttons of a police tunic and the chinstrap of a police helmet, he wore a loosely fastened sack coat and a peaked cap. Nan looked to left and right. This must be the wagon driver.

'Can you stand?' he repeated.

'Yes.'

He relinquished his grip and stood back. Nan looked beyond him, at the horse cropping on the hedgerow, at the dusty lane they had stopped on, a country lane. Birdsong filled the air and there was another sound, growing louder and then fading into the distance. It was the chug of a steam engine. Was she to be put on a train? She opened her mouth to ask the driver but he was ambling way, towards the front of the wagon. He wouldn't just leave her standing here, surely not.

'Where am I?' she called to his retreating back. 'What should I do now?'

The driver ignored her. He was fiddling with something on the wagon. He turned, two bottles in one hand, a bottle opener in the other. Nan's legs weakened, so great was the relief that coursed through her body. She swigged from the bottle he gave her and thanked him. It was the finest ginger beer she had ever tasted. He watched her drink, then took the bottle from her.

'Best get that off, then.'

He meant the prison uniform. Her fingers fumbling, Nan undressed as quickly as she could, revealing her own blue dress beneath. She looked down at her threadbare prison shoes, dismayed.

'It's either them or barefoot,' said the wagon driver.

She kept them on. Taking off her cap, she unpinned her hair so that it fell in a single long plait down her back. The driver bundled up her cap in her prison uniform and dropped it at the side of the road. He looked her over and nodded, satisfied.

'Now, you've got something for me, haven't you? My payment.'

Nan removed one of the two five-pound notes from the pocket of her dress and held it out to him. 'Thank you,' she said.

The man chuckled. 'Oh no you don't. Expensive business, this. Got to make it worth my while, haven't they? You're not the only one that's seen the last of that place.'

Nan handed over the second note. 'What am I supposed to do now?'

'Don't you worry about that.' He held up a finger and walked away again, disappearing around the other side of the wagon. The horse whinnied and Nan went to it, scratching it between its eyes. The animal nudged her with its nose.

'I'm sorry I don't have any food,' said Nan. She had nothing. Her stomach spasmed in fear. Her fate lay in the hands of strangers. How soon would it be before she could reclaim her life? She pressed her face against the shire's flank, which smelled of damp straw and dirt, and inhaled, comforted by the touch of another living creature.

The wagon driver returned with a small cloth bag and gave it to her. He handed her two guineas and a half-crown. 'To pay your next fares.' Nan put them in her pocket – reflecting it was a poor exchange for ten pounds – and looked inside the bag. There was a pair of nail scissors, a small comb and a stoppered bottle of dark liquid. She flinched when the man reached out and took hold of her plait and brought it over her shoulder. The old Nan would have batted his hand away or, depending on the situation, used her charm to extract herself from his grasp. Now, she was helpless.

'Get rid o' this,' the wagon driver said, tugging at and finally letting go of her hair, 'and that's dye.'

'Dye?'

'You wet your hair and you comb it through. All right? The station's that way,' – he indicated a gap in the hedge – 'through the field.' He shook his head impatiently when Nan tried to interrupt again. 'Just listen. There a privy an' a pump. The train's just passed us. You must have heard the whistle, before. That's what we were waiting for. It should be quiet for a bit. You following? Wait on the platform, there's a bench at the end of it. Somebody will come.' He ducked his head to peer into her face. 'Have you got that?'

Nan tried to speak but her throat had closed. She nodded.

'Go on then. Look sharp.'

She finally found her voice. 'Who will it be?'

He shrugged. 'Can't say who because I don't know. I've done my bit. Off you go, now.'

Nan walked towards the gap in the hedge. When she looked back, the driver had set light to the small bundle of clothes. Soon, her prison uniform would be ashes. 'Thank you,' she called. He didn't acknowledge her. 'I hope you stay safe.'

He was now busying himself attaching a nosebag to the horse and spoke without looking towards her. 'Don't you worry about me. Go on, now, before I have to chase you off.'

There were sheep cropping in the middle of the field who ignored Nan as she walked along the boundary fence, heading towards the gate at the far end. She climbed the stile and found herself on another narrow lane. It stretched into the distance on her left and curved around a bend on her right. The wagon driver hadn't told her in which direction she ought to turn. Panic rose in Nan's throat and she was on the verge of running back across the field when she saw a white sliver of a chimney stack and the pot on top, just visible beyond a stand of trees where the road curved. Praying it was the station building, she set off in that direction.

Around the bend, she came across a piece of rutted ground, about a quarter of the size of the prison exercise yard, with a short flight of wooden steps at the far end. Beside the steps was a lean-to shack and the promised water pump above a shallow trough. Nan hesitated, then quickly crossed to the steps and climbed them. She stood on the deserted platform of a small, country station. The station master's office was shuttered. No smoke rose from the chimney pot she'd seen from the road. A crow was perched on the wrought-iron bench beneath the closed hatch of the ticket booth. It cawed at her. There was a second bench at the far end of the platform, greened with mildew. This was presumably the one she had been instructed to sit upon. First, she had a task to complete.

Satisfied she would not be observed, Nan retraced her steps. She lifted the latch on the door to the shack, opened it and immediately closed it again. The stench of the privy was unbearable, but now she realised she needed to empty her bladder. She shoved the bag she'd been given in the gap under the steps, walked to the hedge, lifted her skirt and peed. Then she retrieved the bag and went to stand before the water pump, twisting her long plait in her fingers.

She wished she had a mirror. He had said she should hurry.

Nan lifted the scissors in one hand and her plait in the other, told herself she would not weep and began to saw through the thick rope of her hair. She reopened the door to the privy, held her breath and dropped the plait through the hole in the seat.

–

Nan sat on the wooden bench, her hands stained with black dye. She was bone-tired now, and strangely listless about her fate. All she wanted to do was sleep. As the next train chugged into the station, a boy of no more than twelve or thirteen trotted towards her. This surely could not be the person into whose hands she'd been delivered.

Nan allowed him to pull her to her feet. He shoved a piece of paper into her hand – her ticket – and led her to the back of the train, to the hard benches of the third-class compartment. She sank back in her seat and rested her head against the rough wood panelling, vaguely aware of the boy conversing with another passenger, a burly man sitting across from her. Then her eyes closed, and the last thing she was aware of was a pull in her gut, the tug of the engine dragging her towards an unknown destination.

The next thing Nan knew she was being shaken awake by her fellow passenger. 'This is thine,' he said gruffly.

Nan thanked him and stumbled onto the platform. Painted on a board, the name of the station swam before her eyes. *Headingley & Kirkstall*. It meant nothing to her. She exited the station and stood on the dirt lane behind it, her senses on high alert. The sky was overcast and she had no idea of the time of day, or even what day it was.

The duration of her terrifying journey in the sacks wagon could have been one hour or five or fifteen. She had lost all sense of time during it. And now she had no idea how long she'd slept for on the train. A shudder ran through her body at the thought of being observed while helpless.

But she was here now and there was nothing to do but wait.

After a time, a wagon full of haybales went by, the driver glancing at Nan and away again, giving no indication that his curiosity was aroused by seeing a lone woman standing on the lane, a woman with no covering on her short, dark hair. Perhaps he thought she was wearing a cap. She wondered whether she ought to have raised a hand in greeting. She had simply stood there as petrified as a piece of coal. He might have been the person meant to collect her. Perhaps he had decided two guineas was not worth the risk.

She was startled by the sound of an animal yipping and the panicked bleat of sheep, followed – so near to her! – by the measured tones of a farmer instructing his dog. He must be within yards of her on the other side of the hedge, rounding up his sheep. Ordinary life was going on all around her, while she stood awaiting her fate. Some time later, darkness began to descend, the hedgerows gradually losing their definition to become dark, looming barriers, like the walls of a prison. Nan clamped her arms across her body, tucking fingers numbed with cold into her armpits, and stamped her feet. It occurred to her to try to break into the station master's office and light a fire. Nobody was coming to collect her.

The sky had cleared and stars began to shine, more stars than she had never seen before, their cold light making her shudder.

The sound of horses clopping along at a brisk pace preceded an open-sided wagon coming into view around the bend. A sob escaped her. It didn't matter who they were, she was going to beg a lift to the nearest town. There were two men sitting up front, one holding a lamp, the other controlling the reins. She cried out. 'Please stop!'

When the wagon drew up beside her, the sour stink of hops filled the air. The men's faces were indistinct behind the light from the lamp.

The man with the reins spoke first. 'Sorry, love. We'd have come sooner.'

The second man interrupted him. 'Lost a barrel, didn't we? Right mess. Anyhow, all the deliveries done, except one, and here you are, where they said you'd be. Got summat for us?'

'I think so,' said Nan. Her fingers shook when she removed the guineas from her pocket. The half crown had disappeared. The boy must have taken it. Nan put the guineas in the palm of her hand and held them out for inspection, her gut churning. Was she offering enough or would she be abandoned to her fate in this quiet lane?

'Right you are, then.' The second man patted the bench beside him and reached down, taking first the coins and then her arm. 'Up you come. I'd put you in the back but thanks to this gormless sod you'd soon be drunk on the fumes.'

'Who are you callin' gormless?'

Nan squeezed onto the end of the bench and looked behind her. The flatbed was empty. The man with the lamp tucked the coins into his waistcoat pocket. The driver geed the horses and they set off at a brisk pace. The other man told her they worked for the brewery, but didn't say which one, and didn't offer his name or the name of the driver, or ask for hers. Nan held onto his arm, clutching at the rough material of his coat as they swung along, or she might have fallen off. Again, she drew comfort from the sustained connection. All she'd known for months was the fleeting touch of Sarah's lips on hers, Sarah's fingers squeezing hers and the vicious jabs from Rhoda. She would not think of that.

Shoulder to shoulder, they swayed along, and, in an effort to distract herself from how very cold she was, Nan thought about her last close encounter with a brewery wagon, moments after she had run into Ned's arms. She imagined it was Ned's arm she was hanging onto, his hip pressed into hers. Wherever she was being taken, this was only a stage on her journey back to him.

They drove over a canal bridge where light shone from a warehouse on the edge of the dock, illuminating the low hulks of barges on the black water. The streets became wider, busier with traffic and brightly lit. She had been delivered to a large town. Nan craned her neck in wonder when they passed beneath a wide flight of steps leading to an enormous building supported by a row of tall columns, with stone lions on plinths guarding the entrance and, rising from the middle, dominating an already impressive sight, a tall clock tower topped with a concave dome. The man whose arm she was clutching paid it no attention.

A few moments later, the wagon stopped at the foot of a narrow, paved street lined with terraced buildings and lit by regularly spaced wall lamps.

'Walk down there an' the Rose and Crown is a hundred yards on the right,' said the driver. 'Tell the landlady you've come for the maid's job. You get bed an' board wi' it, an' no questions asked.'

'The Rose and Crown,' Nan repeated. 'A maid's job?'

The other man lifted the lamp towards her face. 'Could be worse,' he said. 'There's an 'ouse of ill repute at the end o' this road. Or would that be better? You might prefer spending all yer time on yer back.' He jumped down and helped her to the pavement. 'Thought of a name for yerself?'

'Yes, I have.' She looked around. 'Where am I? I mean to say, what's the name of this town?'

'It's Leeds, and you're right in the middle o' it.' The driver winked. 'A good place for them who need to disappear. Good luck, lass.'

They left her standing on the paving stones. Aching with exhaustion and numb with cold, Nan turned in the direction of the Rose and Crown. She soon found the pub, sandwiched between the locked and darkened premises of an ironmongery and a bookbinding business. Light shone from the windows of the public house and she could hear the sound of voices and laughter. It was a warm sound, a balm for her nerves. Several heads turned when she entered, then the drinkers went back to their business. Nan stood for a few moments, taking in her surroundings, then approached a young woman serving food to a table of men and asked if she could speak with the landlady. The woman told her to wait where she stood. The men at the table were sizing her up. She moved away. Eventually, an older woman returned, wiping her hands on a cloth.

'What can I do for you?' she said.

Nan took a deep breath. 'I've come for the live-in maid's job. You were expecting me earlier. My name's Ann Baker.'

'Aye, you're late. I thought to start you tonight but no matter. Ann, is it?' The woman put her hands on her hips and looked Nan up and down. 'Who cut all your hair off?' She held up a hand when Nan opened her mouth to answer. 'No, I don't need to know about that. Wages are three shillings a week, free board an' meals an' if you ask for extra food on top o' that you pay for it. Hours are midday to midnight, wi' Sundays off unless we're short-handed, which we often are. You'll be expected to help wi' early mornin' deliveries an' also help the cleaner if she needs it. Ethel comes in at six. If she gets you up, no complaining, understand?'

Nan nodded, and the woman continued. 'I don't tolerate any nonsense. You're out on the street if you can't work extra shifts, if you bring men to your room or if you're disrespectful to the customers. No soliciting. No thieving. Got it, Ann Baker?'

'Yes, I understand you.'

'All right. Let's see how we go.'

She was dizzy with fatigue and relief and could barely manage the bread and dripping and mug of tea she was given to take upstairs. She fell asleep as soon as her head touched the pillow of the narrow bed in the room above the pub kitchen, and dreamed of towering hedgerows and the endless sound of clopping hooves.

—

'Hold out your hand, Ann.'

She obeyed the landlord, who took hold of her wrist, put a one-pound note onto her palm and folded her fingers over it. He patted her closed fist.

'Why'd you look so worried?' he said.

'Well,' Nan said slowly. 'I'm grateful, but I only have fifteen shillings to give you in return.'

She had come to an arrangement with the landlord to exchange coins for notes, whenever her wages reached the value of one pound. The note would be stashed in the pocket sewn inside the waistband of her dress. It was the beginnings of a hoard, but would need to be supplemented or she would be working at the Rose and Crown the rest of Ann Baker's days. Fortunately, this town had a plethora of department stores and trinket shops catering to wealthy ladies and gentlemen, and a correspondingly pleasing number of pawnbrokers and fences. She had already made the acquaintance of a couple of regulars at the Rose and Crown who dealt in liberated items.

The landlord was beaming at her. 'You're a good worker. At least, you try to be. The missus says there's room for improvement and I say give the young lass a bit of time to settle in. So you can consider this a small bonus for the nice way you have wi' the customers.'

She lowered her chin and smiled shyly. 'Thank you kindly.' She raised her eyes as the landlord walked away, whistling a tune. He'd be half-cut by the end of the night, which was a long way off. The cleaner had woken her early and tasked her with scrubbing the saloon room floor, and the twelve-hour shift she was paid for had just begun. Ann Baker would keep her head down and work her fingers to the bone in this job. Nan Turpin had a different plan.

WINTER

Chapter 27

Autumn's glorious canopy had faded. Now, the cold tendrils of winter were exploring every nook and cranny in the house. A fire was lit morning and evening in every occupied room, fuel supplies allowing. The cost of coal had gone up again. Housekeeping had requested more blankets and bed socks.

These thoughts were swept from Hetty's mind by a series of raps on the front door knocker.

A cold eddy of air swirled in when Hetty opened the door. She could not make out the features of the shadowy figure who stood to one side, as if hesitant to make their presence known. They were backlit by the streetlight in the centre of the square that picked out the surrounding cobbles but did not reach the dark corners on the periphery. The shops were closed but there was a glow behind the curtains in most of the upper-storey windows of the buildings that fringed the square, and Hetty could hear the faint sound of fiddle music coming from inside the Q in the Corner. It was nine o'clock at night and she had been called from her desk where she had been writing her weekly report, her thickest shawl around her shoulders, her hands cold in a pair of fingerless gloves.

Her visitor lifted the lamp he was carrying and revealed himself.

'Good evenin' to you,' said Constable Goodlad. 'It's a bitter night, isn't it?'

Hetty stood aside to let him enter. 'It is with the door hangin' open. Come in, come in.'

The constable was alone, on probably the one night in the year a woman in need would have had her pick of the beds. Hetty had bidden farewell to four residents today, two to positions, one poor soul to convalesce in Cleethorpes accompanied by an agent of the house, and one unruly girl to the reform school. 'Whatever's the matter?' said Hetty.

The constable smiled wryly. 'I'm sorry for the lateness of the hour but it'd be nice for once to turn up on a doorstep and not have everybody assume the worst has happened.'

Hetty snorted. 'You'll need to change your profession, then.' She led him down the narrow hall towards the kitchen. 'D'you want tea? I've nothin' stronger.'

'I don't want to put you out,' said Constable Goodlad.

'I'd say if you were.'

She opened the door onto a cosy scene in a room that had been thoroughly warmed by the fire in the range. At one end of the kitchen table, a group of four women were playing a noisy game of Parcheesi, the new board game donated to the house by a benefactor recently returned from America. The game provoked hilarity and the occasional bout of bad language amongst the residents but Hetty hadn't yet had the opportunity to play it. At the other end of the table, two women were frowning at the playing cards fanned in their fingers. Hetty glanced at the tabletop between them. It was clear of coins. Gambling was forbidden in the house. It would only lead to all sorts of trouble if Hetty allowed it.

One of the residents greeted the constable by name and the two of them engaged in conversation, the tall youth standing awkwardly by the table, the young woman pausing in her tale about her new job at a cutlery factory to throw the dice and count a tile across the game board. Hetty busied herself pouring hot water from the kettle, measuring tea into the strainer and finding a teapot and cups. She was reluctant, in front of the women and girls, to ask Constable Goodlad what his business was.

'Let's see who's in the parlour,' she said.

They stopped on their way along the hall when Amelia poked her head out of the ground-floor dorm, saw Hetty's company, nodded to him with a slight curl on her lip and disappeared back into the room. Hetty gestured for the constable to continue and decided to ignore the chagrin on his face. Amelia would not easily forgive being forced to prove she wasn't a thief. She had been to see Mr Brown in his jeweller's shop, to apologise, but the police officer had, in Amelia's eyes, humiliated her.

'How is Miss Barlow?' said Constable Goodlad, as she opened the door to the parlour.

'Recovering,' said Hetty.

In the parlour, a resident sat at the upright piano, playing it badly but quietly. Both the fireside armchairs were taken up, one by Hope whose head was buried in a book and the other by a resident who had a pile of mending in her lap.

Hope raised her eyebrows when they entered, greeted the constable and asked Hetty if they would prefer some privacy. When Hetty agreed that would be a good idea, Hope got up and ushered the women from the room, gently closing the door behind her.

'Well,' said Hetty, once they were alone, 'what brings you here tonight?'

Constable Goodlad set down his cup. 'Nothing of import. I'm on the night shift and thought I'd come by, see how you are, Miss Barlow, and all the ladies of the house.'

'That's kind,' said Hetty. She wondered, irritably, if the opportunity to warm his feet by the fire was the sole purpose of Constable Goodlad's visit. She had a report to finish. 'I did have a run-in the other day, wi' a disgruntled husband, but I saw him off.'

'I'm sure you did.' He scratched the underside of his chin. 'And you know I'm only ever a stone's throw away.' He folded his lips. 'I was wonderin', Miss Barlow, whether Nan Turpin had shown her face here.'

Here was the real reason for his visit. The authorities were still none the wiser as to the whereabouts of a girl who, months earlier, seemed to have disappeared into thin air. The House of Help was the first place Constable Goodlad, in the company of a police investigator, had visited as soon as the news of her escape from Woking jail had been wired. Here he was again, clutching at straws.

'If she ever did show up here,' said Hetty, 'you'd be the first to know but I can guarantee you, Nan Turpin won't want to cross my path again.'

'I'm grateful to you,' he said. 'I have to ask.'

'I know,' said Hetty. 'What about that fiancé of hers?'

The constable frowned. 'He was – is – at the top of our list. Claims he hasn't seen hide nor hair of her. In fact, he's engaged to be married, on Christmas Eve.'

Hetty leaned forward. 'Who to?'

'Frank Prescott's daughter.'

'Oh aye? I've heard of him.'

Constable Goodlad laughed. 'Out of the frying pan and into the fire, eh?'

'Well, I wish the poor lad well. He was that smitten by Nan. Hope told me he took it hard.' Hetty sipped her tea. 'How long has Nan Turpin been makin' fools of you lot, then?'

Constable Goodlad gave her such a glum look that Hetty almost felt sorry for him. 'More than two months now. Stowed away on a wagon right under their noses. The driver's disappeared too. They could be together.'

'She was allus the charmer,' said Hetty.

The constable got to his feet and adjusted his hat. 'Well, you know where to find me if you catch a sight of her.'

'I do,' said Hetty.

It occurred to her, as she saw him out and closed and bolted the door, that Ned Staniforth might not be the only man to have had his head turned by Nan Turpin.

As Hetty turned away, rubbing her arms against the cold, she was surprised to see the door to her quarters swing open. Hope appeared from inside, an urgent frown on her face, and gestured for Hetty to hurry and follow her back into the room.

'Hope? What are you…' The words died on Hetty's lips.

A woman stood in the middle of the room, the black woollen shawl she was wearing pulled up to cover her head, her pale features framed by dark hair. She put her hand over her mouth and crinkled her eyes as merrily as if she'd been caught with her hand in the biscuit tin. Hetty gasped. The hair colour was wrong but she was staring into the eyes of Nan Turpin.

Hetty swung around to glare at Hope. There was desperation in the deputy warden's eyes. 'This is Ann

Baker,' she said. 'She came in the back while you were in the parlour.'

'Pleased to meet you,' said Nan, stretching out her hand. 'I was wondering, have you a bed for the night?' Her voice was full of confidence but her smile trembled at the edges.

Hetty ignored the outstretched hand. She turned to Hope. 'The others?' She meant the residents Nan would have encountered in the kitchen.

Hope shook her head. 'None of them were here then, so there's nobody who'd remember her. As far as they're concerned, this *is* a woman in need whose name is Ann Baker. She's going to a job in a tavern on the Chesterfield Road and she is looking for a bed for one night before moving on.'

In a quiet voice, Nan said: 'I hope you will take that for the truth. I'll be gone tomorrow, and you'll never see me again. I promise you that.'

Hetty stared at her, incredulously. 'Take off that shawl.'

Nan reached up and pulled the shawl from her head. Her hair was mussed up, cut choppily around her jawline. Hetty noted the dark shadows under her eyes and a cut that was healing on her lower lip. She was thinner than the girl who had once unpinned her long auburn hair to drop jewels onto the carpet of the parlour. Her complexion was mottled from the cold, but those strong features and blue eyes were unmistakable.

Hetty glared at her, incredulous. 'Do you know who just left this house?' she said. Both the younger women nodded. 'I should chase after him.'

'Please, don't,' said Hope, 'or I shall be in trouble for allowing her into the house, and going along with the lie about her name and why she's here, in front of six witnesses.'

Hetty shook her head. 'Don't be daft, Hope. We only have to say you brought her inside after Goodlad had left. We can go to the station now.'

'I won't be coming with you,' said Nan.

'No matter,' said Hetty. 'We can tell the police you were here. They'll soon find you.'

'I'll tell them Hope was hiding me away,' said Nan.

'And *I'll* say she was only trying to restrain you.'

'Wouldn't that make you a liar, Miss Barlow? Or do your morals desert you when you care about the person who needs protecting?'

'Stop it, both of you, please,' said Hope. She turned to Hetty. 'Allow her a few hours to warm herself.'

'And then what?' said Hetty. 'What about Amelia, and Clara when she arrives in the morning?'

'I'll be gone by then,' said Nan.

'Where?' said Hetty.

Nan gave her a crafty smile.

Hope spoke quickly. 'That doesn't matter. As far as we're concerned, Ann Baker has set off early, that's all. Least said, soonest mended.'

This was one of Hetty's phrases. It was strange hearing it repeated back to her. Still, it didn't mean that Hope hadn't lost her senses.

'We're committing an offence,' said Hetty, 'by harbouring an escaped convict.'

'If I'm seen leaving,' said Nan, 'I'll say I broke into the house through the coal hole, in the middle of the night, and slept on a chair in the parlour. When you get up in the morning, Miss Barlow, the front door will be unlocked and you'll wonder why, but then you'll get on with your day, and forget all about it.' Her eyes filled with tears. 'I won't go back to jail. I'd rather die.'

'Well, there's no cause to be so melodramatic.' Hetty was wavering, and Hope knew it.

'Allow Nan to remain here until the house has settled for the night,' she said, 'and then leave her in the parlour.' She took Nan's hand. 'I'll stay with her. Whatever her crimes might be, in this moment, standing here, she is a friendless girl.'

—

Hetty lay watching the embers of the fire until the glow faded to black. At half past four, she rose, took a lamp, and went quietly into the hallway, her breath pluming in the cold air. If Nan had spent the night out of doors she might have frozen to death and Hetty had not wanted that on her conscience. Nor had she desired the inevitable drama involved in turning Nan over to the police, even if Hetty could have prevented her from running off again, could have somehow held her captive in the house. Paradise Square would be rife with gossip if Hetty reported a sighting of the escaped convict, and Mrs Calver would mount her warhorse, no doubt. In short, Nan had got her way again.

In the parlour, Nan and Hope were crouched on the rug, a lamp beside them, examining the contents of a valise. It was the same embroidered bag that Mr Wallace had donated to the house, the one that had belonged to his late wife. He had presented it to Hetty before she embarked on a trip to the seaside with a girl recovering from smallpox. She recalled with a wave of affection his awkwardness when he had presented her with the bag.

'You're givin' her that?' she said, softly.

Hope looked up. 'You don't mind, do you? It's so that she can carry a few items of clothing and some money. I've donated them,' she added hurriedly. 'I have more than I need. Nan has nothing.'

Hetty couldn't, and didn't, argue with that. The valise would add to the innocent picture of a young female traveller, once daylight revealed her to the world.

Nan rose to her feet. She wore a long, buttoned-up black cape, a few inches of her blue skirt visible beneath the hem, pale blue gloves, a matching scarf around her lower jaw and an old-fashioned black hat on her head with wings that would hide her face from anyone who wasn't standing directly in front of her.

'I'll go now,' she said, her voice muffled. She embraced Hope and held out her hand to Hetty, who shook it.

'I hope to never see you again,' she said.

'The feeling is mutual, Miss Barlow.'

An hour later, the first house resident showed her face in the kitchen, where Hetty and Hope sat warming their hands around mugs of tea. Mabel Hargreaves started work at six and wouldn't be back from her job as a buffer until six in the evening.

'Tha pair's up early,' she said. 'Nice to have the fire lit, though.' She disappeared into the pantry, returning with the tin snap box she'd packed the night before. 'Si thee later, loves.'

By half past seven there was no room to spare around the kitchen table. Amelia leaned on her hip in her usual place against the kitchen sink, listening to the women's chatter. Hope had pleaded a headache and gone to her bed, and Hetty sat at her little table for one in the corner of the room, drinking her third cup of tea and wondering whether she, too, ought to try to get some sleep. A task for later would be to make an entry in the ledger on the off-chance Ann Baker's name was raised. She sipped her tea. *Ann Baker, age twenty-seven, no fixed address, no family, on her way to a position on the Chesterfield Road, arrived needing somewhere warm and safe for the night. Left early the following morning.* There was also her report to finish, for delivery to the treasurer's office tomorrow. Mr Wallace had been absent lately and Hetty's last three warden reports had been left with his secretary, a cadaverous man who took the papers from her with his index finger and thumb as if he was afraid of catching poverty.

By three o'clock Hetty had finished her report and her head was nodding. She would take a nap and make up for the night's sleep she had lost over Nan Turpin. She read the report over. A shortage of bed spaces was a recurring theme, although Hetty had been told that a move to bigger premises was on the cards. Gratifyingly, eighty per cent of those women and girls who came to the house friendless and destitute, and would have been destined for the workhouse, had gone into service, or to factory jobs or shop work. There were a couple of cases where nothing could be done. One woman had stayed at the House of Help on three separate occasions, and every time had gone back to her abusive husband. She would reappear days or weeks or months from now, her eye or cheek or mouth bruised, her arm in a sling or a bandage around her head. Hetty would find her a bed and the husband would be locked up for a while, and she would return home. Then he'd be released and the rigmarole would begin over. Hetty wondered how Nan Turpin had come by her split lip, and whether she would ever come back to the house, or be caught and flung back into jail.

Hetty found herself hoping that Nan would continue to foil the authorities.

She smiled to herself. Wild horses wouldn't drag that truth from her.

There was a tap on the door. Before Hetty had time to answer, Amelia came in, slightly out of breath and with a wide smile on her face. 'You've a visitor,' she declared.

Hetty reached for her cap, reluctantly. 'I was about to have forty winks,' she said.

'Don't bother with that,' said Amelia, impatiently. 'It's not an official visit. The opposite, I'd say.'

'What're you talkin' about?'

'*Some*body has asked for a private audience, like you're the Queen or summat.'

'A what?'

Hetty followed Amelia into the parlour, where Mr Wallace was standing in front of the mirror over the mantlepiece, straightening his necktie in the mirror. 'Here she is,' announced Amelia cheerfully and left the room, closing the door behind her.

Mr Wallace turned to greet Hetty with an anxious look on his face. Hetty sat on the edge of the chaise longue and folded her hands in her lap. Perhaps Nan Turpin had been captured crossing the path of Constable Goodlad on night patrol and confessed her recent whereabouts. Hetty was too exhausted to deny it, if Mr Wallace asked. Or the trustees had changed their minds about her position and Mr Wallace was here to tell her that her tenure as warden was at an end. Although Mrs Calver would want to be present for that. Hetty wiped her eyes. She was bone-tired.

'Miss Barlow, am I disturbing you?'

'I'm always happy to see you, Mr Wallace.' She yawned. 'Excuse me. Will you sit?'

To her surprise, instead of seating himself in a chair, he crossed the room to sit beside her on the chaise longue, with only a hand's breadth between them.

'Did you walk?' said Hetty.

'Yes, I walked from my office.' He seemed about to speak again, then folded his lips and shook his head.

'Would you like a cup of tea?'

Mr Wallace shook his head in a gesture that seemed impatient. He took off his hat and gloves, placed them beside him and, to Hetty's astonishment, put a hand over hers.

'Miss Barlow. May I call you Henrietta?'

'You can call me Hetty, if you like.'

'Of course. Hetty.' He took a breath. 'I want to apologise for my absence of late. There has been a matter of some delicacy to discuss with Mrs Calver. We have our widowhood in common, as you know, and Mrs Calver did confide in me her loneliness along with her desire to be married again. There was a conversation to be had.'

He was trying to tell her that he had proposed to Mrs Calver. Hetty wanted to say that this was none of her business. The dull feeling that was spreading through her body was due to physical exhaustion. She looked down at his hand and he withdrew it with a mumbled apology.

'I am all at sixes and sevens,' he said.

'Go on,' said Hetty. Amelia had always believed Mr Wallace carried a candle for Hetty. The girl would be disappointed. Hetty would miss their friendship, for now the future Mrs Wallace would be with him whenever he came to call. That thought made her suddenly want to weep. She really ought to take a good long nap.

Mr Wallace cleared his throat before continuing. 'I wanted my daughter's blessing, and she asked for some time to consider my proposal. My Flora has been through so much, losing her mother at a young age.'

Hetty nodded sympathetically. All she wanted to do was wrap herself in the coverlet of her bed and sink her head into the pillow.

'But she did give me her blessing quite readily and it is my own fear, my cowardice, that has kept me silent, and away from you, for so long. Will you permit me to ask a question, and answer truthfully?'

Perhaps Hetty's weariness was affecting her ability to make sense of what Mr Wallace was saying. She stroked her temple with her fingers. 'We are friends but surely you're not askin' for *my* permission to marry Mrs Calver.'

'My dear.' Mr Wallace took her fingers gently away from her face, and folded her hand between his. 'You misunderstand. I have come to ask, would you consider doing me the honour of becoming my wife?'

Chapter 28

He found her everywhere he looked.

She was the girl sitting on the top deck of the tram bus as it passed him by, her auburn hair teased by the breeze. She was the woman with the husky laugh entering the Blue Pig on the arm of another man, and she was the woman in the green dress reaching with long fingers for an orange on the fruit stall at the market. She was everywhere he looked, and nowhere to be found.

Ned recalled he had laughed in Constable Goodlad's face when the man first turned up with the news of Nan's escape. It had been a shout of joy that escaped his throat before he could stop it. He'd happily acquiesced when the police told him they would need to search his cottage and the business premises, although they balked at entering the furnace room. They wouldn't find his flame-haired girl there. Nor was she in the room behind the spattering wheel where Goodlad, and a man Ned assumed must be his superior because of the way Goodlad deferred to him, hovered uneasily beside the fist-sized links of the iron chains that supported the tilt hammer. One of Jacob's men was inspecting the frame, using a sledge hammer to knock tight any loosened wedges. Goodlad flinched with every solid wood-on-wood blow. 'Wait 'til the hammer starts up,' Ned had said, with a smile. 'Lift yer off yer feet.' It was only a little sport.

In any event, Ned had nothing to hide, except his heartbreak that Nan had not sought him out. He wished she had gone to him. He would have found a place to hide her, although Ellie would be none too pleased. That, as Ned's grandmother might have said, was a bridge to cross once they got to it.

The days passed and eventually it was Ellie who made him see sense. He had to accept there was no bridge beyond which Nan would be waiting for him. 'I'm here,' Ellie had said. She had laid her hands against his chest and kissed him on the lips. 'Stop actin' the fool.'

When Constable Goodlad showed up again a few days ago he'd had Ellie to contend with. 'Ned's wi' me now,' she told him. 'We're gettin' wed soon and she'd better not be back, if she knows what's good for 'er.'

Privately, Ellie told Ned he should thank his blessings for the life he had, that he should forget about the past and devote himself to the woman he was with. It was, he was forced to admit, the same advice his grandmother would have given him. Still, the idea that Nan was out there in the world nagged at him like a missing tooth, a gap he could not help exploring, all the while knowing there was nothing to find.

Ned walked across the yard with Jacob, the sweat on his brow and arms from the intense heat of the furnace room cooling quickly, making him shiver.

'Too hot in there, too cold out 'ere,' said Jacob. 'An' never the twain shall meet.'

Ned removed his neckerchief and wiped his face with it. He slapped the haunch of one of four horses tethered to a tarp-covered wagon and greeted the driver, who was picking tobacco out of his teeth and nodded disinterestedly, before turning to Jacob. 'What's up wi' thee, then?'

Jacob had been out of sorts all morning, his face screwed up into a scowl, snapping at the men, complaining to Ned about a faulty control on the boiler and generally looking liable to explode like a blocked valve at any moment.

'I do 'av summat to say,' said Jacob. 'Let's get dinner down us first.'

'Tell me now,' said Ned, struggling to match his cousin's pace as they strode towards the cottage.

'After dinner,' said Jacob. 'I'm starvin'.'

Jacob stopped abruptly and folded his arms, his scowl deepening as he watched Alfie Prescott emerge from the clerk's office carrying a large satchel. The youth acknowledged the two men with a brief salute as he swung himself onto the wagon, perching on the bench beside the driver who twitched the reins. Straining forward, the horses began to move. The driver was making a delivery to the canal basin and Ned assumed Alfie had hitched a ride to bank the week's takings, and the extra on top.

'It's all goin' like clockwork, lad, an' isn't that grand?' Mr Prescott had said the Saturday before when he'd delivered Ellie to the cottage in his horse and trap. She'd smiled at her father when he peeled a bank note from the stack he was carrying and handed it to her. 'Buy summat nice wi' this, next time tha's in town.' He'd given Ned the rest. 'Get our Alfie to put this lot through the books, all right, lad?' said Mr Prescott. Ned had hesitated and Mr Prescott peered at him. 'What's good for the family is good for thee. I'll leave you pair o' lovebirds to it.'

The woman who cooked for Ned had left a meat and vegetable stew simmering on the range. Ned got out a loaf of bread and a block of butter while Jacob ladled the stew into bowls.

'Looks tasty,' said Jacob. 'This'll set us up for the rest o' the day.'

Ned sat down opposite his cousin, who tore a piece of bread from the loaf and dipped it into the stew. 'What's up, our Jake?'

Jacob held up one finger, stuffed the bread into his mouth and commenced to chew. Ned set about his own meal, but the roiling in his gut had robbed him of any appetite. He suspected what was coming, and had for a while. He put down his spoon.

'I would've never got a loan from the bank,' he said. 'Tha thinks I'm reckless, that I think nowt through.'

'No,' said Jacob. He swallowed. 'It's more tha's too trustin', thinkin' everyone's a decent sort, like thee.'

'Prescott's brought us along further than we'd be,' said Ned.

Jacob shook his head impatiently, although the look he gave Ned was sympathetic. 'What's tha rush?' he said, then held up his hand to forestall any answer Ned might give, not that he had one.

They ate the rest of their meal in silence, a silence freighted with unspoken words. Finally, Jacob sat back. He patted his belly.

'That were lovely,' he said. 'Let's hope Ellie Prescott will cook as good a dinner for thee.'

Ned sighed. 'Aye, well.'

'What?' said Jacob. 'Not all rosy in the garden? Still pinin' for that other one?' He got up and left the table, returning with two bottles of ale. 'Sorry, Ned. I shouldn't be takin' this out on thee.'

'Whatever it is,' said Ned, 'we can sort it out.'

Jacob shook his head. 'He threatened me, tha knows. Your pal Prescott. I've a family, little 'uns. Toe the line, he said to me, or tha'll get what's comin' to thee.'

Ned's gut contracted in shame. But he was angry too. 'Don't tar me wi' the same brush,' he said. 'I'd never… I'll have a word wi' him.'

'Don't bother.' Jacob swigged from his bottle. 'I weren't expectin',' – he waved his arm around – 'none o' this. I can't be doin' wi' it, Ned. Tha's put us in bed wi' a crook. Anyhow, I'll say no more except there's a foreman's job goin' at Atlas Works.'

'But this is ours, what we wanted,' said Ned. 'Me an' thee.' Even to himself, his voice sounded weak, and unconvincing. He coughed. 'Let me talk to 'im.'

Jacob put the bottle down on the table and looked away, towards the door.

'No point,' he said, and finally met Ned's eye. 'I'm sorry, lad. I've taken the job.'

–

On a bright but bitterly cold Sunday afternoon, Ned helped Ellie onto the omnibus that would transport them from Malin Bridge to Hillsborough, where they'd take the Infirmary Road tram bus to get them to the middle of town and only a short walk from the Prescott family home. They sat across from each other on the lower, enclosed deck, their feet resting on the damp boards, shoulder to shoulder with the other passengers. The bus smelled of wet wool and muddy boots. Ellie's cheeks were pink with cold beneath the brim of the black plush hat she wore. It was decorated with a wide green velvet ribbon, tied under her fox's chin, that matched the cape she wore.

The shade was forest green, Ellie had informed him, and the hat was the newest style. Ned could hear Mr Prescott in his head. *Only the best for my Felicia.*

Ned stuffed his hands into the pockets of his greatcoat. He could see himself walking down the aisle and traipsing all the way to his grave while always falling short of Ellie's expectations. He had failed Jacob. He had failed Nan. A shiver ran down his spine when he thought about Nan's mouth against his ear at the foot of Snig Hill. *Don't tell,* she had whispered and kissed him on the cheek. That old woman who had come to the magistrates' court with Hope had called her *incorrigible*. The warden of the House of Help had called her *that girl* and told Ned he was being led by the nose.

Nan could lead him through the gates of hell. He'd follow.

'What,' said Ellie, leaning forward and lowering her voice, 'are you smiling about?'

'Nowt,' said Ned. He wiped his hand over his mouth. 'Wonder if Frank'll be there?'

Ellie pouted. 'So you pair can run off to the pub after dinner?'

She sat back and turned her head deliberately away from him and gazed into the distance, her mouth set, holding herself stiff against the swaying of the bus. Observing her, Ned saw his life mapped out in the sharp lines of her jaw and cheekbone. After a while, he looked away too.

Frank let them into the house and strode off towards the kitchen. 'Ma's cooked up a feast,' he said, 'wi' a side o' ham procured for her by her darlin' son.'

'Tha's in a good mood,' said Ned, following him. ''Ow do, Mrs Prescott, Mr Prescott. 'Ey up, Samson.'

He fondled the ears of the hound that had jumped up and pressed his paws against Ned's chest, pink tongue lolling.

'Leave him,' said Ellie, 'or he'll not stop pesterin' thee.'

'I don't mind,' said Ned.

'Samson! Come 'ere.' Mr Prescott shooed the dog out of the back door. 'Reight, lad. I want to know all about that cousin o' thine. Oh, I've 'eard. Does that surprise thee?'

Mrs Prescott took Ned's coat from him and patted his arm. 'I'm dishin' up in five minutes. It can wait 'til then, can't it, Frank? Ellie, you look smashin' in that hat. Where'd you get it from?'

Ned went to stand by the window over the kitchen sink. The dog was in the yard, sitting on its haunches, facing the house. Samson's ears pricked up when he saw Ned at the window. A light rain had begun to fall and the dog's fur was already bedraggled. 'Wish I could let thee in,' whispered Ned, and thought, but did not say the words: *And me out.*

After dinner, Ellie gave him a knowing look when Frank suggested to Ned that the two of them go for a pint. Mr Prescott had already disappeared on some mysterious business, leaving mother and daughter to clear the plates away.

'We've nowt else to do,' said Frank, 'except sit round 'ere wi' the women.'

'Thanks for the grub, Mrs Prescott, it was lovely,' said Ned.

'Tell thee what,' said Frank. 'I'll come halfway towards thine. Five Alls on Infirmary Road. Tha knows it, corner o' Gilpin Street. I can get me head down there, an' all, an' you can hop on a bus 'ome.'

'It's rainin',' said Ned.

'Well, tha's goin' to get wet, regardless.'

Mrs Prescott followed them out of the kitchen. 'What place is this, then, where tha can get thee head down?'

Reaching for his coat, Frank kissed her on the forehead. 'None o' tha business, Ma. I'm thirty-odd, did tha know that?'

'Aye.' She pushed him away. 'And no lass on thee arm. Not like our Ned, here.' She smiled at him. 'Go an' say bye to Ellie, love, while I get thee coat for thee.'

A horse bus took the two men from Snig Hill to a stop some two hundred yards from the Five Alls. Collars turned up and caps pulled down, they hurried towards the glowing windows of the public house like moths to the flame. Ned glanced up at the sign above the door as they reached the corner. The five disembodied heads painted on it — a lawyer, a parson, a soldier, John Bull and the Queen — were barely visible in the gloom. He recited the mantra in his head. *I plead for all. I pray for all. I fight for all. I pay for all. I reign over all.*

Frank nudged his shoulder and pointed to the upstairs window of the house next door, where, in place of net curtains, a dress hung on a hook. 'Me luck's in,' he said.

The pub was warm and noisy, filled with soldiers from the nearby barracks. Ned and Frank shouldered their way to the counter, purchased pints of porter and found a place to stand near the roaring fireplace.

'Here's to thee,' said Frank, chinking his pint pot against Ned's. 'Well done, lad.'

'What d'you mean?' said Ned.

'Well, tha's offloaded that whinin' cousin o' thine.'

Ned frowned. 'That's not what I wanted, though.'

'Me father'll see thee straight. Pay off the cousin, find somebody to fill his place.' Frank gulped down his drink.

'I wun't worry about it, if I were thee. It's a good thing. Another? I'll get 'em.'

'It were our business. We were in it together,' said Ned, but Frank was already walking away.

He only realised he was staring at, without seeing, a table of red-coats when one of the soldiers, huddled close by a young woman with a painted face, asked him what he was about. Ned shook his head and looked away. The soldier muttered something that made everyone around the table laugh.

Frank returned, a pint pot in each hand.

'Tha's got a face like a slapped arse,' he said. 'Drink up.'

'What's the rush?' said Ned. He'd raised his voice to be heard over a swell in the volume of the chatter around him, and now he was shouting. 'Tha dragged me 'ere and now tha wants to sup up and go?'

The same soldier who had ragged him looked over, frowning. Ned glared at him. His blood was up and he was spoiling for a fight. A small voice in the back of his mind told him to get a grip on himself. He ignored it. All the injustices of the past year clamoured in his chest.

Frank laughed. 'Did tha see that dress in the window or not? Open invitation, that.' When Ned didn't respond, Frank clapped him on the arm. 'It's all reight for thee,' he said, 'tha's got it on tap.'

Ned clenched his jaw. 'Tha's talkin' about thee own sister, like that?'

'What's got into thee?' Frank supped his ale, unperturbed. 'I know what it is.' He nodded his head vigorously. 'Tha's worried about that cousin o' thine spilling tha secrets.'

Ned was caught off guard. Was Frank talking about Nan? He had confided in his cousin but since Ellie had come on the scene Ned had kept his sorrow to himself. 'What secrets? What's tha on about now?'

'Look,' said Frank, 'if he knows what's good for him he won't blab about our Alfie's little business on the side. Tell you what, I'll pay Jacob a visit, eh?'

Ned bristled. 'What d'you mean?'

Frank's smile was sly. 'Nowt too harmful, just a warnin', a bit o' horseplay.' He made a fist and gently bumped Ned on the chin. 'Enough so he'll know to keep his trap shut.'

Ned's pint pot was in his hand, then it was falling to the ground and his fist connecting with Frank's nose, sending the other man staggering backwards, an almost comical look of surprise on his face. There was a cheer from the table of soldiers, then Frank's brow darkened and he launched himself at Ned. They hit the ground, rolling in a furious embrace, each trying to land a punch. Ned could hear muffled shouts through the high whine in his ears. He gasped when something hard hit the back of his skull, his hand finding the iron rail that ran around the edge of the hearth. It was enough for Frank to gain the advantage. Ned was on his back, Frank straddling him, the blade of a knife glinting in the firelight.

Two things happened at once. A white-hot pain sliced down his cheek at the same time as Frank was lifted off him by the scruff of the neck, his arms twisted behind him by two of the soldiers who had been sitting at the nearby table. He roared when the knife was shaken from his grasp to land on the wooden boards near Ned's face. A boot appeared and sent the knife spiralling away across the floor. Frank was roaring at him, spitting out incomprehensible words.

Ned staggered to his feet, touching his face where the knife had cut. His fingers came away wet with blood. He looked around, aghast. What had happened? Frank had three men on him now, wrestling him to the ground. A hand gripped Ned's shoulder. He shook it off, and ran.

He leaned against the back wall of the cottage, pressing his sleeve to his cheek, unsure how much of the wetness was rain and how much his own blood. He had run some of the way, propelled along by the adrenaline that coursed through his veins, and walked the rest when dizziness overcame him. Beneath the knocking of his heart and the pounding in his head he could hear the river rushing by in full spate at the bottom of the garden and water dripping from the gutter above his head. Eventually, with fumbling fingers, Ned reached for the key he kept on the lintel of the back door, his fingers exploring the rough wood.

In the darkness behind him, a throat was cleared.

Ned spun around, and the world spun with him. He dropped to his hands and knees with a painful jolt. His cap fell from his head. He was aware of a female voice calling his name from a great distance. 'Ellie?' he said, then the black void descended.

Chapter 29

She tugged him onto his back – it helped that he had slumped down on his side or she would not have managed it – and dug her fingers into his shoulders and shouted his name, her voice hoarse with fear and exasperation. She put her face close to his. There was no smell of drink coming off him, only the musty odour of wet clothes and tobacco smoke.

He was getting soaked. The driver waiting in the lane might lose patience and turn his gig around and leave. At a loss, she clenched her fists in frustration. Her eyes fell on the black outline of the metal watering can on the edge of the patio. She lunged for it and threw the contents into Ned's face.

He spluttered awake, staring up at her without really seeing her.

'Are you there?' she said. 'Wake up, Ned Staniforth.'

Even in the dark, she could see recognition dawn in the widening of his eyes and the slackness of his jaw. Ned sat up, his leg splayed before him. He lifted his hand, then dropped it. She took hold of the lapels of his coat and clung on, afraid he would fall back and bang his head on the paving slabs. The absurdity of the situation hit her and she laughed. 'You're a weight.'

'Nan?'

'Who else would be lurking in your garden in the middle of the night?'

'Nan?' He used the wall to scramble upright, and leaned against it.

'Can you walk, Ned?' Saying his name, speaking his name back to him, filled her with joy, but there was no time to savour their reunion. 'Ned, we need to get going. Do you understand?'

She moved away to try the handle of the back door. It remained just as locked as it was when she had arrived a few minutes earlier.

'Here,' said Ned, reaching up again to find the key. Their fingers brushed when he gave her the key, their eyes locking. Nan broke the spell, turning away to open the door. Pushing it wide, she returned to Ned and put her arm around his waist, wedging her shoulder into his armpit.

'Lean on me.'

With Ned shuffling and Nan using every ounce of her strength to keep him on his feet, they reached the sitting room beyond the kitchen. Ned fell onto the settee, his legs hanging over the end, and Nan put a cushion under his head. She left him there and went to find a lamp. Returning to sit on the edge of the settee, she brought the light close to his face. Now she could see the cut on his cheek, seeping blood mixed with rainwater, but only a little. His skin was as white as a clean sheet.

Nan made to rise but Ned grasped her wrist.

'I'm going to find a cloth,' she said.

'Wait.' His voice was guttural, thick with emotion. He touched a strand of hair that had escaped from her bonnet and frowned. 'It's your face.'

Nan laughed. 'It is my face.'

Ned smiled, then winced. 'I've missed that sound,' he said. He ran his thumb over the cut on her lip, sustained when she had resisted the advances of the chef at the Rose and Crown. It had been the signal for her to leave that place. She took his hand away gently and kissed his fingers.

'Looks like we've both been in the wars,' she said. 'What a pair we are.'

She unfastened her bonnet and took it off. Ned glanced at her hair then back into her eyes. Nan leaned down and gently kissed his lips. She put her face against his uninjured cheek and whispered in his ear. 'Will you pack a bag and come with me?'

This was the moment of truth.

Her gut swirled with fear and hope as Ned sat up, consternation on his face. 'I never 'eard from thee. Nowt at all. Not a single letter.'

'It wasn't permitted,' she said. The gig was waiting, might even now be turning to trot away, but she couldn't resist asking the question. 'Did you write to me?'

His eyebrows shot up. 'I were postin' a letter a day, or thereabouts.' He laughed. 'They were rubbish, though. Best tha never got to read 'em.' He gulped and her heart was wrung by the hurt in his eyes. 'I came to the cells, though, and the court, to see thee, to support thee. Seemed like tha'd given up on me.'

'I never did,' said Nan. She could have told him that he was the one who had given up on her. Hope had told her about Frank's sister. The retort died on the tip of her tongue. None of that mattered now. 'Who did this?' she said instead, taking his chin in her fingers and gently turning his head. 'Who cut you?'

'Frank. We had words.' His mouth twisted. 'It were my fault.'

'Will the police be coming?'

'Nah, not if the family has owt to do wi' it.'

The family. Nan shivered. 'They're not your family,' she said. 'I am.'

Ned shook his head, as if to clear it. 'Have you really come back to me, Nan? I took a knock to the skull, tha knows. I could be dreamin' all this.'

'You're not dreaming,' said Nan. She smiled at the wonderment on his face and bent to kiss him. There was a loud mechanical-sounding click and whir and Nan sprang to her feet.

'It's all right,' said Ned. 'He left it, the old man. It does that. Needs fixin'.'

As he spoke, the grandfather clock in the corner of the room began to chime the hour.

'It's a bit too big to take along with us,' said Nan. 'It'll have to stay broken.'

'Daft apeth,' said Ned.

A sob rose in Nan's throat. She sank down beside Ned and took his hands in hers. 'I've come to fetch you away with me. I've got a driver waiting outside to take us to the railway station at Stocksbridge. We're going north, to Scotland.'

'Scotland,' said Ned, disbelievingly.

'Why not?' She would tell him about Sarah later, explain her obligation to the woman who had gifted Nan back her life.

The twelfth chime died away, leaving a silence deeper than the sea. Ned was staring at her, a naked frankness in his eyes that pierced her heart.

'I don't know, Nan.' He shook his head. 'Anyhow, where've you been, these past two months?'

She forced a smile. 'Gathering nuts for winter.'

When he opened his mouth to speak, she put a finger against his lips. 'Add your hoard to mine, Ned. Come away with me.'

'Now? A midnight flit?'

'It has to be now. Pack a bag, bring all the money you have. Forget about the grandfather clock.'

'An' everything else.'

'And everything else.'

'Never comin' back then?'

Nan laughed. 'This is me helping you escape.'

She stood and tugged at Ned's hands. He shook his head, but got to his feet and embraced her, folding his coat around her. Nan laid her head on his chest, her arms around his back, listening to the beat of his heart.

She had never felt so alive.

Chapter 30

Hetty was drawn towards the open door of the parlour by an insistent set of notes from the piano, a melodic march she had heard before, in a church, perhaps, in a different time of her life.

She entered to find Hope playing and Amelia in the act of turning a page on the sheet music. Both women looked up and smiled at her, somewhat mischievously, she thought.

'That's rousing,' said Hetty. 'What is it?'

Hope finished with a flourish. She was an excellent pianist, a skill she had kept hidden during her early days as a resident at the house. 'It's Mendelssohn,' she said.

Amelia interrupted her. '"The Wedding March".'

Both young women burst into laughter.

'Well, I'm only here for your amusement,' said Hetty.

'Have you decided?' Amelia said. 'When is he comin' back?'

'This afternoon.' Hetty took a deep breath. 'I'm to give my answer this afternoon. He's arrivin' at three.'

'An' are you wearin' that?' said Amelia. She crossed the room to sit in the chair facing Hetty. 'What about that dress you wore to the botanical gardens?'

Hetty looked down at the white bib of her warden's uniform. 'I had this on yesterday, when he… well, I was wearin' this.'

'Aye,' said Amelia, 'but you had no idea what was comin' yesterday, did you? Don't you want to titify yourself up a bit?'

Hope replaced the lid on the piano. 'I think Mr Wallace has more on his mind than your mother's attire.'

Amelia stuck out her tongue at Hope as she pulled up a chair to sit by the fire and put out her hands to warm them. 'Have you decided,' said Hope, 'or are we not permitted to ask?'

' 'Course we are,' said Amelia. 'An' I want to know.'

Hetty's heart fluttered in her chest. She hadn't been able to eat breakfast nor the dinner Cook put in front of her. She had let two cups of tea go cold and had to keep apologising for her cloth ears whenever anybody tried to speak to her. Her day, thankfully, had been busy enough. She had settled in a new resident, assigning the woman along with two others to laundry chores for the rest of the day, and helped Amelia sort through a trunk of donated clothing: women's clothes and girls' smocks and stockings and boots. They had discovered a porcelain doll in the bottom of the trunk, dressed in stiff silk and gauze, and with a delicately painted face, obviously a collector's item. Hetty had taken it up to the twelve-year-old girl lying in the attic bed with a fever and tucked it in beside her. It would be the first thing the girl saw when she woke.

'Hetty,' said Amelia impatiently. 'What will you tell him?'

Hetty brushed imaginary crumbs from the bib of her uniform.

'D'you know, I haven't had chance to play Parcheesi yet,' she said. 'Will you fetch it, Hope, and Amelia bring the card table? You can teach me.'

The game was straightforward enough. Each player started with four tokens and the aim was to move them around the board, the number of moves dictated by a pair of dice, until they reached home, and safety. A player whose token landed on a space containing an opponent's token could send them back to the start. That was the most satisfying part, Amelia told her.

Hetty threw the dice and moved one of her tokens two spaces forward and pushed another five spaces on. 'Amelia,' she said, 'tell me what you think.'

Gratifyingly, her daughter understood she was not talking about the game. 'I've allus liked him. He's a bit older than you, though, is our Bertrand.'

Hetty nodded. 'By twenty-odd years,' she said. 'He's asked me to disregard the discrepancy in age. It's not something I've ever paid notice to, when we've been together.'

She felt her cheeks colour.

'Will you call him Bertie?' said Amelia. 'Oh, Bertie. Take me in your arms.'

'Stop that,' said Hetty.

'Do you like him?' said Hope.

Hetty sighed. 'I do, very much.'

'Do you love him?' said Hope.

Hetty cooled her cheeks with the palm of her hand. 'It's not summat I've had to think about.'

'Let me put it like this,' said Hope. 'Are you happy that Mr Wallace has asked you to marry him?'

'Or,' said Amelia, making claws of her hands, 'does it fill you with dread and fear?'

Hetty ignored Amelia's cackle. She bit her lip. 'It makes me feel happy,' she said.

Hope beamed at her. Amelia leaned forward and moved a token on the board.

'It's your turn to throw the dice, Hetty.'

At the appointed hour, she stood at the window in her quarters, watching people browse the Christmas market that had been set up that morning on the cobbles. The gaily painted stalls would remain in place all week. Amelia was amongst the shoppers, wandering around under a bruise-coloured sky, and Hetty hoped that she would buy a trinket for herself. Amelia had already declared that she would have the warden's quarters when Hetty went to live with Mr Wallace. Hetty would stay on as warden, and Amelia as housekeeper – but with a room of her own. Hetty smiled to herself. Amelia had it all mapped out before Hetty had even given her answer. It was a relief to see her beginning to emerge from the grief that had consumed her.

A group of carol singers were organising themselves on the pavement at the foot of the square. Hetty glanced at the clock on the wall. It was ten past three. When she returned her attention to the square, Mr Wallace was hurrying towards the house. His head was down and he could be any gentleman negotiating the crowds except that she recognised his gait. He reached the door and was raising the knocker when he caught sight of Hetty at the window.

He replaced the knocker soundlessly, his face lighting up. A bubble of joy rose in Hetty's throat and she found herself smiling widely back at him, like a stupid girl in love, like the girl she had once been. He tilted his head to one side and put a hand to his chest and Hetty laughed and copied him, placing her hand against her heart, which was full.

She went to let him in.

Chapter 31

Ned walked along the platform until he reached the foot-plate of the impressive beast that served the Carlisle to Glasgow line. He stopped to watch the fireman shovel coal into the box at the end of the locomotive's long plum-coloured snout, then retraced his steps to the last first-class carriage and stood, his hands in his pockets, gazing through the window into the expensively decorated interior. Nan sat upright in the carriage, her face hidden by the wings of her bonnet, leaning forward slightly as if to will the train into motion. Ned blew air from his cheeks and looked up and down the platform. A guard came out with a flag. Ned's heart quickened in his chest. They had come this far. It was nearly time.

He willed Nan to turn her head, to see him standing there. She did, her lips parting slightly in surprise. The sight of her always lit a flame in his belly. How he wanted to kiss that mouth, to run his fingers through her crop of hair that was already beginning to show its original fire. A whistle blew, and Nan's eyes widened in alarm.

Ned twisted the door handle and stepped inside the carriage. He sat down beside her.

'I thought you were going to miss it,' she said. 'What were you doing?'

'I got these,' said Ned, unwrapping a waxed paper parcel to reveal half a dozen small custards. He lay the paper on the embroidered cushion of the empty seat opposite him. 'Travelling in style, eh? In a carriage all to ourselves.'

He leaned his head against the antimacassar on the back of his seat. There was a tasselled lampshade above the high seatback, windows where walls would be in the lower-class carriages, wood-panelled clerestories to boot. First-class tickets had depleted the pot but it guaranteed a degree of privacy. People tended not to question the rich.

Another whistle blew and the train jerked forward, the pistons beneath the great engine grinding into motion.

'We're off,' said Ned.

Nan was grinning at him.

'What?' he said.

'Don't look so anxious,' said Nan. 'Let's enjoy the journey.'

The shrill sound of the steam whistle heralded an increase in speed. The carriage rocked and Nan took off her bonnet and lifted his arm up so she could nestle into the side of his body. There was no going back. His fate had been sealed the moment he had stepped foot outside the cottage and they had hurried up the lane to find the gig still waiting.

Ned gazed out of the window at fields and hills and valleys he had never set eyes on before, and wondered what would await them in the city of Glasgow, and beyond. Nan had talked about pressing even further north, to find a house she knew about that sat on the edge of a loch. He bent to rest his almost-healed cheek on the top of her head, and raised his eyes to the pale blue dome of the world. Was his grandmother looking down from the heavens, shaking her head in disbelief? It had been so easy, in the end, to leave everything behind. Perhaps wanderlust was in his blood, after all.

Nan squeezed his hand and Ned looked down at their linked fingers and squeezed back.

'Allus an adventure wi' thee,' he whispered. 'Allus an adventure.'

Author's Note

The walls of my office are covered in maps. Some are of far-flung places I've visited, but most are maps of Sheffield, where my sagas are set. There's a modern-day map dominating the wall behind me, with red lines for the main arteries radiating from the ring road that encircles the city centre – like a spider's web spinning outwards, encompassing the hamlets and villages of yesteryear. Over my desk are older maps and illustrations charting the growth of Sheffield from a cluster of buildings around St Peter's Church – today's cathedral building – with street names that have survived for centuries: Snig Hill, Norfolk Street, Campo Lane, to name a few.

Maps tell a story. There are many Sheffield roads – like Tenter Street, Furnace Hill and Love Street – that inform us about the people who lived on them long ago. Modern developers carry on the tradition – kudos to whoever snuck Letsby Avenue[1] past the planning authority. Often, place names evolve over time, and this can be tricky when you're trying to be historically faithful to an area. Prompted by a correction made by my copy editor, I spent far too long trying to establish precisely when Shales

---

[1] Yes, there really is a police station on Letsby Avenue.

Moor and Crookes Moor – names that reflected the local topography – became Shalesmoor and Crookesmoor (I lived on Crookesmoor Road as a child so this one felt personal). In the end, we went with the modern spelling.

When did Far Gate become one word and Saville Street drop an 'l'? My old maps and sketches, some compiled years before they were printed, some perhaps containing spelling mistakes, fail me here, so apologies for errors of this nature that creep in, especially if you, like me, grew up on one of Sheffield's historic streets. Names are important. They give us our sense of belonging.

Acknowledgements

As ever, thanks to my lovely editor, Emily Bedford, and all the team at Canelo, especially Alicia Pountney and Catriona Camacho, to Kate and Saskia and everyone at the Kate Nash Agency, to Asha, Carly, Emma and Sarah, to cherished friends and family, and avid readers everywhere – 'There is no frigate like a book to take us lands away.'